TAKEN AT THE FLOOD

NENE ADAMS

Bella
BOOKS

2016

Bella Books, Inc.
P.O. Box 10543
Tallahassee, FL 32302

Printed in the United States of America on acid-free paper.

First Bella Books Edition 2016

Editor: Ruth Stanley
Cover Designer: Sandy Knowles

ISBN: 978-1-59493-478-0

"There is a tide in the affairs of men,
Which taken at the flood, leads on to fortune.
Omitted, all the voyage of their life
Is bound in shallows and in miseries.
On such a full sea are we now afloat,
And we must take the current when it serves,
Or lose our ventures."
-William Shakespeare, *Julius Caesar*

CHAPTER ONE

Meredith Reid lifted the bottle of Red Stripe to her lips, hesitated, and took a drink.

The restaurant was a little too noisy, a little too crowded, a little too touristy for her tastes, but she had a great view of the marina from the terrace. She enjoyed the breeze coming off the water and the smell of salt in the air. Sitting here also gave her more privacy for the meeting with her new client, who was—she checked her watch—fourteen minutes late.

"You should try the oysters," said an unfamiliar female voice from behind her chair. "I hear they're so fresh, they practically jump in your mouth. It's one of the things I love about Miami. The seafood is to die for."

"I don't care much for oysters," Meredith replied, concealing her surprise. She put the beer bottle on the table as a woman sat down opposite her. "Ms. Stanton, right?"

"Please, it's Fairuza—my Turkish grandmother's fault—but you can call me Rue."

"In that case, I'm Meredith. Or Mer, if you're feeling particularly informal."

"Not Captain Reid?"

Meredith's mood instantly darkened. There had been a time, before she resigned her naval officer's commission, when she'd taken pride in the title. "Just Meredith is fine," she said coolly, taking a drink of beer. Swallowing past the knot in her throat took an effort.

"I'm sorry. I didn't mean to offend you."

"No offense taken."

The harried waitress arrived, took Rue's mojito order, offered to bring Meredith another bottle of Red Stripe, and hastened back inside the restaurant.

Rue picked up the menu and studied Meredith over the edge.

Meredith knew her appearance wasn't impressive: rawboned, suntanned, with a mop of curly brown hair, brown eyes and a souvenir from a bar scuffle during her Annapolis days in the form of a crooked nose. Her clean T-shirt and jeans weren't as businesslike as Rue's designer power suit—which probably cost more than her yearly marina slip rental—but the woman wanted to hire her boat, not negotiate a corporate merger.

In turn, she took the opportunity to size up Rue more closely. She knew nothing about Rue other than her stated desire, via their telephone chat, to charter a boat to an unspecified location for an unknown purpose. Under the circumstances, she might've been suspicious, but Rue didn't ping her radar as the criminal type.

Rue was so well groomed she practically shone. Her dark auburn hair was swept back smoothly in a French twist. No jewelry. Just the right amount of makeup. Beautiful. Almost too beautiful, in fact. Her face showed signs of cosmetic surgery.

Definitely cheekbone implants, Meredith thought. Nose job. Facelift too, judging by the pale scarring in front of her ears, though Rue seemed kind of young for the procedure. She snorted quietly. Superficial, vain women started self-improvements early, before time had a chance to leave its mark. Why would a woman like that want to hire a boat like hers? she wondered, finishing her beer in time to accept the second bottle brought by the waitress.

Rue broke off her scrutiny to order a dozen raw oysters from the waitress. She glanced over. "Do you mind? Or would you prefer to go straight to the entrée?" she asked.

"I'm good," Meredith replied. Noticing the waitress's impatient shuffling, she went on, "Go ahead and enjoy your appetizer. I'll order something later."

The waitress scurried away.

"Well, as I told you when we spoke the other day," Rue said after taking a sip from her mojito, "I'm looking to charter a boat, no questions asked or answered." She wiped the lipstick smudge off the cocktail glass's rim with her thumb.

Meredith shrugged. "You don't seem the type." When Rue's eyebrows rose, she added, "My usual charters are deep sea fishing. Sometimes I head down to the islands. But let me be clear, *Lady Vic* is no party boat. I don't tolerate drugs or liquor. And if you're into something illegal, like smuggling, I'll take a pass right now."

"I have no contraband to declare. If you can make the arrangements, I'd like to leave tomorrow morning." Rue held up a hand to forestall her protest. "I'm more than willing to pay extra for the inconvenience. Say, half again your usual fee?"

Meredith snapped her mouth closed. Frankly, she needed the money. Her charter business had run dry. She loved *Lady Vic*, but a twelve-year-old, forty-two-foot lobster boat cruiser couldn't compete with the bigger, fancier, faster yachts for hire. The best she'd scraped up lately had been a quick run to Kingston.

"Suppose I agree," she offered. "Where are we going?"

"Mexico."

"Whereabouts in Mexico?"

"I prefer to keep our destination private until we're underway. It's on the Caribbean side, if that's what you're worried about."

The waitress returned bearing a tray of freshly shucked oysters on a bed of ice and rock salt. Rue squeezed a lemon wedge over the oysters before picking up a shell and slurping the contents. Her expression suggested she'd found paradise.

Meredith ordered a glass of sparkling water to dilute the beers she'd drunk. "Why Mexico? And why the hush-hush?" she asked.

"I'd rather not say," Rue replied while choosing another oyster. "No questions answered, remember?"

Meredith scowled. "I'd rather not have my license yanked or face jail time because my passenger's into something hinky she kept under her hat."

"Ms. Reid…I mean, Meredith." Rue dabbed her mouth with a napkin. "I don't know how else to assure you of my intentions except give you my word: nothing I want to do in Mexico is illegal, immoral, or even breaks any of the Ten Commandments. To be honest, you're a last-minute substitute for the person I'd previously hired. He had to cancel the charter due to an accident. Since it's prime tourist season in these parts, I didn't have a lot of choice when it came to boats. You were the last call I made."

Knowing Rue felt she was scraping the bottom of the barrel stung. Meredith bristled on *Lady Vic's* behalf. Rue gulped another three oysters in the time it took her to wrestle her immediate furious reaction down to irritation. "Be that as it may, I won't tolerate being kept completely in the dark," she said, her tone coming out more clipped than she'd intended. "Either tell me right now what this is about, or I'm walking—"

White lightning flashed in her vision, followed by a deafening roar and a wave of immense pressure. The world ended. She ended, too, apart from a single thought following her into the darkness: the word "bomb."

CHAPTER TWO

What seemed like a long time later, Meredith opened her eyes to fire, smoke and chaos. She lay on her side on the terrace, partially shielded by the upturned table. Sounds stuttered and echoed hollowly in her skull as if coming from the bottom of a well.

A person stumbled past her. A man. One shoe on, the other off, his socked foot leaving a blood trail through glass and debris. She fought to remember what happened. A heavy charred smell lingered on the air. Had a gas stove exploded inside the restaurant?

Her sluggish wits left her in a semidaze. She tried taking a mental inventory to figure out how badly she'd been injured. No broken bones, she decided, but she had bitten her bottom lip and her right arm felt like a loan shark's enforcer had taken a baseball bat to it. She pushed herself up, careful of her sore arm, and glanced around.

The wall of glass on this side of the restaurant was gone, blown outward and scattered like glittering diamond confetti over the terrace. Patrons stayed where they had fallen or wandered the area like hollow-eyed zombies. She seemed poised on the edge of shock herself and felt relieved she hadn't been injured worse. Then she remembered Rue Stanton.

She checked the area where she thought Rue had been sitting and found no sign of the woman. Alarmed, she started to call out Rue's name. She felt a touch on her shoulder. Her neck cracked loudly when she turned her head.

"How are you?" Rue asked, squatting next to her.

"Been better," Meredith replied, hoping like hell her hearing returned to normal soon. "Been worse too." Her stomach lurched. She clenched her jaw, breathing through the nausea. A glance at Rue showed no blood or obvious signs of injury.

Rue gave her a tight smile. "Come on, we need to get out of here." She gripped Meredith's arm—thankfully not the bruised one—and tugged hard, trying to pull her upright.

"Okay, okay, give me a sec." Meredith cooperated and finally stood on her feet, swaying when her knees wobbled and nearly dumped her back on the floor.

Rue didn't appear to notice. She looked frazzled, her hair hanging in clumps around her face. "Hurry, hurry, hurry," she chanted under her breath.

Meredith let Rue lead her across the terrace and down the steps, around the side of the building, through an alley, and out to the street. Not until Rue pushed her into the passenger seat of a compact black sedan did she think to protest.

"Hey, we shouldn't leave the scene," she said, repeating herself when Rue slid behind the steering wheel, slung a briefcase under the driver's seat, and stuck a key in the ignition. Her tongue was too thick, fumbling on the words in her mouth. "People need help. And we'll have to give a statement to the police."

"Where's it docked?" Rue asked tersely.

"What?" Meredith rubbed the side of her head, wishing she could reach in and tear out the cotton wool swaddling her thoughts.

"Your boat. Where's it docked?"

A fire truck wailed past, followed by four police cruisers flashing blue and red lights, and a couple of ambulances. People began gathering on the other side of the street, most holding cell phones aloft to take pictures and videos of the burning restaurant.

Meredith gave up and told Rue the name of the marina and the slip number.

The journey took longer than usual due to rubberneckers slowing their cars to a crawl to gawk at the fire. Rue drove intently, both hands white-knuckled on the wheel. She didn't pause for yellow traffic lights, but floored the gas pedal and flew through intersections with blatant disregard for other vehicles. Meredith hoped they survived the trip.

After arriving at the marina lot, Rue parked the car, turned off the engine, and shifted in the seat. "We need to leave as soon as possible. Are you good to go?"

"Not exactly." Meredith closed her eyes to block out the too-bright sparkle of sunlight on the water. She rested her head against the headrest. At least her hearing had improved. She clearly made out the impatient grinding of Rue's teeth.

"I'm not kidding," Rue said, poking her upper arm.

Meredith sighed. "What's the rush?" she asked, opening her eyes and focusing on Rue. "And I already told you, until you tell me what's going on, my boat stays put."

"There's no time. We should get underway right now," Rue insisted. "When we're in open water, I'll tell you everything you need to know."

"No deal."

Rue sat quietly, staring into the middle distance as if debating with herself. At last she said, "All right, fine. I want you to take me to Los Dolores, a fishing village on an island south of Cancún called Isla Azul. Satisfied?"

"What's in Los Dolores?"

"My business, not yours." Rue remained tense. "Nothing illegal, like I said. All you need to know is I'll pay you for your time and trouble. Hell, if we leave within the next ten minutes, I'll double your fee. Sound good?"

Meredith wasn't reassured by Rue's generosity. In her experience, people only offered a lot of money when they were desperate to get away from something—or someone—or get to a place in a hurry. The cause of their haste was rarely legitimate. "Why are you so hot to leave Miami so quickly?" she asked. As soon as the question left her mouth, a possible answer struck her. "Are you a fugitive?"

"No. I'm just someone who wants to pay you in exchange for the temporary rental of your boat and your sailing expertise." Rue yanked the briefcase out from under her seat, opened it, and withdrew a stack of money.

Three or four thousand dollars, Meredith noted when the wad fell in her lap. "A charter costs about nine grand for a round trip from Miami to Cancún."

"I can get more money and it's not a round trip. Drop me off in Los Dolores and we're done, okay? I'll make my own travel arrangements from there."

The deal still sounded extremely shady, but Meredith had a headache, she wanted to put some ice on her bruised arm, and she was desperate for aspirin. "Make it ten grand."

"Done."

"You have a valid passport on you?"

"Yes."

Meredith gathered up the money, opened the car door, and stepped outside, glancing at Rue over her shoulder. "Are you coming or not?" she asked, beginning to head to the dock.

She heard Rue scrambling out of the car.

CHAPTER THREE

Sitting at the *Lady Vic*'s helm station three hours later, staring out at the wide, impossibly blue expanse of ocean stretching to meet the cloud-streaked horizon, Meredith should have felt peaceful and calm. Instead, her insides griped as if she'd eaten barbed wire.

Not that Rue Stanton was a bad passenger. The woman gained her sea legs quickly and without complaint—few things worse than green-faced, puking lubbers—but to go with the suitcase she'd taken from the trunk of her car, she'd brought brand-new scuba equipment aboard.

The diving gear troubled her. Questioning Rue resulted in no adequate answers, only evasions that seemed to confirm her darkest suspicions. She'd never liked being kept in the dark by her superior officers when she'd served in the navy and she sure as hell didn't like it now. Somebody always got screwed when it came to need-to-know status, and what she didn't know might boomerang around to bite her in the ass.

As a distraction from her pessimistic thoughts, she double-checked the boat's heading. From Miami to Cancún, their route skirted the northern tip of Cuba, a somewhat tricky feat of navigation. She had to ensure the boat stayed outside the communist country's territorial waters or she risked trouble with the US Coast Guard.

After setting the autopilot, Meredith went belowdecks to find Rue sitting on the L-shaped settee on the starboard side of the salon.

Rue sat with her legs tucked under, her head bent over a book in her lap. Sunlight from a porthole turned her auburn hair to fire. On sighting Meredith, she slapped the book closed and asked, "How are we doing?"

"We're getting there. *Lady Vic* may not be built for speed, but she's safe and stable." Meredith sat down on the settee about an arm's length from Rue. "You're lucky I stocked up on food, water and fuel the other day."

"I take it we won't run out of any of those things before we reach Mexico."

"That's right. As for tonight's meal, I'm no gourmet chef, but the pantry's full of staples and I can rustle up a sandwich whenever you want some dinner."

"Thanks, sounds great." Rue's smile didn't quite touch her eyes. Her gaze drifted to the book in her lap. After fidgeting slightly, she glanced up.

For the first time, Meredith realized Rue had heterochromia. Her left eye was a cool, steely blue, almost matching the settee's upholstery, while the other eye was brown, the color of fine Spanish sherry. The effect reminded her of a Turkish Van cat she'd once owned.

"What do you do for a living?" Meredith asked.

To her surprise, Rue answered readily. "I'm an art recovery specialist. People hire me to investigate art thefts and retrieve the stolen items."

"Sounds exciting."

"Not necessarily. It's not all cloak-and-dagger stuff, you know. Most of the time, I negotiate with the thieves on behalf of the painting's owners. A lot of my clients are private collectors who just want their property returned without a hassle, and they're willing to offer rewards and unofficial amnesty from prosecution to get it."

"And insurance companies and the police aren't likely to offer anything to thieves except a prison sentence, which is why you get called instead," Meredith guessed.

"Exactly. I usually get results."

"What you do…is that legal?"

Rue looked cagey. "Let's just say I often skirt a fine line and leave it at that."

Meredith nodded toward the book. "Part of a new case?" When Rue said nothing else, she firmed her expression and went on. "You said you'd tell me what our trip to Mexico is about when we were in open water. Well, it doesn't get more open than this." Her gesture encompassed the ocean outside the ship's hull.

"How about we save my story for after dinner?" Rue asked. "Please tell me you have a shower. I feel positively grubby." She pinched her blouse between her thumb and forefinger, pulling the soiled fabric away from her body. The restaurant explosion had left dark, briny-smelling stains on her clothes from the oysters. "I think I might still have glass in my bra."

"The head—the bathroom—is behind this door," Meredith said, pointing to port. "Toilet, sink and shower, but don't count on the hot water. I wouldn't linger if I were you."

"Thanks." Rue rose and went into the head. She took the book with her, much to Meredith's disappointment.

While waiting for Rue to finish showering, Meredith walked above decks to the mid-galley, opposite the built-in dinette. Thank God she had gone grocery shopping before her meeting, otherwise they'd have been reduced to a jar of peanut butter, a bottle of hot sauce, and a box of stale saltine crackers.

The pair of drawer refrigerators under the helm seats were crammed full with an assortment of sliced meats and cheeses from the deli and a few other perishables, like half-and-half, yogurt, butter, and a well-wrapped package of red snapper fillets given to her that morning by a neighbor at the marina. She also kept a supply of her sole vice: whole roasted Guatemalan coffee beans costing sixteen dollars an ounce. Serving in the navy had spoiled her for civilian coffee. She deemed these beans an adequate substitute.

"What's on the menu?" asked Rue, walking into the mid-galley and rubbing her wet hair with a towel. She had changed from her soiled business suit to a boatnecked shirt and navy blue shorts that showcased her legs. Unlike many redheads, her skin tone was warm rather than pasty, hinting at gold. Her bare feet made no sound on the deck.

Meredith caught herself staring at the elegant turn of Rue's calf and cleared her throat. "Sandwiches, right? I've got turkey, ham, pastrami, cappicola, soppressata, roast beef, provolone, Swiss, pepper jack, Havarti—"

"Sorry I asked!" Rue laughed. "Everything sounds good. I'm not a picky eater. Is there a place outside we can sit? The sun's gone down a little, it's not so bright now."

"Sure, there's a seating area just behind here in the stern. I'll make dinner and bring it through. Want something to drink?"

"I'm good."

Meredith quickly built a couple of turkey and Swiss sandwiches on whole wheat bread with a smear of lemon mayonnaise. The sandwiches went on nonslip plates, along with a bright Florida orange each. She carried the plates out and handed one to Rue.

They ate in silence. When Meredith finished, she said, "I'm ready to listen if you're ready to talk." She didn't add that if Rue put her off one more time, she'd alter course and haul ass back to Miami. The threat was implied by her tone, she hoped.

Rue made a face, but nodded. "First thing is…well, I don't know quite how to put this so it won't sound too alarming."

Meredith leaned forward, her skin prickling despite the heat. "Go on. I can take it."

"You remember the explosion in the restaurant?"

"Yes."

"That wasn't an accident. Someone's trying to kill me."

CHAPTER FOUR

"Oh, really?" Meredith's skepticism bled into her question. Rue's eyes narrowed. "Yes, really." She sighed. "Look, it's kind of a long story."

"The sun's going down," Meredith said. "We've got all night. And we'll sit right here until you tell me the truth. Nothing but the truth, mind you. I have an excellent bullshit meter, Ms. Stanton. Keep pinging it and you won't like the consequences."

Rue glared and snapped, "I don't appreciate vague threats."

"Would you rather I be more explicit?"

"Go to hell."

Meredith waited.

Muttering under her breath about bullies, Rue finally sat back, crossed one leg over the other, and began peeling her orange. "You want to know what's going on. Okay, I'll tell you, but I'm not going to share the recovery fee with you, understand?"

"I'm not interested in your fee. Get on with it."

"I'm after a German U-boat."

Struck speechless, Meredith sat still and quiet while Rue continued peeling her orange. The strong citrus tang of the fruit almost overcame the sea's salty odor. "Did you say U-boat?" she finally asked in the vain hope she'd been mistaken.

"Yes."

"As in World War II German submarine?"

"Yes."

Meredith wearily rubbed her eyes. "Care to elaborate?" she asked. "Especially the part where this U-boat connects to people trying to kill you."

Rue tossed bits of peel over the side. "It's simple. I'm looking for a Type XXI *Elektroboot* built in 1944, and someone doesn't want me to find it. That's the truth, the whole truth, and nothing but the truth." She popped an orange segment into her mouth.

Meredith let her doubt show. "That's obfuscation at best."

"The truth is the truth." Rue shrugged. "Sorry. In my line of work, it pays to be discreet. I'm not used to explaining myself."

"I understand discretion," Meredith said, "but these people who want to stop you from finding the U-boat...they seem willing to set off an explosive device in a crowded restaurant because the intended target happened to be in the area. That's crazy. Who are they?"

Rue threw the rest of the orange overboard. "I don't know. I'm sorry for the people in the restaurant. Believe me, I had no idea the situation would escalate that much."

"But you were aware a threat existed."

"Yes and no. Ever since I took this assignment, I've gotten warned off by email, over the phone, even a letter, but nothing suggesting what happened today."

"You have no idea who might be targeting you?"

"I've thought about it. Look, I understand why another recovery specialist might try scaring me off. The estimated value of the cargo is more than twenty-five million and my fee is ten percent plus expenses. Still, a bomb goes way beyond business rivalry."

"Which is why you wanted to leave Miami in a hurry." Meredith considered the woman seated opposite her in a new light. Not quite the kind of fugitive she'd first suspected, but definitely on the run. "Tell me about your job. What's so special about the U-boat? Is that what your diving equipment is for? Why we're headed to Mexico?"

Rue winced, as if each question dealt her a blow. She rose from her seat and went to stand with her back against the rail, her arms crossed over her chest. "We're going to Los Dolores to pick up a lockbox. I need the scuba equipment to reach it."

"Why a lockbox? I thought you were after a submarine."

"Because I believe the box contains clues that will help me find the U-boat."

Meredith mouthed a startled obscenity. "You don't even know the U-boat's location? That sub could have been sunk by a torpedo, or scuttled after the war for all you know."

"No, U-3019 exists." The sun hovered just above the horizon behind Rue's head, the fading light veiling her face in shadow. Her rigid stance spoke eloquently of her certainty. "I've done my research. The sub's out there. I have to find it. Will you help me?"

"What's the U-boat's cargo? Is it worth your life?"

"Worth taking a calculated risk? Definitely."

"What about other people? Innocent bystanders?"

Rue didn't answer.

Suddenly needing a moment to herself, Meredith stood and paced to the helm station, glad when Rue didn't follow her. She stared blindly at the instrument panel, her fingers drumming on her thigh while she considered what she'd been told.

If she were a prudent woman, she'd turn *Lady Vic* around this minute and return to Miami. The tale of a lost U-boat worth $25 million sounded like fiction, yet every instinct she owned told her Rue was not lying. As for the U-boat, she knew many secrets lay deep in the ocean's belly, preserved by the dark and the cold.

She frowned, her thoughts going to the restaurant bomb. Whoever threatened Rue meant business. It had been years since she was an officer and a gentlewoman, so to speak, but she found it impossible to turn down someone in need. She decided to stick with Rue for the time being and see how matters unfolded. If at any point she determined the situation had become too hazardous, she would overrule Rue's protests and pull the plug.

Her mind made up, she returned to the stern seating area. Rue remained at the rail, but she had turned around to face the sea. When she heard Meredith approach, she glanced over her shoulder, an eyebrow raised in mute inquiry.

"I'm in," Meredith told her.

Rue's smile was blinding.

CHAPTER FIVE

"Don't break out the champagne yet," Meredith warned. "I still want the whole story."

"I can't give you the whole story, but I'll tell you what I know." Rue left the rail and took a seat, gesturing for Meredith to follow suit.

"The Nazis looted Europe," she said. "Millions of dollars in artworks and jewels, not to mention gold and silver, relics, other valuables. Some of the art ended up in museums or private collections after the war. It's not easy for survivors or their families to make a claim for their stolen property. A claim needs proof of ownership. Provenance is everything, and many times, ownership papers were lost or destroyed."

Meredith nodded. She'd studied World War II and Nazism during her military history classes at Annapolis. The information wasn't new to her.

Rue went on, "One of the men responsible for raids on Jewish families in Antwerp was Hugo Krause, a colonel in the Schutzstaffel—the SS. He primarily targeted diamond dealers.

It's been rumored Krause kept records on every raid he and his men committed, but his papers were never found. He fled Germany just before the end of the war, changed his name, and lived in a small fishing village in Mexico until his death in 1988."

"Los Dolores on Isla Azul," Meredith guessed.

"Correct."

"What's the connection between Krause and U-3019?"

"Ah, that's where the story gets interesting." Rue sat up straighter, her mismatched eyes shining with excitement. "One of the last raids performed by Krause was on the home of an Antwerp diamond dealer named Schilders who'd concealed some jewels and other goodies in a hidden room. Nobody knew about the room's existence except Schilders and his brother-in-law. Unfortunately for the family, the brother-in-law sold them out. Krause rounded up everybody, young and old, and shipped them off to Breendonk.

"The SS raiders took cut and uncut gems, some paintings, some heirloom silver pieces. For himself, Krause kept a necklace Schilders had been commissioned to make before war broke out in Europe. The necklace featured a rare, twenty-three carat, blood-red diamond with blue-white diamonds in a platinum setting."

"What about the U-boat?"

"I'm getting there. Toward 1945, Krause guessed which way the wind was blowing and wanted to get out of Germany. At his instigation, his nephew was given command of U-3019, an experimental *Elektroboot*, one of the last submarines to come off the factory line. Krause and his nephew loaded loot into the sub and headed for parts unknown."

"And this necklace is worth $25 million?"

"No, that's probably worth $8 to $12 million at auction, maybe more given the rarity of the center stone. The rest comes from a painting in Krause's personal collection—"

Meredith stopped listening to Rue. The wind had freshened, now blowing from the south-southeast. Night had fallen, but the sky had turned a strange, flat black without visible stars. While she watched, the moon disappeared behind racing clouds, reappeared, and was swallowed again. *Lady Vic* rocked a little as waves slapped the hull. On the horizon, she caught a flash and a thin, electric fork of lightning clawed down to illuminate the ocean.

She stood. "Rue, there's a storm coming," she interrupted. "Go below to the salon, the stateroom, and the head, make sure everything's secure. Nothing loose, okay?"

"A storm?" Rue shot to her feet. "Will we be okay?"

"*Lady Vic*'s built for heavy weather. You'll see."

Meredith went to the mid-galley and put everything away, giving their used dinner plates a quick wash and dry before returning them to their places in the cupboard. She considered brewing a pot of coffee and filling a thermos, but decided to wait.

After checking the National Weather Service broadcast, she decided the storm was likely a commonplace squall, nothing out of the ordinary for the time of year and the place, and put the engine in neutral. She went out to the stern. The smell of ozone had grown stronger. She estimated the wind had sharpened to twenty knots. The waters around the boat were white-capped and choppy. As a precaution, she moved the seat cushions indoors.

"I'm done," Rue said, coming up from belowdecks to stand next to the dinette. "Anything else?" She appeared nervous.

"We'll heave-to and ride out the storm. Do you have any medicine for seasickness?"

"Oh, God."

"Just in case, I have transdermal patches in the first aid kit."

A few scattered raindrops pattered on the windshield; the next second, the squall hit.

The boat pivoted until it lay ahull and began rolling back and forth, buffeted by wind and a churning sea. Rue let out a squeak and sat down abruptly. Chuckling under her breath, Meredith took the necessary steps to pay out the sea anchor on a hundred-foot line.

The effect was immediate. When *Lady Vic* fetched up on the line, the bow swung into the wind, the pitching motion calmed, and she rode the peaks and troughs of waves as neatly as Meredith had ever seen. She blinked rain out of her eyes, grinning.

She visited the head belowdecks and dried her short hair with a towel before joining Rue in the salon. To her relief, the woman didn't appear seasick. "You holding up?"

Rue glanced at her. "This isn't too bad. It's actually kind of pleasant."

Meredith stepped up the ladder to the mid-galley. Time for the coffee she'd promised herself. Rue followed.

"Wait until you get hammered by a strong gale." Meredith put the water on to heat and began grinding coffee beans. "Heavy swells, high waves, cross seas, wind gusts to fifty knots. I've had rain blowing horizontally in my face. Lightning strikes a few feet away."

"Dangerous."

"So's driving a car," Meredith pointed out, putting several tablespoons of freshly ground coffee in the bottom of a French press pot. "You need to know what you're doing, sure. Obey safety precautions. Be ready for anything. But it's beautiful, Rue. Alone in a boat with nothing but the stars above you and the sea rocking you to sleep."

Rue made a noncommittal noise. "That's how I feel when I'm hunting a piece of art," she confessed. "Alive and ready for anything."

Meredith added hot water to the pot. A glance toward the bow showed the squall was already abating. "Even when people try to blow you up?"

"I've been beat up, shot at, stabbed, run over by a car, knocked down the stairs twice, and nearly flattened by a wrecking ball." Rue absently brushed her fingertips over her cheekbone. For a moment, she stared at nothing. She rallied herself. "Recovering stolen art is a tad more unhealthy than, say, wrestling alligators, but there are perks to the job. For one, I get to travel a lot. I have more frequent flyer miles than the Pope." Her smile seemed brittle. "But most of the time, I'm stuck in dusty old archives chasing a paper trail."

"Ten percent terror, ninety percent boredom. Sounds familiar. Hey, I was thinking..." Meredith plunged the filter straight down, freeing the coffee from grounds. Taking a mug out of the cupboard, she filled it. Rue refused her offer with a shake of her head. She went on, "You take the stateroom tonight. I'll sack out on the settee."

"No, I can't take your bed. It's not right," Rue protested.

"I have to keep an eye on the boat," Meredith assured her. "I'm used to napping. You should try to get a good night's sleep. We'll be in Cancún tomorrow morning."

"Only if you're sure."

"I'm positive."

"Okay, I'll see you in the morning. Good night." Rue went belowdecks.

Meredith sipped her coffee. Perfect.

As soon as the storm ended, she finished the mug standing at the rail on the stern deck, watching the night sky clear and the bright pinpricks of stars return. She went to raise the sea anchor, wondering how to reconcile her initial impression of Rue as a vain, superficial woman with the warm-blooded reality.

CHAPTER SIX

"Do we really need to put in at Cancún?" Rue asked the next morning.

"I have to visit the Port Captain for clearance, we both require tourist cards from Immigration, and I'll need an import permit from Customs." Meredith shifted the wheel between her hands, altering *Lady Vic*'s course around a shrimp boat with its nets out. Seagulls dipped and wheeled around the vessel, flashes of white feathers against the blueness of sky and sea. "The whole shebang can take a while."

"I mean, can't we just skip all that business and go straight to Isla Azul?"

"Only if you want to be arrested for entering the country illegally. What's the hurry? We can be at Los Dolores tomorrow morning."

Rue grimaced. "I hate bureaucracy."

"Understandable." Meredith resumed the boat's original course toward the marina. "We'll get there. Don't worry. Just have your passport ready."

An awkward silence descended.

A feeling of foreboding swept over Meredith. She turned her gaze on Rue, who flushed. "Before we left Miami, you told me you had a passport."

"Well, I didn't exactly have time to pack the essentials, did I?" Rue swept a hand at her clothing, the same scoop-neck shirt and shorts she'd worn last night.

"I saw you bring a suitcase on board."

"My suitcase contains reference materials crucial to my search. There wasn't room for much else. This is my only outfit and my last clean pair of underwear."

"And no passport. Jesus Christ!" Meredith muttered. She continued guiding *Lady Vic* to the marina, avoiding a panga fishing boat cutting across her ship's bow. "Here's what we're going to do. I'll rent a slip and make arrangements for fuel, then we'll head to the market and buy you some kit. Do you need a loan?"

From the rear pocket of her shorts, Rue produced a platinum credit card.

Meredith whistled. "I didn't take you for an heiress."

"Did I mention expenses?" Rue waggled the card. "This little baby draws on one of my client's corporate accounts. I'm authorized to spend up to a quarter million dollars if necessary. More than that, I need to call for permission first."

"Who's your client, Donald Trump?"

"Hardly. Let's just say my client is richer, better mannered, and has more hair."

Meredith spent the next several minutes navigating *Lady Vic* to the marina's fuel dock. "Go below and hang tight," she said, plucking the credit card out of Rue's hand. She grabbed her licenses and papers, and hopped off the boat to enter the marina office.

The young man behind the counter brightened at the sight of platinum. In practically no time, Meredith put down a $500 deposit, arranged for fuel, sorted out her vessel's entry requirements, and refused a number of offers including free bait, laundry service, bicycle or car rental, taxi, ice, beverages, and a baggie of marijuana the young man produced discreetly, and at her refusal, whisked out of sight as if by magic.

She asked for and received a slip assignment at the outer edge of the marina, away from the office—a necessity since she made no mention of having a passenger aboard. When she exited, she saw an employee already topping up *Lady Vic*'s tank with diesel.

Impressed by the service and speed—no doubt lubricated by the implied promise of a rich American skipper with money to spend—Meredith returned to the *Lady Vic*. As soon as the fuel tank was full, she quickly moved the boat to the assigned slip.

Rue came up the ladder from below and joined her at the helm station.

"Keep that safe," Meredith said, handing her the credit card. "If you buy at the market or in small shops, better pay in cash. Credit card fraud is rampant."

"Grandmothers, eggs, the sucking thereof," Rue replied, sticking the card down the front of her shirt and, Meredith assumed, securing it inside her bra. She squirmed around as if having trouble, creating some interesting movements inside the garment.

Meredith realized she'd been staring at the swell of Rue's breasts beneath the clingy fabric. She felt her face grow hot. "Excuse me," she murmured, going to the stateroom for a baseball cap and a backpack. Behind her, she heard Rue chuckling, and blushed hotter.

Leaving the boat, she and Rue walked to a nearby bank to exchange money and afterward caught a bus to Mercado 23, a scruffy, open-air local market located across the street from the main bus terminal. Vendors hawked fresh fruits and vegetables, dried and fresh herbs, beans and rice, meat, spices, street food, and stacks of tortillas. Little shops in the area sold everything from clothing and leather sandals to hammocks and piñatas.

Rue swept through the clothes shops like a whirlwind. She ended up purchasing a few inexpensive shirts and a wraparound denim skirt prettily embroidered around the hem.

"I still need a bathing suit. And underwear. And other stuff," Rue reported.

Meredith paused in bargaining for corn tortillas still warm from the grill. "That's okay," she said, turning to Rue. "There's a big mall, Plaza Caracol, over by the convention center." She wiped the sweat from her forehead with the back of her hand. "I hear they've got air-conditioning." Paying the stallholder for the tortillas, she put them in her backpack to join the fresh pineapple, chili peppers, cilantro, and other items she'd already purchased.

Flagging a taxicab in the street took mere moments. Getting the driver to turn down the Mexican ska music blasting from the radio seemed to take forever, but the ride to the convention center actually lasted only twenty minutes.

Inside the mall, Rue gravitated immediately toward Benetton, where she unleashed the power of her platinum credit card on casual clothes, mostly jeans, shorts and T-shirts.

Meredith found herself carrying more and more shopping bags as they made their way from shop to shop. "I didn't sign up to be your rented mule," she groused.

"Hush," Rue said, drifting toward a beachwear store with an avaricious gleam in her mismatched eyes. "I'll buy you an ice cream later."

Meredith refused to let Rue purchase another item. "At this rate, *Lady Vic* will founder," she said firmly. "Let's go. You've given that card enough of a workout."

"But I still owe you an ice cream," Rue said.

"What I need is a drink," Meredith groaned, but she allowed Rue to pull her along to the second floor and the Häagen-Dazs shop.

Before she and Rue reached the counter, a thin man wearing sunglasses approached them. Colorful tattoos covered his neck to the underside of his chin. Meredith noticed he kept his right hand in the pocket of his hoodie.

"You come with me," he said in an undertone. From his pocket, he flashed a glimpse of a Colt .45 snub-nosed revolver, and slipped the gun back into its hiding place. He jerked his chin to the right, clearly expecting them to obey.

The US Navy trains its officers to keep a cool head in emergencies. Meredith didn't hesitate. She swung the heavy shopping bags at his head and his hand. The bags connected solidly, knocking him off balance. The gun fell from his grasp and spun across the tiles.

"Run!" she shouted to Rue, grateful when the woman obeyed by dashing to the escalator a heartbeat behind her.

Once on the ground floor, she spotted two more men in hoodies lurking near the main entrance. She had no idea if they were connected to the armed man upstairs. A glance to the left showed uniformed security guards approaching. They didn't appear to be in a hurry.

Rue tugged on her shirtsleeve and nodded in a direction away from the waiting thugs.

Walking as fast as she dared without calling further attention to herself, Meredith moved to the exit. To her mild surprise, she hadn't dropped any shopping bags.

"If you lose my new clothes," Rue said in an urgent tone, "I'll kill you."

"Those guys back there may save you the trouble," Meredith retorted.

The exit was locked, damn it. Feeling trapped, she searched for another way out. The mall was crowded with people, a likely mix of tourists and locals milling around, chatting, eating, shopping, admiring the art, and talking or texting on their cell phones. Suddenly, like a gift from heaven, across the space she saw the white and red glow of a sign: *Salida*.

"Come on," she said to Rue, steering her in the direction of the newly discovered exit.

Her pulse jumped. Freedom was close, if only they could avoid getting shot.

CHAPTER SEVEN

After glimpsing a man in a hoodie close by—too close for her comfort—Meredith pushed Rue ahead of her and quickened her steps. Something of her urgency must have communicated to the crowd since people jumped out of her path.

Rue banged through the door first. Meredith stuck close. The instant she was clear of the mall, she glanced around the sunny parking lot. A couple of buses zoomed past them, belching exhaust. A taxi idled nearby, the driver watching a man struggle to remove a foldable baby carriage from the backseat while juggling a wailing infant on his hip.

Aware that any moment, gun-toting assailants might burst through the door, Meredith shoved the shopping bags into Rue's arms, stepped over, and after a few words with the sweating man, removed the carriage and unfolded it. He babbled grateful Spanish at her. In the meantime, Rue got into the back of the taxi, spreading her bags over the seat beside her.

The driver impatiently gunned the engine. Meredith waved away the father's gratitude and hopped into the passenger seat. She barely had time to close the door before the taxi shot through the parking lot to the palm-lined street and careened into traffic.

Heavy metal blared from the radio, the powerful, guitar-rich music banging inside Meredith's head like a hammer. Glancing at the driver, she noticed he seemed young, maybe eighteen or nineteen years old. His fingers were covered in black ink. The Aztec designs continued scrolling up his hands and wrists until the markings disappeared under the sleeves of his tracksuit jacket. A teardrop tattoo marked the corner of his eye.

Her gaze dropped lower, to the TEC-9 machine pistol cradled in his lap. *Aw, hell.* She looked out the windshield. The taxi wasn't headed toward the marina, but deeper into the city. Her heart thumped. She turned her gaze back to the driver.

He grinned.

In a split second, the scene inside the mall ran through her head. Their pursuers had herded her and Rue to that particular exit. The man and the baby might be part of the setup. The driver was definitely in on the plot. Was this connected to the threat against Rue?

Her adrenal response kicked up a couple of notches, clearing her head of everything except a single survival imperative: remove the threat.

She snatched at the TEC-9's grip. The driver uttered a startled oath. The taxi skidded into the next lane to a chorus of honking horns. He took hold of the pistol with one hand, trying to wrench it out of her grasp while steering the taxi around a pickup truck stalled in their lane. The struggle continued until she braced her foot against the dashboard and used the leverage to tear the weapon out of his clutching fingers.

"La Sirena Marina," she ordered, pointing the muzzle at him. When he gave her a sidelong glare, she thumbed off the safety and pulled the bolt back to chamber a round. With her other hand, she turned off the radio. She repeated her demand.

"What the hell, Meredith?" Rue cried from the backseat. "What's wrong?"

"We're going to the boat right now," Meredith replied, not taking her eyes off the driver. "Everything's under control—"

The driver stomped on the brakes and jerked the wheel to the side. The taxi slewed around violently.

Meredith was thrown hard against the door, cracking her head on the window and biting the inside of her cheek. Scarlet light exploded in her vision. The world faded to squealing tires and the stink of scorched rubber.

When the taxi came to a shuddering halt, she found the driver pointing the TEC-9 at her. Metallic-tasting saliva filled her mouth. The arm she'd bruised earlier throbbed. Over the ticking of the engine, she heard Rue's indrawn breath.

Meredith read the driver's murderous intent, prompting her to reach out and slap the gun's muzzle upward just as his finger tightened on the trigger. A burst of deafening, semiautomatic gunfire stitched the taxi's roof.

Rue's shout filled the cab. She threw herself forward, almost sliding over the back of the car seat. Her fingernails raked across the driver's face. He fell back, bleeding and cursing.

Meredith yanked the pistol from him, not caring about the muffled pop of his trigger finger dislocating. Meeting his furious gaze coolly, she pointed the TEC-9 at him. "Looks like it's déjà vu all over again," she said, freeing a hand to help Rue return to the backseat. "I won't tell you again. La Sirena Marina or I'll put a bullet in your head and drive myself."

To her relief, he seemed cowed, if smoldering with resentment. Rue had clawed him like an angry cat, leaving his face marred with four livid, bloody scratches from his eyebrows to his mouth. He tried to cover his hatred behind indifference. The attempt failed. Starting the engine, he pulled the taxi sedately into traffic and turned in the direction of the marina.

"You okay?" Meredith asked Rue, who snorted.

"My manicure will never be the same, but I'm fine."

Meredith risked a glance behind her. Rue looked pale except for twin spots of hectic color burning high on her cheeks. Sweat dotted her brow. She trembled slightly.

Shock. Nothing she could do about it except give some advice. "If you feel faint, put your head down between your knees and breathe."

Rue scowled. "Like I said, I'm fine."

The drive to the marina was accomplished in silence. When they arrived, Meredith eyed the driver, wondering what to do with him. He kept his hands on the steering wheel, but as the moments ticked by, she knew he wouldn't remain compliant for long. Taking him on the boat wasn't an option. Neither was leaving him there. What if he had other weapons inside the cab? What if he ran his vehicle into *Lady Vic* before the boat cleared the dock?

She heard the rustling of a paper bag. Something blue flew over the back of the seat to land in her lap. A dainty pair of ladies panties, as it turned out.

"Think you could manage with those?" Rue asked. "I'm fresh out of handcuffs."

With grave misgivings, Meredith handed the TEC-9 to Rue, who held it at arm's length but at least kept her finger off the trigger. She knotted the panties around the driver's wrists and asked for a second pair to lash his wrists to the steering wheel.

"Damn it, I really liked those," Rue complained. "Next time, use your own." She returned the TEC-9, collected the shopping bags, and managed to maneuver out of the taxi without dropping anything. She stood on the dock, waiting.

Meredith poked the driver with the pistol. "Who hired you?" She repeated the question in Spanish. He shook his head mulishly, his mouth drawn into a tight line.

She reconsidered taking him on board *Lady Vic*. Perhaps in another atmosphere and with the proper threats, he might be more forthcoming. Finding the person behind the attacks on her and Rue had become a priority. However, she had neither the means nor the inclination to torture the truth out of him. She'd learned how to captain a ship, not interrogate suspects.

She tried once more. "Who's paying you? Tell me!"

He said nothing, merely stared at her and smirked, his dark eyes unfathomable.

Dissatisfied but unable to do anything about it, she left the taxi and walked down the dock toward the slip she'd rented. On the way, she tossed the TEC-9 into the water.

"Don't you want to keep that?" Rue asked, hurrying behind her. "I mean, what if we need a gun for self-defense?"

Meredith thought about the superior weapons she kept below in a gun locker. "Trust me, we don't need it." She led the way onto the boat.

As soon as Rue went belowdecks, she cast off and set *Lady Vic* on a course to take them out of Cancún harbor.

CHAPTER EIGHT

"Here." Rue pointed to a shopping bag on the dinette table. The other bags had vanished, presumably into the stateroom.

"What's that?" Meredith asked over her shoulder. She sat at the helm station where she'd been checking navigation charts for the local waters.

Rue beamed. "I bought you some shirts."

Meredith didn't know what to say. "Oh. Thanks. That's very, um, thoughtful." She swiveled back to the marine GPS and chart plotter. Something soft struck her in the back of the head. She spun around to see Rue shaking another cushion at her.

"Hey, I risked life and limb in that mall. The teenaged girls in Benetton's were vicious," Rue said. "I got so many pointed looks, I almost bled to death."

"Why were they giving you the stink eye?"

"To those girls, anyone over the age of thirty has one foot in the grave."

"And the other on a banana peel?" Meredith grinned. "What do they know? They're kids. Wait until they hit middle age and gravity starts to be their obsession."

"Damned straight," Rue replied, dropping the cushion on the settee. "Where are we?"

"We'll be at Isla Azul in about four hours. I was planning on anchoring in this cove just off the coast on the east side of the island." Meredith indicated a point on the chart plotter. "We'll have to walk about a quarter-mile to get to the village. Is that okay?"

"Fine by me, but the spot I want later is north of Los Dolores."

Meredith squinted at the screen. "You said north? There's nothing there."

"Oh, yes, there is. Know much about blue holes?" At Meredith's shrug, Rue came closer. She'd taken the time to freshen up and change into newly purchased clothes. By some miracle, the orange and red tie-dyed sundress she wore didn't clash with her dark auburn hair, which she'd fastened into a knot at the crown of her head. Curly tendrils had escaped the pins to stick to her sweat-dampened skin. "Blue holes are underwater sinkholes," she explained. "There's one in the Bahamas over six hundred feet deep. El Zacatón in northeastern Mexico is over a thousand feet deep. Well, there's a blue hole north of Los Dolores that hasn't been discovered by the diving and free diving communities yet. That's where we're going."

"Why?"

"I told you Hugo Krause kept very good records of the property he seized from Jewish diamond merchants in Antwerp. I have reason to believe I'll find at least some of those records in a lockbox at the bottom of our mystery blue hole."

Meredith asked her most burning question first. "How do you know?"

Rue seemed startled. "Beg pardon?"

"How do you know Krause's records are in a lockbox? For that matter, how do you know the box is in this blue hole you're talking about?" Meredith asked, pointing out the obvious flaws. "What draws you to this conclusion? Where's your evidence?"

"I'm not on trial here," Rue said flatly. "I don't have to convince a jury."

"No, but unless you can convince *me* the risk is worth the reward, you aren't diving anywhere." Meredith watched Rue's expression close off. The woman's mismatched eyes snapped with fury. "Before you have a tantrum," she added, "may I remind you if you're so sure of your facts, all you have to do is share them with me."

Rue inhaled deeply, opened her mouth, and said nothing. She turned on her heel and marched away, going down the ladder belowdecks. She reappeared several minutes later carrying a tablet PC and a couple of books, including the volume she'd been reading yesterday in the salon.

Meanwhile, Meredith moved to the mid-galley to begin preparing dinner: red snapper tacos with pineapple salsa. "I hope you're not expecting Wi-Fi onboard," she said, continuing to finely dice chunks of pineapple into squares. *Brunoise*, her chef on the *USS Prescott* had called the technique. She smiled to herself despite the pang the memory caused and returned her full attention to Rue, now perched in a helm seat.

"It's okay, I don't need an Internet connection." Rue tapped the tablet PC with her fingernail. "Our story begins with Hugo Krause, who, as we all know, was a horrible human being. I told you he escaped with a bunch of loot at the end of the war and ended his days living in Mexico under an assumed name, right?"

"My short-term memory's still pretty good for an old lady," Meredith said mildly.

"Don't sass me. You're the one who wanted to hear my reasons, so just listen," Rue grumbled. "Besides, you're not old." She stared at something on the tablet, grimaced, and swiped her finger across the surface. "Anyway, according to Krause's journal—"

Meredith paused the knife midchop. "You have his personal journal?"

"Right here." Rue patted the book she'd been reading. When she moved her hand, the tablet tilted, showing a solitaire game in progress on the screen. "Why are you frowning? Oh, I see. Yes, I like to play solitaire, it helps me think."

"If that's what does it for you…"

Rue gave her a heavy-lidded glance. Her voice dropped to a sultry purr. "Mer, honey, you have no idea what does it for me." Meredith chuckled and reached for a chili pepper. Rue couldn't be serious. "Quit flirting, you hussy. Go on with the story."

"As I was saying, according to his journal, Krause made arrangements in the event of his death to have a certain lockbox he'd carried with him from Germany dropped into the blue hole off Los Dolores. The locals call it *El Ojo de Dios*."

"God's Eye," Meredith translated. "Sounds like the plot of an Indiana Jones movie." Setting the finished salsa aside, she bent to open the refrigerator drawer located below the helm seat where Rue sat. Murmuring, "Excuse me," she reached for the drawer handle while trying not to bump her chin on Rue's knee.

Rue hiked up the sundress a bit and spread her legs apart so they dangled on either side of the drawer. "Go ahead," she drawled, a glint of challenge in her eyes.

After a moment's hesitation spent wondering if Rue really was flirting with her or just messing with her head, Meredith pulled open the drawer. A refreshing breath of coolness crept out, raising gooseflesh on her arms. As close as she was to Rue's legs, she couldn't help noticing how the smooth, sun-kissed skin drew taut at the first touch of cold air.

Pulling up the sundress left the long length of Rue's legs free, but shadowed the area between her thighs. Meredith tried not to look as she reached inside the drawer, tried not to stare under the dress, but her gaze was inexorably drawn to the shady, secret place and the dim white triangle of Rue's panties. She felt like a voyeur, a pervert, but the sight mesmerized her. She couldn't help imagining what lay beneath the lace and nylon. She turned her head a little, just a little, and sniffed the side of Rue's knee in what she hoped was a discreet manner. Rue smelled delicious, like sunlight and heat with a trace of lemongrass soap.

Her inner muscles clenched.

Rue's laughing voice came from above her. "Are you going to leave the drawer open all day? Feels good." She made an obvious full-body shiver.

Snatching at the package of snapper fillets, Meredith almost slammed the drawer closed in her haste to get out of temptation's way.

CHAPTER NINE

Meredith spent several moments regaining her composure before saying, "You were telling me about Krause." Her voice didn't shake, which was good since her insides probably registered 7.5 on the Richter scale. She shook off the surge of lust heating her blood and concentrated on making dinner. Whether Rue had been flirting with her or not wasn't the point. She had to exercise better self-control.

"Right." Rue cleared her throat. "If the lockbox is in God's Eye, and I don't suppose Krause would have reason to lie in his private journal, then I'm going down there to get it."

Meredith began cooking the snapper in a grill pan while warming the corn tortillas in the toaster oven. She added chopped cilantro to yogurt, thinly shaved half a head of iceberg lettuce, cut a lime into wedges, and opened a bottle of chilled sauvignon blanc. She surveyed the components, ticking off a mental checklist, and turned off the flame under the fish.

"Do you want to eat at the dinette or outside?" she asked.

"I guess in here is fine," Rue replied, sliding off the helm seat. After depositing the books and tablet PC on the dinette table, she returned to collect the wine and wineglasses while Meredith assembled fish tacos on two plates.

"How'd you get hold of Krause's journal?" she asked, bringing dinner to the table and taking a seat.

Rue poured the wine. "I make a lot of contacts in my work. One is a former Mossad agent living in New York. When I told him about the Krause assignment, he sent me the journal. Seems a Nazi hunter almost caught Krause back in '68 during the Summer Olympics in Mexico City. Somehow Krause got wind of the operation and skipped town. He had to leave in a hurry though. The journal was found in an abandoned suitcase in his hotel room."

"Wait a second," Meredith said, holding a taco poised halfway to her mouth. "If Krause hasn't updated the journal since 1968, how do you know his instructions about the lockbox were followed? For that matter, how do you know the journal is genuine?"

"I don't know anything for certain. I'll only find out the truth when I dive into God's Eye. If I don't find the lockbox, then Krause lied and I'm a gullible idiot. But if I do find it, the records inside that box will get me a step closer to U-3019."

"Speaking of the U-boat, if Krause and his nephew left Germany together, how'd Krause end up in Mexico and his nephew and the sub nowhere in sight?"

"I don't know." Rue took a bite of taco, chewed, and swallowed. She followed with a mouthful of white wine. "Wow, that's seriously good."

"Thanks." Meredith finished her meal, satisfied her cooking lessons hadn't been a complete waste of time. Rue's obvious pleasure in the food woke an answering happiness in her, a glow of satisfaction she rarely felt these days.

"If nothing else, whoever's after me clearly believes the lockbox exists," Rue said after a while, returning to the previous topic. "Otherwise, why bother?"

Picking up her wineglass, Meredith took a sip of the sauvignon blanc. Cool, fruity, not too dry. Delicious. "If they know the lockbox is in the blue hole, why haven't they gone after it themselves?"

"No idea." Rue shrugged.

Meredith considered the matter. She'd always had a knack for problem-solving, one of her strengths as a naval officer. "When did the threats begin?"

"About a month after I accepted the assignment, I got a letter in the mail. An actual letter, can you believe it? Posted from London, England. Before you ask, it was typewritten, no signature, no return address. Basically, I was told to drop the investigation or else."

"Or else what?"

"I don't know. Nothing like unspoken, open-ended threats to raise a girl's hair, but I have six brothers. I'm not easily intimidated. I figured the letter was probably a competitor trying to scare me off. It's been known to happen."

"And after that?"

"A couple of phone calls, a close call with a hit-and-run driver, an email. The most serious attempt was the restaurant bomb in Miami. If we hadn't been sitting on the terrace…"

Meredith nodded and drained her glass. She refused a refill. "What about—"

"Know what?" Rue interrupted. "I'm tired of answering questions. How about you answer one for a change: how long till we reach God's Eye?"

"A few hours," Meredith said after checking her watch. "You in a hurry?"

"No. Yes. Damn it, I want to get the dive over before the sun goes down."

"We may have to wait until tomorrow."

Without another word, Rue stood, tossed her napkin on the table, gathered her tablet and books, and vanished belowdecks.

After cleaning the kitchen and putting everything in order, Meredith joined her.

"Do you read German?" Rue asked abruptly when she came into the salon.

"No." Meredith sat on the other end of the settee. "Why?"

"Because I wish you could read Krause's own words. This is not the journal of a haunted man. He sounds confident, unashamed, and doesn't mince words. It's clear he never intended the journal to be read by anyone other than himself." Rue thumbed through the pages. "Like right here, an entry from early 1939 when he criticizes Hitler's decision to invade Poland. Later, he has some cutting things to say about Germany's failure to capture the Allied army at Dunkirk. I could go on, but you get the idea. This book's filled with treason. Any one of these comments could have gotten him court-martialed and shot."

"So?"

"So if he planted the journal as a red herring to draw away the Mossad, why'd he mention God's Eye in later passages? Why'd he mention Los Dolores at all? Why not just say he was living the good life in Brazil or anywhere else in the world?"

"I get your point." Meredith frowned. "Why didn't the Nazi hunters grab him in Los Dolores if they knew where he lived?"

"Ah, because he didn't name the village outright. There's a kind of code here—not an actual code, but you have to read between the lines."

"Still, wouldn't the Israelis have figured it out?"

"Maybe they did. Maybe they didn't. Would you go poking around in Mossad business? Not me. I have a healthy regard for my own skin, thank you very much."

"Okay, okay, next question: if Krause didn't get a chance to update the journal once he lost it in '68, is the information still accurate?"

"He died in Los Dolores. I'm assuming he kept his lockbox where he lived and it was disposed of as he planned. Like I told you before," Rue said, closing the journal, "I'll only find out by diving the blue hole. If the box isn't there, I'll know the journal's a dead end."

Meredith had been thinking about Rue's proposed dive while she cleaned the kitchen. "There may be another way."

"If you're going to try the tyrant act and forbid me to make the dive, forget about it." Rue shook her head. "You're not my mother."

"No, I was thinking of something else." Feeling slightly devilish, Meredith paused until Rue squawked with impatience. Relenting, she went on, "Krause lived in Los Dolores for years. He died there. Surely somebody from the village or the island would have had to row a boat to God's Eye and dump the box after his funeral."

Rue's mouth formed an O of astonishment.

"Just talk to the villagers," Meredith added smugly, "and I'll bet you find out whether Krause's lockbox exists or not."

CHAPTER TEN

With Rue seated in the bow, Meredith rowed the dinghy toward the beach. *Lady Vic* lay anchored behind them in the cove she had chosen, a well-protected and calm spot with very few wave reflections from reefs or rocks colliding with the oncoming swells.

The sea was a clear, sparkling turquoise, almost lighter than the sky. Definitely lighter than Rue's steel-blue left eye, she thought. The brown right eye had no comparison here, unless she counted the color of the feathers on the pelican bobbing on the waves nearby. She found Rue's heterochromia an intriguing imperfection and somewhat endearing.

Meredith worked the oars, her arms aching and shoulders protesting, until she felt the dinghy's keel bite sand. "Here we go," she said to Rue. She jumped over the gunwale and landed with a splash in knee-high water.

Rue followed her lead, clearly intending to help.

"It's okay. Head to the island, you can pull the dinghy from there," Meredith said.

A wave slapped her on the back, wetting her shirt to the neck. The tide was coming in.

Rue waded to the beach, but Meredith didn't wait. She gave a mighty heave, sending the dinghy sliding through the water, over the white sand to the shore. The effort made her gasp out a curse. Her fatigue reminded her she wasn't in peak condition. Setting her jaw and her footing, she heaved a second time, pushing the dinghy further onto the beach and above the high-water line. She had no desire to swim to *Lady Vic* if the incoming tide sucked the little boat out to sea.

"Hey, I wanted to help," Rue complained. A freshening breeze caught the brim of her floppy straw hat. She slapped a hand on the crown to hold it in place. The bottom half of her sundress was wet and clung to her legs.

"I'll remember you said that when it comes time to row back," Meredith said, stripping off her red sleeveless shirt and wringing seawater out before pulling the garment over her head. She'd worn a pair of khaki Bermuda shorts that would dry quickly in the heat. Reaching into the dinghy, she removed her tennis shoes and slipped them on her bare feet.

Rue let out a shrill wolf whistle. "Looking good, Mer."

Meredith followed the line of Rue's gaze and found herself staring at her own chest, at her firm breasts where they pushed against her shirt's damp fabric. She'd worn a threadbare sports bra, which did little to conceal her hardening nipples. "Oh, please, don't even go there," she scoffed. "Nobody cares about that."

"I happen to enjoy *that*, as you put it," Rue told her pertly. Her wink seemed exaggerated, as did her leer. She dropped the act when Meredith scowled. "Where's the village?" she asked.

"A quarter-mile west."

"*Vamanos chica.*" Rue led the way.

Meredith remained content to let the woman pace ahead. On the short walk, she had time to admire the landscape. Isla Azul was a picture of tropical perfection, a paradise of palms, lime trees, banana and papaya trees, and dense vegetation in a hundred shades of green made more brilliant by flocks of wild parakeets. She was surprised by the island's apparently pristine state. Let the tourism companies and investors get wind of an untouched jewel in the Caribbean and there'd be hotels and time-share condos spoiling the beaches in no time. She thought of the hokey souvenir shops in Cancún with a shudder and walked on.

The fishing village of Los Dolores appeared typical of its type: a collection of well-kept whitewashed houses, a church, dogs and children playing in the shallows, boats drawn up on a broad beach, fishermen smoking cigarettes and mending nets, women hanging out laundry. If any of the citizens had money, they kept their wealth to themselves.

Meredith stopped to greet a wide-eyed, curious boy, about eight or nine years old, who ran up to her. In Spanish, she asked him about the church, thinking the local priest would have attended Krause in his dying moments.

Of course he could take her to the priest, the boy told her proudly. Padre Ignacio Velasquez was the finest priest on the island. The finest priest in Mexico! He would take her and the other lady to him at once. And did she know Padre Ignacio had served in Mexico City until criminals kidnapped him last year? Yes, that is what happened. Padre Ignacio's ransom had been twenty thousand *pesos*. He'd heard his grandmother talking about it. And when he grew up, he would go and shoot those criminals. Bang! Bang! Bang!

Meredith smiled and let the boy chatter while he led them to a small dwelling beside the church. A bench stood to one side of the door. On the bench sat a rail-thin man wearing a black shirt with a white clerical collar. He read the Bible, but glanced up at their approach.

Rue walked over to Padre Ignacio, offering him her hand. In halting Spanish she said, "We hope to find more information about a Señor Jerardo Guzman who lived here."

Meredith had been told Krause's alias on the boat. She waited for the priest's reaction. He didn't seem to recognize the name.

"Can you help us, Father?" Rue went on.

He shook his head. "I'm very sorry, miss, the señor must have died before my time," he wheezed. "I came here only last year, after the old priest passed away. I know very little except Señor Guzman lived for many years and died after a long illness." He crossed himself.

Seeing the pink healing scar slashing across his throat, Meredith understood the reason for his desire to exchange Mexico City for a sleepy fishing village.

"Does your church keep records?" Rue asked. "Or perhaps there's someone in the village who remembers him well."

The boy piped up, "Señora de Perez, she will know. She knows everything."

Padre Ignacio chuckled. "Go on, Jaime. Go help your father." When the boy sprinted away, he continued, "Señora de Perez is a widow, a very good and devout woman. She has lived in Los Dolores all her life and does much charitable work for the island's sick and elderly. Perhaps she can tell you more about the gentleman."

After thanking the priest and getting directions to the widow's house, Meredith and Rue went to visit Señora de Perez, a white-haired woman who appeared neither frail nor dim-witted. Rue explained why they had come to the island.

Señora de Perez regarded them with glittering eyes before stepping aside to allow them inside her home. "Yes, Señor Guzman, I remember him," she said, settling in a chair and picking up a smoldering cigar from a dish on a table at her elbow.

A small, wizened, hairy dog of unknown breeding made his creaky way onto Rue's knee and sat there, drooling and smelling fouler than the cigar.

After glancing at Rue's struggle to maintain a straight face, Meredith kept her amusement to herself.

"I was a girl when he came to the village," Señora de Perez said, puffing her cigar with obvious enjoyment. "It was after the war. He said he came from Spain, but his accent was terrible. My parents knew he lied, everyone knew, but they said nothing because he paid for their silence. I remember my mother bought for me a white dress with lace, and my brother a red bicycle. Guzman's money built the church and paid for the priest's house. He had masses said for men lost at sea. He was not a good man in his heart, but he did good works. And he had much trouble with his lungs, poor man, always coughing. His health was not good."

Meredith nodded. "Did Guzman live in the village?"

"Not until the last few months of his life. He built a house by the Playa del Beso, lived alone, kept to himself, never took a wife, and when he became too ill to stay there, he came here to my house. My children were grown, my dear husband gone to God, so I cared for him. He never went to church, but with the help of the Blessed Virgin and the saints, he made a confession to old Padre Alejandro before the end." She crossed herself.

Rue surreptitiously tried to shove the dog off her leg, but his guttural growl stilled her. "After Señor Guzman died, were his wishes carried out?" she asked.

Señora de Perez knocked ash off the end of her cigar and frowned. "*Sí, sí*, his body was taken to the mainland and cremated as he wished."

"That's not what I mean," Rue said. "Did he have a box in his house?"

"The señor had many boxes."

"A box with a lock on it."

The widow shrugged.

Meredith decided she'd better step in. "What happened to Guzman's ashes?"

Another shrug. "They were returned here. One of the men—Jesús Aguilar—rowed his ashes out to *El Ojo*, God rest his soul. It was his final request."

"Only his ashes?" Meredith persisted. "Nothing else?"

"Nothing else."

Meredith turned to Rue. "Dead end," she said, burning with disappointment despite her earlier doubts.

Before she could say more, Señora de Perez spoke up. "Guzman's ashes were put into a box from his house as he wanted," she said thoughtfully. "A box with a lock. And as I recall, it was full of a great many papers. Perhaps this is the box you mean?"

Rue's face shone with triumph.

CHAPTER ELEVEN

Rue was on fire to go to God's Eye immediately. She jiggled on the thwart like an excited toddler while Meredith rowed the dinghy to *Lady Vic*. "Oh, my God," she breathed. "It's so close. We're almost there."

"Yep, we'll be on the boat in no time," Meredith said blandly.

"I don't mean—oh, yes, very funny, I see what you did there. The lockbox! Of course, it has Krause's ashes in it, which is gross, but on the other hand, so was that woman's dog." Rue brushed at the drying drool on her sundress.

"There won't be any diving today. It's too late."

"Tomorrow, then. First thing."

Meredith made no reply, simply continued rowing to *Lady Vic*. She brought the dinghy behind the stern and hooked on to the stainless steel davit. Rue boarded the boat before her. Once aboard, she used an electric winch to haul the dinghy out of the water.

Everything secure, she went below to the salon where Rue still bubbled with enthusiasm. "I'm going to check my gear, if you don't mind—"

"Actually, I do." Meredith brushed off Rue's immediate objection and went on, "Sit down. We need to talk."

"But you heard the woman, Krause's lockbox exists. It's full of papers. It's in the blue hole. How much more evidence do you want?" Rue sat down on the settee, clearly upset.

"Listen to me. Even seasoned divers wouldn't go down there alone. You can't dive by yourself, Rue. Too dangerous."

"Well, I'm not letting anybody else do it."

"What if I go with you?" Meredith smiled at Rue's surprise. She'd considered the problem and come up with a solution. With any luck, Rue would accept. "I'm certified. And I have an old buddy who lives on Isla Mujeres nearby. Clay was in Navy Special Ops before he retired. I'm sure he'll let me borrow some scuba equipment."

"Isla Mujeres. Is that the island across the bay from Cancún?"

"That's the one. So it's settled. We'll dive God's Eye together."

Rue shook her head. "I'm sorry, Mer, I'm really sorry, but you can't—"

"You can't go alone," Meredith interrupted. "I suspected you weren't being entirely truthful with me. How deep do you plan on diving?"

"I don't know. As deep as it takes."

"And if God's Eye is a few hundred feet deep or more? What will you do then?"

"I'll think of something." Rue sounded equal parts confident and uncertain.

Meredith shook her head. "No, we'll plan our approach. Clay will help out. He's a good guy." She tried not to think about the last time she'd seen Master Chief Cochrane and the gut-wrenching disappointment in his expression when she'd resigned.

"I am not letting another person in on my assignment," Rue protested.

"You will if you want to continue."

"I'm paying you for your services. Or have you forgotten that fact?"

"Have you forgotten you don't have a passport? Good luck getting into the United States without papers," Meredith said calmly. She had no desire to stir up trouble, just a strong imperative to keep Rue safe, even from herself. "There's no need to tell Clay what we're after. He probably won't care anyway."

"Fine," Rue said grudgingly. "I'll think about it."

"Great. Let me know what you decide." Meredith knew she had won. She also knew better than to gloat. "How do you feel about a trip to Isla Mujeres tonight?"

Rue appeared to consider the idea. "All right, you get us there, and I'll shower and change since I don't have anything better to do." She paused. "Are you sure this Clay character will be okay with us dropping in on him unannounced?"

Meredith recalled the man she had known so many years. "He's sociable," she carefully answered. Not quite a lie either. Hopefully, Cochrane would be polite enough to hear what she had to say before throwing her out on her ass. "I'm sure he won't mind."

She waited until Rue left the salon before heading above decks to the helm station to plot a course to Isla Mujeres—the Island of Women.

The trip took a couple of hours. Meredith stayed at the wheel alone, drinking water with a splash of lime and privately reminiscing about Clay Cochrane and her navy days.

Finally, Isla Mujeres loomed nearer in the water, a long, green streak of land fringed in white sand beaches, dotted with buildings and hotels, and punctuated by a high rocky cliff— the Cliff of the Dawn with its Mayan ruins—on the island's southeastern end.

She guided *Lady Vic* through the harbor to the marina. The sun hovered on the horizon, a flaming copper ball painting the sky in dusky reds and purples. A ferry churned the gilt waters as it pulled away from the island, no doubt returning visitors across the bay to neighboring Cancún. She sighed. Although she and Cochrane hadn't parted on the best terms, he had been her friend once. For Rue's sake, she would try convincing him to help.

After renting a slip from the marina office and docking her boat, stern in on the chance they might have to make a quick getaway, Meredith went below to let Rue know they'd arrived at their destination. She found the woman in the stateroom, dimly lit by the cool, dying sunlight filtering through the ceiling hatch/skylight.

An obviously nude Rue lay sleeping on her side on top of the bedspread, her tousled auburn hair spilling across the pillow and over her bare shoulder. A spare white sheet covered just her torso, leaving her calves, thighs, and the bottom curve of her buttocks exposed.

Standing in the doorway with her tongue thick in her mouth, Meredith let her gaze linger on what seemed like acres of gold-tinted skin.

The sun dipped lower in the sky. Rue murmured and shifted, flexing her toes and curling further around the pillow. The sheet slipped off her breasts, giving Meredith a brief glimpse of a rosy nipple before Rue turned further onto her stomach.

Involuntarily, Meredith took a step into the stateroom and another to the queen-sized bed, stopping when her knees touched the mattress. Her heart fetched a heavy, thudding beat, stealing her breath. Desire tightened her throat. She wanted Rue. Without permission, her hand crept out. Her fingertips touched the fragile-seeming anklebone.

In the next second, she saw the scars. She froze.

Silvery scar tissue covered Rue's left knee. A further three inches of precise surgical scarring ran below and above the joint. Old, discolored, crinkly burn scars marred her hip and meandered down the side of her thigh, ending in small, scattered pale specks.

She became aware Rue was awake and gazing at her.

"Automobile accident," Rue said matter-of-factly, making no move to cover herself with the sheet. "Well, not really an accident. More of a hit-and-run. Thank God for airbags." She rolled over and sat up, dislodging Meredith's tentative touch. "But the car caught fire and the door was jammed. A good Samaritan pulled me out before I roasted alive. My knee got messed up and I had some burns. Since I wasn't wearing a seat belt at the time, my face became intimately acquainted with the steering wheel, requiring reconstructive surgery."

"Sorry." Meredith winced at how lame she sounded.

Rue didn't appear to notice. "In case you wonder why I wasn't wearing a seat belt, at the time I was trying to get away from some guys armed with machetes and a machine gun."

Meredith felt her eyes widen. "Jesus, your job really *is* dangerous."

"Oh, no, nothing to do with my profession. I just seduced the wrong girl, got caught *in flagrante*, and her family took exception." Rue's teeth gleamed in the graying twilight. "All those months of recovery? Totally worth it. She was hot."

"Well, try not to seduce the wrong girl on this trip," Meredith mock admonished with an answering grin.

"Mmm, how about the right girl…would that be okay?" Rue purred, sloe-eyed and kittenish. She hooked her toes in the sheet and pushed it further down. Her palms were planted flat on the bed. She arched her back to make her breasts stand proudly.

Meredith's desire resurged at Rue's clear invitation. She forgot about Isla Mujeres, Clay Cochrane, and everything else except the naked woman in her bed.

CHAPTER TWELVE

Meredith crawled onto the big bed, a sudden aching need between her legs.

Rue scooted up further until she lay propped on pillows, watching avidly. In the encroaching darkness, the difference between her eyes was erased. "You're wearing too many clothes." Her toes traced a line over Meredith's thigh, still clad in faded jeans.

"Don't care," Meredith muttered, but she knelt on the bedspread, pulled her T-shirt over her head, and flung it away. She moved to kneel at Rue's side.

Reaching out, Rue grabbed the back of Meredith's head and pulled her down for a kiss. She and Rue met with a shock of wet lips, and heat surged like ball lightning in her veins. She groaned when teeth lightly tested her lower lip, and opened her mouth to Rue's tongue, so sweet, so deliciously soft.

Meredith's face felt hot. The flush flowed down and down, through her neck, her chest, her rib cage, and lower still to pool molten in her belly. Breathless, she tore her mouth away only to artlessly kiss Rue again and again, unable to control her hunger. It had been too long since she'd allowed herself to feel this needy.

Greed overcame her. She gasped against Rue's cheekbone and somehow found air enough for another kiss before she had to stop, the pulse pounding in her head.

Rue's warm hand slid down her spine, coming to rest on her bra clasp. Clever fingers undid the hook-and-eye fastening. "You drive me crazy. Sit up a second," she said. When Meredith obeyed, Rue slid the bra straps down her arms, releasing her breasts. "Lovely."

Under the appreciative gaze, Meredith's nipples tightened. She leaned over to switch on a light, having no patience for fumbling in the dark.

Rue tugged at the waistband of her jeans. "Off!" she demanded.

Though she could hardly bear to leave, even for a moment, Meredith complied, getting out of bed to wriggle free of the garment and get rid of her panties at the same time.

"Wow, you're a real sailor, aren't you?" Rue asked, her admiration clear. Her fingernails lightly traced the half-sleeve tattoo covering Meredith's upper arm.

"I had it done after graduation from the Naval Academy," Meredith replied. The octopus with its oversized head and writhing tentacles made a splash of orange and red against the background of curling, blue waves inked into her skin.

Turning on her side, Rue pressed against Meredith, her body firm yet yielding. "God, yes, shut up already." Her voice sounded low, rough, and edged with need.

Meredith kissed Rue hard and deep, wringing a surprised whimper out of her. She had nothing else to say. She wanted to feel, not talk.

Rue melted under her touch, growing more pliant as Meredith kissed bruises into the smooth flesh, using her lips and tongue to soothe the sting of teeth. She traced patterns over the scars on Rue's hip and thigh, smiling when Rue sobbed and fisted the bedspread. She took her time learning the different textures of scarred and unscarred skin. Heat bloomed everywhere she touched Rue, soon turning into sweat and salt.

Lady Vic rocked in the wake of a larger boat passing by the slip. A muted roar from the engine outside penetrated the hull, growing louder and slowly ebbing into the distance. At last, the only sounds remaining in the stateroom were Rue's thready moans when Meredith finally slipped a finger through the dark red curls covering her sex.

Time stretched as if the world paused on its axis and held its breath.

Inside, Rue felt creamy, slick and startlingly hot. Meredith's mouth watered. She pushed her finger deeper into the heated passage, withdrew, and pushed inside again. Rue was silent, her body quivering with tension.

Meredith quickly established a rhythm and added a second finger when Rue tilted her hips. She bent forward to dip her tongue into the top of Rue's sex and stroke the swollen clitoris over and over. The taste of arousal excited her, tempting her to indulge. She slowed her movements, lapping slowly until Rue yanked on her hair. She glanced up to see Rue move her hands to her own breasts, plucking and pinching her nipples to little red points.

The sight made Meredith want to straddle Rue's leg and grind until she exploded, but she knew waiting would make the moment sweeter. She added a twist to each thrust into the burning heat, working as deeply as possible at every roll of Rue's pelvis.

"Right there," Rue panted. "Yes, like that, exactly like that."

A little gush of musky fluid flowed over Meredith's tongue when Rue's climax struck. Grunts and cries bounced off the bulkheads. Internal muscles clenched hard and fluttered against her fingers. She continued teasing Rue's clitoris until the spasms ceased.

Rue sank back on the pillows, her eyes glazed, sweaty tendrils of hair clinging to her face. In that moment, she resembled nothing so much as a smug and well-satisfied cat who had not only gotten the cream and the canary, but everything else it wanted too.

Meredith rested her forehead against Rue's thigh, her breathing harsh in her ears. Her hand was tacky and smelled like Rue. She lifted her fingers and licked them, enjoying the bittersweet traces of intimacy.

A hand touched her leg. She shifted to give Rue a kiss, fitting their mouths together perfectly. Strands of Rue's hair stuck to her sticky cheeks when she pulled back to stare into eyes that weren't matched in color, but held the same sharpening expression.

"Do you want me to touch you?" Rue asked. "Like this?"

Meredith's inner core pulsed when Rue's fingers found her sex and slid to her entrance, teasing before penetrating and rubbing her walls. She felt loose and open, but her clitoris had drawn tight in anticipation. Her thigh muscles bunched.

"God," she groaned, spreading her legs wider apart until she felt the burn. "That's it, baby. That's it. Come on...fuck!"

"I'm inside you, Mer," Rue crooned, her tongue flicking out to swipe across Meredith's lips. "I'm making you feel so good... now I want you to come for me. Can you do that? Can you come for me?"

Reaching down, Meredith pinched her clitoris. Her nerves sizzled. "Yes," she managed in a high, breathy whine.

Rue pumped her passion higher and higher while she rubbed her clitoris more frantically. She climbed closer to climax with every stroke. Hot and cold swept her body from head to toe. Her muscles clenched. She became distantly aware of Rue saying filthy things to her, promises of depravity making her hotter. She shouted and convulsed when the orgasm rolled over her in a wave of the purest, most satisfying pleasure she had ever known.

Sated and boneless, she fell to the bed to lie next to Rue, content just to breathe.

CHAPTER THIRTEEN

Clay Cochrane's flat, unreadable stare unnerved her.

Meredith had no problem admitting the fact to herself. After years of silence, she'd shown up at his house at nine o'clock at night with a strange woman in tow. Had he welcomed her with open arms and the metaphorical fatted calf, she'd have searched for a pod. But the way he stared at her, so cool and polite with about as much expression as a brick wall, made her wonder if she'd seriously overestimated their former friendship.

On a sofa, Rue stuck to her side, practically clinging despite the muggy heat.

"Let me get this straight," Cochrane said in a slow, deliberate fashion, which Meredith vividly remembered preceded one of his legendary dressing-downs. "You two ladies want to dive *El Ojo* over by Isla Azul."

"Yes," Meredith replied, bracing herself for verbal impact. She had once witnessed a crusty USMC gunny bursting into tears of joy on hearing Cochrane's creative invective.

"And you need to borrow scuba equipment."

"That's right."

"From me."

"Clay, do we really need to do this?"

"Of course we do."

"Carry on."

"You come here to my house asking for my help even though it's been...let's see...eight years since you walked out on me."

At the end of Rue's shocked gasp, Meredith said with a feeling of genuine relief mixed with exasperation, "You son of a bitch."

He wore an unrepentant, toothy grin.

Meredith felt the corners of her mouth twitch. "Rue, this amiable bastard is retired Master Chief Petty Officer Clay Cochrane. He may be a terrible practical joker, but I promise he doesn't bite."

"Only on invitation," Cochrane said, shaking Rue's hand and giving her a frankly appreciative look.

"Nice to meet you," Rue replied, not turning a hair.

"Clay, do you need a minute to empty your drool cup?" Meredith asked sarcastically. A possessive part of her leaped up snarling at his interest in Rue. She pushed the unwarranted jealousy aside and said, "Down, boy. The lady's spoken for."

"Sorry, didn't mean to poach." Cochrane shrugged and took a swig from a bottle of Mexican beer. "How the hell have you been, Captain?"

The title struck Meredith to the heart. She tried to cover her instinctive flinch by standing to give Cochrane a slap on the back. Her palm stung. The man was solid muscle and built like a tank despite passing his sixty-fifth birthday. In eight years, he'd gotten more silver in his black hair, more creases around his pale eyes, but he remained largely the same.

"Running charters out of Miami," she told him. "Eating a lot of peanut butter sandwiches."

He raised an eyebrow. "And is Ms...?"

"Rue Stanton," Rue supplied, right on cue.

Cochrane thanked her with a smile before returning to Meredith. "Is Ms. Stanton one of your charter customers, or are you lovebirds here on vacation?"

"Age has made you nosy, old man." She meant no offense.

He clearly took none. "Just sussing out the lay of the land, that's all." He stood and went to a small refrigerator in the corner of the room. "Beer? Bottled water? Or soda? I keep the sweet stuff around for the kids."

Rue shook her head.

Meredith hesitated—a cold beer sounded tempting—but finally refused. She sat back down next to Rue.

He returned to the other battered sofa and sank down on the colorful woven throws. "Well, that's about the extent of my hospitality at this time of night." He finished his beer in several swallows and set the empty bottle on the floor by his foot.

Meredith leaned forward, propping her elbows on her knees. "Kids? Did you get married, or are you living in sin?"

"Neither. I volunteer to teach diving classes to the local children." He eyed her and Rue. "Why *El Ojo*? Nobody dives that hole."

"Why not? It sounds like fun." Rue acted altogether too pert.

Meredith shot the woman a warning frown and a silent message: *don't overdo it.*

Cochrane fixed Meredith with a serious gaze and clasped his big, callused hands together. A bead of sweat rolled down the side of his lined face. "Getting a boat out to *El Ojo* is tricky. You've got shallow reefs and shoals for miles. No clear channel."

"*Lady Vic* has a tad less than a four-foot draft," Meredith said.

He thought a moment. "In some places, you'll have less than two feet of water under the keel," he said at last. "The hole is six hundred feet across and circled by a rim of coral. If there's a storm, you'll have a hell of a time navigating out, especially if you're in a hurry."

"My boat can handle it."

"Maybe, but can you?"

Meredith bristled. "What the hell do you mean, Cochrane?"

"I think we both know, Captain," he replied evenly. He turned to Rue. "She ever tell you why she got kicked out of the navy?"

"Clay!" Meredith gasped. She started to jump out of her chair. What she'd do when she got to her feet, she wasn't sure, except the need to silence him sent crazy ideas flitting through her brain, from physically gagging him, to bribery, to downright assault.

"Okay, I admit my statement wasn't quite accurate. See, she voluntarily resigned her commission." He sounded bitter. "Voluntarily, my ass. Best captain in the fleet let herself be bullied into running away like a goddamn coward."

Rue's restraining hand prevented Meredith's desperate lunge. "I want to hear this story," she said. "If you'd really rather I didn't, I'll leave."

Meredith slowly relaxed until her butt hit the sofa cushion. Forcing her racing heart to calm, she glanced at Rue, who watched her with a combination of curiosity and concern. Cochrane, on the other hand, looked as sternly judgmental as ever.

She took a deep breath and considered where to begin. "Fleet exercise," she said, deciding to keep her tale short, if not-so-sweet. "Sixteen of my people died."

"Oh, there's more to it than that," Cochrane said, grimly triumphant. "There's enough to fill a damned book," he went on to Rue. "First female captain of the USS *Prescott*. Brilliant military strategist. The Navy War College named the 'Reid maneuver' after her."

"Please, Clay. Please stop," Meredith choked around the constriction in her throat. She gripped the edge of the cushion so hard, her hands hurt.

Cochrane shook his head. "No, the truth has to be told. You didn't say a thing eight years ago, just packed up and took off. Now I'm going to have my say." He returned his attention to Rue. "During an exercise, there was an explosion in the Number Three gun turret. Sixteen crewmen died, another thirty-five were injured."

"What happened?" Rue asked.

"Officially, according to the navy, cause unknown. But not everybody agreed with the result of the investigation. There was a lot of hoo-ha with the Government Accountability Office, the House Armed Services Committee, the Senate, Congress... all those assholes were scared of political fallout and needed a scapegoat. The navy couldn't bump Captain Reid down a grade so they took her command and offered her a promotion to desk duty instead. She resigned rather than fight the sons of bitches." He looked disgusted.

Meredith closed her eyes. At that moment, she hated Clay Cochrane for dredging up the past. She'd worked hard to put the USS Prescott behind her, to create a new life separate from her old one, even when the smells of gunpowder and burning flesh haunted her dreams.

"It wasn't an accident," she said at last, opening her eyes. "I knew it when I felt the explosion. I knew who sabotaged the gun and I knew why, and when I made a statement during the NCIS investigation, the truth went over like a lead balloon."

"What truth?" Cochrane asked.

Meredith let the words tear out of her throat, clawing their way out of the darkness where she'd hidden them many long years ago. "I'm guilty. The explosion was my fault."

CHAPTER FOURTEEN

"What the hell?" Cochrane blurted, rearing back as if she'd slapped him. "You? Sabotage?" He rallied. "I don't believe it. Not for a second."

"Do you remember Lt. Maya Patel?" Meredith asked him.

"Cute little thing, decent officer, pretty good rep belowdecks, hell on heels if you crossed her," Cochrane said, blinking in confusion. "What's Patel got to do with it?"

"How about gunner's mate second class Sullivan Hayes? Don't glare at me, just answer the question, Clay."

"Yes, he was assigned to the Number Three turret. Hayes died in the explosion. So did Lt. Patel, for that matter."

Meredith hesitated.

"I remember reading about the explosion on the ship in *The Washington Post* at the time," Rue said, filling the gap in the conversation, "but I don't recall the details."

Meredith did. She hoped she wouldn't puke. Whoever said confession was good for the soul had neglected to mention how tough it was on the digestive system. "I'm sure you didn't know

Hayes became obsessed with Patel," she said to Cochrane. "Sent her explicit love notes, hung around her berth, ordered flowers sent to her whenever the ship was in port."

"Wait a minute. How come I never heard about any stalking?"

"Because Patel felt sorry for Hayes. He reminded her of her kid brother. She tried to let him down easy. But she got real tired, real fast when she found out he'd hacked into her email accounts. She came to me privately because she didn't want to make a formal complaint and be considered a whiner. She just wanted a transfer off the ship." Her head hurt. "I should have had more sense, Master Chief, but I let a pretty young woman persuade me not to open an investigation against my better judgment. So when the rejected, obsessed, and unstable gunner's mate Hayes found out about her upcoming transfer and decided to commit murder-suicide by overramming powder bags into the breech of the Number Three gun, the flareback took fifteen other people with him, including Patel, and injured other crewmen for life." She covered her face with her trembling hands. Christ.

"No way was that your fault," Rue said, touching her shoulder.

Meredith dropped her hands, needing to see Rue's face. She couldn't take pity, not from this woman, not now, but thankfully, all she read was worry.

"Everything on the *Prescott* happened on my watch. I was the captain," she stated bluntly. "I could have tried harder to talk Patel into filing those charges. I could've asked my XO to keep an eye on Hayes. With his problems, he was a security risk. Instead, I decided to deal with the matter later and did nothing while the clock ran out.

"Believe me, Patel wasn't cute after the explosion ripped her to pieces, Clay. I saw her body, and all the other bodies, and all the victims with blast injuries in sick bay, and all the wounded on cots crammed in the passageways…and the worst, the very worst, happened after the NCIS investigation ended. I couldn't believe the report didn't mention Hayes at least. They concluded the cause was undetermined. Nobody in the chain of command took my calls. Then Rear Admiral Bryant came to see me just ahead of the GAO. The man practically had 'cover-up' tattooed on his forehead. He ordered me not to leak a word to the press, keep my mouth shut, accept my promotion like a good sailor, and God bless the US Navy."

Cochrane growled deep in his throat.

She went on, "Turned out Hayes was a senator's nephew. Uncle Moneybags greased the way for Hayes since the family has an old navy tradition. The senator had a lot of juice in Washington and he leaned on the SecNav to bury the scandal. The promotion was supposed to be a reward, Clay. More pay, more perks, you know the score. And in return, all I had to do was lie by omission." She shook her head. "I resigned instead."

Silence.

At last, Rue spoke. "Are you culpable in the tragedy? Yes. You could have done something about Hayes before he blew up the turret. Are you solely responsible? No. Listen to me, Mer. People don't turn obsessive and suicidal out of nowhere. There were signs. Everybody in Hayes's life had a chance to send up a red flag over his behavior and didn't, including Lt. Patel. The burden of guilt isn't on your shoulders alone."

"Patel didn't take him seriously," Meredith said.

"She should have," Rue said darkly. "There've been enough stories in the media about women harassed and murdered by their stalkers. She should have taken action."

"She did, Rue. She told me." Meredith was tired of explaining herself. "I should have reported Hayes myself. Look, I'm done debating, and no, I'm not wallowing in guilt. Not anymore. I made my grand gesture and burnt my bridges by resigning. That was my decision. I don't regret it. What I do regret is my inaction led to loss of life. Period."

"But—"

"No more. We're done."

Rue subsided.

Cochrane stood, his expression solemn. "I consider you the most honorable person I've ever met in my life, ma'am, and also the most goddamn stubborn." He saluted her, his arm snapping up sharply, his rigid hand set at a precise angle to his brow.

Meredith did not let herself cry, but her eyes burned.

He relaxed. "Why'd you drop me like a hot potato, Reid? We were friends."

"Association with me would've tanked your career, and if I told you what happened and you punched the SecNav in the face, you'd have lost your pension too. Best to cut off everyone and disappear." She made a face. "No need to drag you down with me."

"Hey, I earned my living. I paid for my rank with sweat and blood. Not one of the brass did me any favors, so screw 'em. We're friends." Cochrane smiled. "Tomorrow, since you've got your heart set on it, us friends are diving *El Ojo* together."

Rue opened her mouth to speak, but Meredith broke in quickly. "That's nice of you, Clay, but not necessary. You've got your own job to do, I'm sure."

"Nah, it's fine." He waved a hand. "I'll get Jorge to tend the dive shop. He's better at dealing with the tourists than me anyway. Your boat or mine?"

Meredith gave up reasoning with him. Further protests would only fire his curiosity. "Preferably mine." She ignored Rue's hiss for attention. "Do you have a chart?"

He left the room, muttering under his breath.

"The more fuss we make, the more bullheaded he'll become," she said to Rue in an undertone, not sure how far Cochrane had gone. "It'll be okay."

Rue's mouth twisted into an unhappy line, but she made a short, sharp nod.

"It'll be okay," Meredith repeated, staring at Rue until the cold left her eyes.

"Just don't say anything about the box," Rue warned.

Meredith settled down to await Cochrane's return. She thought he'd done pretty well for himself after retirement. His house was a modest single-story in the Spanish style, but the Caribbean ocean sparkled just feet from his front yard. He owned a dive shop. She felt sorry they'd lost touch. She and Cochrane had been very close until the end.

Cochrane came into the room bearing a rolled-up chart. He seemed excited.

Meredith kept most of her mind on the chart while she and Cochrane plotted a course through the reefs and shoals, bantering back and forth as if the years hadn't interfered in their friendship. A smaller, darker part of her wondered if Rue would end their association as abruptly as she'd ended hers with Cochrane, and send her back to Miami, aching and alone.

Feeling Rue's gaze on the back of her neck, she tucked her misgivings away.

CHAPTER FIFTEEN

El Ojo de Dios—the Eye of God. Meredith shuffled through the pictures Rue had downloaded from the Internet and printed out at Cochrane's house last night.

The blue hole was an irregular circle punched out of the reef and rimmed in coral, the water in the basin a striking indigo much darker than the surrounding aquamarine lagoon. Eons ago, God's Eye had been a cave in the reef, but time and perhaps a geologic event had collapsed the ceiling, leaving behind a bluer-than-blue sinkhole deeper than the lagoon.

After studying the chart last night, she understood Cochrane's caution. The waters hereabouts were treacherous. Taking *Lady Vic* beyond the rim of God's Eye would require tricky navigation. The greatest dangers lay in holing the boat's hull on the coral formations jutting below the surface in the shallows or catching on a shoal, but Cochrane had volunteered to go ahead of *Lady Vic* in the dinghy to mark a safe channel with inflatable buoys.

She owed Cochrane a lot. Instead of rebuffing her as she'd half feared, he had lent her the necessary gear, inspected Rue's equipment, and made sure they had everything needed for the dive. A tension she hadn't known she'd been carrying had dissolved under the renewal of their friendship, providing a welcome breath of relief.

Rue emerged on the stern deck looking sleek and mouth-watering in a fuchsia bikini that flattered her curves. "Do I seriously have to wear a wetsuit?" she asked, gathering her auburn hair into a ponytail at the crown of her head.

"Blue holes sometimes contain layers of hydrogen sulfide. Do you want to be poisoned through your skin?" Meredith asked, trying to sound firm, but afraid her wide smile ruined the effect. "Besides, you're beautiful no matter what you wear."

"Flatterer." A light pink flush stained Rue's cheeks. She quickly fastened the ponytail with an elastic band and patted her hip. "Well, I hear black is slimming."

"As if you need to worry about that," Meredith scoffed.

Rue grinned. "Zing! You're really racking up the brownie points." She paused and turned serious. "Will we be able to reach the bottom?"

"Maybe, maybe not. I don't know how deep we'll have to go. But Rue, if we can't, if it's too dangerous, promise me you'll abort the dive."

"Damn it, Mer."

"Damn it, Rue, we are not going through with this dive if I have to worry I'll be bringing your corpse out of that cave."

"You know I'm not here to admire the scenery." Rue crossed her arms over her chest and lowered her voice. "If I don't have a chance to find the lockbox, what's the point of diving at all? If you're getting cold feet, just say so. You can stay on the boat."

Frustrated, Meredith tried to run a hand through her hair, but her fingers caught painfully on wind-tangled black curls. She blew out her breath, ran a litany of curses through her head, and finally addressed Rue with relative calm. "If either Clay or I orders you back to the boat, you go to the boat, understand? Or we'll drag you by the ankle. Not to thwart your ambition, honey, but to prevent your death. Why do you think I didn't want you to go alone?"

"It's just a hole, for Christ's sake."

"It's a sub-marine cave. Pieces of the walls in such caves have been known to fall off. Like I said, there could be layers of hydrogen sulfide. You might get lost or run out of air. Or bitten by a shark. Or suffer nitrogen narcosis. A thousand things can go wrong."

For the first time, Rue seemed less than confident. "I thought it was just a hole full of water. In and out like that." She snapped her fingers.

"No. What we want to do is somewhat more complicated." Meredith turned to speak to Cochrane, who sat on one of the helm seats checking the rubber seal on a dive mask. "Hey, how deep is God's Eye, any idea?"

"About a hundred and thirty feet in some places, but where we're going, about sixty feet or so," Cochrane answered. He regarded Rue with good humor. "There's no need for wetsuits. *El Ojo* is clean. Besides, it would be a criminal shame to cover up that tan."

"I thought nobody dived God's Eye," Rue said, her glance at Cochrane decidedly jaundiced. "Isn't it an undiscovered blue hole? That means we're the first, right?"

He chuckled. "Let's call it a well-kept secret by local divers like me. I hope things will stay that way, but with Mexico chasing American tourist dollars, *El Ojo* will become an attraction before too long, and then it's adiós to peace and quiet for Isla Azul."

Meredith wondered if she should tell Cochrane about the lockbox, but the barely contained disappointment on Rue's face changed her mind. She asked in her most casual tone, "Anybody find anything down there? I heard a couple of divers ran across a body in one of the Bahamas caves last year. Fossilized bird carcasses in another."

"I don't think so," he replied. "Nothing interesting, anyway."

"Daylight's burning, Master Chief," Meredith reminded him. "We going or not?" Out of the corner of her eye, she saw Rue relax.

Cochrane put the mask aside. "You lower the dinghy, I'll get the buoys from below," he said as he disappeared down the ladder.

Meredith took advantage of the opportunity to lean over and kiss Rue. The woman tasted like black coffee and the sweet rolls they'd eaten for breakfast, and smelled like sunshine and sunscreen. Her hands dragged over the skin at Rue's waist.

"Promise me," she said against the parted lips—a shared breath, she thought, warmer than the air. "If anything happened to you…" Her voice trailed off. She closed her eyes, rested her forehead against Rue's, and listened to the slap of waves on the ship's hull.

"I promise," Rue whispered, embracing her.

Their bodies fit together beautifully.

With great reluctance, Meredith broke away, releasing Rue when she heard Cochrane's tread on the ladder. She spent a few minutes lowering the dinghy with the electric winch, aware of Rue's stare like a hot brand between her shoulders. She forced herself to focus on the dive and not let her thoughts wander into lustful territory.

As Cochrane had told her, navigating the lagoon surrounding the blue hole was tricky. The depth varied from twenty-five feet to just five feet, but with his help she avoided steering the ship onto shoals or into any elkhorn or staghorn coral formations. Once past the shallowest part of the lagoon, she anchored *Lady Vic* close to the encircling reef.

Rue practically hung over the side gazing into the clear, crystalline water. "I see lots of fish," she reported with delight. "Even an angelfish. No sharks, though."

"Not yet," Cochrane said, coming aboard after securing the dinghy to *Lady Vic*'s stern. "The tourist boats around Belize usually chum to attract sharks, but you might see one or two cruising around here anyway. These are prime hunting grounds."

Meredith went below to put on her bathing suit, a bright turquoise one-piece. She didn't bother with sunscreen. An olive skin tone inherited from a Greek grandmother ensured sufficient melanin to make sunburn unlikely. Moving to the head, she ran a comb through her mop of wild curls, gave her armpits a sniff, and checked her reflection in the mirror.

She'd never really cared much about her appearance. Her body had always done what she required of it—that was good enough. But now she regarded herself with a more critical eye, taking in the imperfections like the ten pounds she'd put on in the last six months, the slightly sagging skin here and there, and the creases fanned at the corners of her eyes.

Rue didn't seem to have a problem with the way she looked, she reminded herself. Her skin was smooth and brown, her breasts still firm, and her crooked nose gave her character. Satisfied, she left the head and returned above decks to the stern.

Rue whistled when she appeared. "Hey, *mamacita*, the suit suits you."

Cochrane shrugged, but his glance sparkled with mischief. "I've seen her in a lot less, you know," he said slyly. "Remember the massage lady in the red-light district in Manila?"

"Dog that hatch under your nose, sailor," Meredith replied, ignoring the flush creeping up her neck. To Rue, she explained, "I had a stiff neck and he swore the woman was a nurse. Turned out 'massage' has a different meaning depending on context."

"That's okay. I'm just hoping he's got a Speedo." Rue jabbed her thumb at Cochrane. "Body like that...yum!" At Meredith's snort, she added, "What? I have an aesthetic appreciation for a man who takes care of himself."

Cochrane's grin flashed white in his tanned face. "I appreciate your appreciation."

Meredith sighed. "Please, Rue, don't encourage him."

"All right, ladies!" Cochrane scrubbed his hands together briskly and stood to strip off his T-shirt, revealing a broad, muscular, hairy chest. Dark hair also peppered his forearms and his firm belly. "Enough with the mutual admiration society. Let's get this show on the road."

Rue let out an enthusiastic yell, while Meredith tried to quell her concerns.

CHAPTER SIXTEEN

After steering *Lady Vic* through a break in the reef at Cochrane's direction and anchoring close to the center of the blue hole, Meredith stood up to settle the BC—buoyancy compensator vest—and the air tank she carried on her back. The vest fit snugly around her chest like a cumbersome backpack. The equipment's combined weight made her feel ungainly, but she knew she'd hardly notice it in the water.

Cochrane tugged the primary and secondary regulators to hang over her right shoulder, and did the same for the pressure gauge and BC inflator hose on her left. She took a few breaths from both regulators to ensure they were functioning and saw Rue do the same.

"Remember, we'll have forty-five minutes at depth," Cochrane said.

Rue's eyes widened. "Why? I thought we'd have more time."

"The deeper you dive, the greater the pressure of the water, the faster you burn through your tank," he explained. "Maximum time is sixty minutes, maybe a little longer, but we can't deplete our air supply completely unless you plan to grow gills for the return trip."

"Oh! Oh, yes, sorry, I guess I forgot," Rue stammered, flushing.

Cochrane glanced at Meredith, suspicion lurking in his pale eyes. She shook her head to forestall any questions she dared not answer.

"We'll be descending fast to depth, so you may have trouble equalizing," he said to Rue. "If you need help, ask for it. And if you start to feel a little loopy, give me a sign."

Rue mouthed "loopy" at Meredith with a questioning look.

Using the excuse of washing gunk off her face mask, Meredith took Rue into the mid-galley, away from Cochrane and his keen hearing. "A symptom of nitrogen narcosis," she explained softly, though she didn't hide her exasperation. "You told me you were a certified diver. You should know this stuff."

"I am, but it's been a while," Rue protested. She sounded sincere, but kept her gaze focused on the counter by the sink.

Meredith wasn't sure whether to believe Rue or not, but she realized Cochrane had donned his fins and vest. He stood by the dive platform, obviously waiting for them.

She snagged Rue's arm, drew her closer, and whispered in her ear, "Sure you don't want to stay on the boat? I can bring up the lockbox—"

"No!" Rue pulled away, setting her teeth in a tense smile when Cochrane looked their way. She lowered her voice. "I can do this, Mer. I have two experts with me, don't I?" She went out on the stern deck to pull on her fins.

Meredith couldn't do anything else than follow Rue. Foreboding rose from her stomach to kick her in the ribs before seizing her by the throat. She pushed her feelings aside and remained resolute. If at any time she or Cochrane deemed the conditions too dangerous to continue, they'd all return to the boat. If that meant earning Rue's anger, so be it. She slipped a pair of fins on her feet.

"Ready?" she asked Cochrane, peering at the waves crashing on the coral fringe enclosing God's Eye. The indigo blue circle seemed bottomless, mysterious, almost alien, and certainly terrifying. A darker shape slipped under *Lady Vic*'s keel. She recognized the silhouette: a hammerhead shark. Her heart jumped.

"Stick together," Cochrane said, fixing Rue with a stern look. After checking her diving watch, Meredith put the regulator in her mouth and jumped off the platform with a hand flattened on her face mask. The sensation of falling, always prompting a brief instinctive fright, ended a split-second later in a splash when she plunged into the warm Caribbean ocean. Thousands of quicksilver bubbles billowed around her body. She inflated the BC and bobbed to the surface to give Cochrane the all-clear signal.

Removing her face mask, she spit on the glass, rubbed the spittle around, and rinsed it out—a necessary step to prevent fogging. She donned her mask and let some air out of the BC to submerge a few feet. A moment later, she heard the dull, muffled booms of two more bodies crashing into the ocean, one right behind the other.

Lazily treading water she waited for Cochrane and Rue while they defogged their masks. Below her, she saw nothing but darkness. Above her, the surface of the water reflected faint shafts of sunlight in shades of blue and green. Her anticipation heightened.

Feeling a tap on her shoulder, she turned to see Cochrane close by. Rue hovered just behind him. At his thumbs-up, she turned on her belly and released the air in her BC. The weights in her belt began dragging her down, deeper into God's Eye.

After equalizing the pressure in her ears and sinuses, Meredith enjoyed the free fall. She spread her arms out like she was flying. At nearly three feet per second she *was* flying, moving fast past a rough, irregular, lumpy wall pitted with holes and small caverns.

A school of small jacks darted off at her approach, the fish flashing like silver coins turning this way and that in unison, a mutual pattern of escape from predators. She allowed herself a moment of fascination.

At thirty-two feet, the seafans, coral heads, anemones, and tube sponges vanished. A near constant rain of calcium carbonate flaked off the walls. Her ears popped. Light dimmed. Colors changed as reds and oranges faded in the increased depth. The bright yellow dive computer strapped to Cochrane's wrist lost much of its color. His red swimming shorts and Rue's fuchsia bikini appeared blue. She thought her tanned skin and turquoise swimsuit might appear almost invisible to her companions.

At fifty feet, she tapped the button to reinflate her BC with compressed air. Her descent slowed. She tapped once more. Finally, her weight equalized.

She hung motionless in blue space in front of a massive overhang studded with stalactites resembling the jagged teeth of some fantastic sea predator. She paused to wait for Cochrane and Rue to join her, but Rue didn't stop. The woman continued plummeting to the bottom, her hair streaming behind her in serpentine ribbons.

Meredith followed. What else could she do? But Rue apparently got the hang of the BC in time to avoid smacking into a huge, squat stalagmite jutting from the sea floor. Once she was assured of Rue's safety, she glanced up. The surface couldn't be discerned. A few darker shadows circled overhead, most likely bull sharks.

Fat air bubbles rose from her regulator, flattening a little to shimmering disks wobbling like jellyfish as they rose in a column in her peripheral vision. She caught Rue's wide-eyed gaze and gestured to the space by the overhang. The lockbox should be in this area, provided it had not bounced off any coral projections on its way to the bottom.

Rue nodded. She swam slowly around, using a knife to stir the sediment.

Cochrane touched her ankle. Meredith shrugged at his frown, made a vague gesture, and joined Rue in her search for the lockbox. He'd no doubt interrogate her later.

Keeping an eye on her watch made her a less effective searcher. So, too, did the unwelcome realization that each flap of her fins stirred up a fine powder from the bottom and decreased her visibility. The sediment layer seemed quite thick. She found nothing, but remained aware of Cochrane circling above them much like the restless sharks.

At last, she went over to Rue when forty-five minutes had elapsed, but the woman stubbornly shook her head and continued stabbing at the sediment.

Anger ignited in Meredith's chest, a feeling like the worst heartburn she'd ever experienced. She waved her watch in front of Rue's mask to emphasize time had run out.

Again, Rue shook her head.

Clearly losing patience, Cochrane intervened by simply grabbing Rue's upper arm and reinflated his BC with enough air to send them both up several feet. Meredith swam to join them. Cochrane's scowl was apparent behind his face mask, as was Rue's stubborn grimace. A silent argument went on between the pair before Rue sheathed her knife and began reinflating her own BC to start the ascent to the surface.

The water seemed to grow colder as Meredith rose in stages. Cochrane swam stiffly, giving her sidelong glances. Rue refused to look at her. She pushed down the nervous fluttering she felt, concentrating on a safe ascent and staying alert. The wall anchored her on the left. On her right, the endless ocean. She tried not to fret.

At last, ripples of light flickered through the water, growing brighter and brighter until she broke the surface. She spat out her regulator. Saltwater rushed into her mouth, brackish and nauseating, which may have been due to the discouragement curdling in her belly. Krause's lockbox was gone, swallowed by the sea.

No lockbox, no submarine. No submarine, no diamonds or artwork.

She could only imagine how Rue felt at the setback.

CHAPTER SEVENTEEN

Climbing the steps to the platform at the back of the boat took a wrenching effort, as if the ocean were reluctant to loosen its sucking grasp on her body. Meredith managed to get aboard *Lady Vic* without too much hassle and turned to assist Rue.

Assuming Cochrane could take care of himself, she turned away to shrug off her BC, sit on a seat, and remove her fins and face mask. She grabbed a towel off the stack she'd laid out previously and began to rub her short hair dry, freezing when she heard the distinct squeak of tennis shoes on the deck. Rue and Clay were also barefoot. She yanked off the towel.

First, she focused on the man behind the gun. She recognized him—the taxi driver in Cancún. She'd know those Aztec tattoos anywhere. He no longer wore a hoodie, but had changed into a sleeveless shirt and loose cargo pants. The long scratches Rue left on his face were scabbed over, but still looked puffy and red around the edges. He held a .357 revolver in a gangster grip, the weapon pointed at her sideways.

On the opposite side of the deck, Rue held her face mask clutched to her chest. Next to her stood a stranger, a burly, scruffy man in a T-shirt and jeans. He wasn't visibly armed. She didn't know where Cochrane had gone, but prayed he'd stay out of sight.

The taxi driver made an abrupt gesture with his gun. "*Dámelo!*"

Give him what? she wondered, trying to understand why he'd followed her and Rue out to the reef. Not just to kill them, she thought, or he would've taken a shot already. He wanted something, but what? How had he gotten here? Where was his boat?

He repeated the demand. When she failed to answer, the scruffy man grinned, took hold of Rue's hand, and wrenched her index finger back.

At the sound of Rue's strangled scream, an eerie calm descended over her, blotting out fears and anxieties. The world leaped into sharper focus. Through the blood pounding in her ears, she heard the buzz saw noise of a motorboat engine coming closer.

"*Dónde está?*" the taxi driver practically screamed. He came forward, his scabbed face flushed with thwarted rage, and drew the revolver back as if he intended to whip it across her face. The scruffy man's hoarse, pain-filled cry made him spin around instead.

In the instant of his distraction, Meredith swung her foot up with force, trying for a crippling kick to his thigh, but he'd already turned too far. The blow struck him lower than she'd intended. Nevertheless, he dropped his gun and fell forward to sprawl on the deck.

She jumped off the seat to stomp hard on his hand when he reached for the revolver. A primal part of her triumphed at the feel of delicate bones crackling under her heel. He cursed and tried to scrabble away. Bending over, she grabbed the back of his head and slammed his forehead against the deck several times until he managed to buck her off. She rolled, staggered up, and made a grab for the revolver, but someone's foot struck it. She watched the weapon slide across the deck and disappear over the side, out of reach. She sucked in air, part of her savagely glad she'd have to kill him with her bare hands.

The sound of another scuffle drew her attention. Her gaze flicked to the other side of the deck. To her astonishment, the scruffy man was bent almost backward over the rail. Rue stood too close to him, her face a picture of fury while she flailed her mask on his head.

Beyond Rue, she spotted an approaching motorboat skimming the waves. Whoever piloted the fast boat was their enemy. The fight needed to end before reinforcements arrived.

Before she could act, the taxi driver threw his arms around her knees, pinning her in place. Tiny pinpricks of heat rushed across her skin, leaving sweat in their wake. She swept her cupped hands back and forward to clap over his ears. The painful, simultaneous strike loosened his grip, allowing her to shove him away.

He lurched to his feet, his balance gone. She fisted his shirt and used his momentum to rush him off the dive platform and into the ocean. Not waiting to see if he swam or drowned, she turned to help Rue and found the scruffy man slipping overboard, his shoes kicking at the air until he vanished with a splash.

Cochrane swarmed over the rail in the man's wake shouting, "Go! Go!"

Meredith ran to the helm station. She spared a second to verify Cochrane raising the sea anchor and started the engine roaring to life. She took the wheel to send *Lady Vic* flying forward, away from the motorboat, out of the coral reef circling God's Eye, and into the dangerously shallow waters of the lagoon.

Fortunately, the buoy markers remained. She steered *Lady Vic* around the shoals and other hazards, each moment expecting gunfire or the crunch of a coral growth holing the boat. The moment her chart indicated clear water under the keel, she gunned the engine to its maximum thirty knots and chose a random course that left the motorboat far behind.

The knot of tension in her gut slowly eased.

After putting on the autopilot, Meredith returned to the stern. Cochrane sat on a seat clutching his elbow. Rue seemed fine until she noticed a bloody footprint. Glass from the broken face mask littered the deck.

"Whacked my funny bone when I slipped," Clay said, waving her off. "It's fine."

Rue grimaced. "I've got a piece of glass in my foot."

Meredith fetched the medical kit. Using tweezers, she extracted the slender sliver of glass from the ball of Rue's foot, made sure no more debris remained, cleaned the cut, and applied antiseptic ointment and a bandage. The whole time she treated the minor injury, she felt somewhat distant, as if the hands manipulating the tweezers didn't belong to her.

When she finished, she put the supplies away and sat down, drained and numb. She continued sitting when Cochrane got up and headed to the helm station. *Lady Vic* slowed to cruising speed. She shivered, suddenly cold despite the heat of the sun.

Cochrane returned with a blanket, which he put around her shoulders. "Smooth moves, Reid," he said in an undertone. "You make an old man proud."

Meredith nodded. Cochrane had taught her every dirty fighting trick he knew. She attempted a smile but the expression felt false, crumbling at the edges.

"What's wrong?" Rue asked, perching on the arm of the chair.

"She's in shock," Cochrane answered. "Why don't you go make us some coffee? We could all probably do with a cup."

"Do I look like your barista?" Rue grumbled, but she went to the mid-galley.

Sadly, Meredith could muster only a distant enthusiasm for the way the rounded globes of Rue's buttocks moved in the fuchsia bikini bottom.

"I guess the life of a charter boat captain is a lot more exciting than I thought," Cochrane said, sitting on the seat next to her as soon as they were alone.

She felt his keen gaze on the side of her face and didn't know what to say.

Cochrane snorted. "I'm going out on a limb here, Reid, and guess those two assholes weren't interested in deep sea fishing. What the hell have you done?"

"None of your business," she croaked, clutching the edges of the blanket closer.

The smell of coffee wafted across the deck.

"C'mon, kid, don't play coy with me." When she declined to answer, his gaze narrowed toward the mid-galley. "I knew it!" he muttered, a muscle in his jaw working. "Goddamn it, Reid, what's little Miss Va-Va-Voom up to and why are you neck deep in it?"

"It's not my secret to tell, Clay," she replied, finally throwing off the blanket. Her blood stirred, whipped by burgeoning anger. She didn't need a shield to deal with him. "Look, I'll drop you off at Isla Mujeres. Thanks for loaning us the equipment."

Cochrane shook his head. "You don't get away that easy."

"I think I do."

"You drop into my life after disappearing for years, dump a mystery in my lap, and then clam up? Forget it. I'm not moving a muscle until you spill."

The tense silence was interrupted by Rue, who walked onto the stern deck carrying a tray with three cups of coffee on it and announced to Cochrane, "I was looking for a lockbox belonging to the late Mr. Jerardo Guzman of Isla Azul."

"The box wasn't in the blue hole, so we're done," Meredith added when she'd recovered from her surprise.

Rue had insisted on secrecy from the beginning, but since the lockbox was absent, she supposed there was no harm telling him the truth. She doubted further searching in the sinkhole would do any good. In the years since Krause's death, the box must have been swallowed by the thick layer of sediment.

Cochrane scratched his stubbled cheek and stared at a low, dark hump of land on the horizon while he drank his coffee.

Meredith tried her mug, found the coffee well brewed and very hot, and gave Rue a smile of approval. She'd just taken a second tentative sip when Cochrane spoke.

"The box wasn't there because it's sitting in my closet at home," he said.

Startled, Meredith gulped, scalded her mouth, choked, and spit coffee on the deck.

CHAPTER EIGHTEEN

At Cochrane's house a few hours later, Meredith forced herself not to pace the living room while the man searched through his closets. The suspense was killing her.

Rue sat on the sofa with her legs crossed. One sandaled foot bounced up and down, a sign of her impatience. She had braided her hair into a single tail falling over the shoulder of her thin, sage-green cotton shirt. Now she fiddled with the end of the braid, twisting the curl at the end to and fro until Meredith's throat hurt with the effort not to yell.

A fly buzzed through the open window and made a lazy circuit of the room. Chafing at the delay, Meredith shooed the insect away with a fishing magazine and considered mayhem. Her frayed nerves were fast approaching the breaking point.

Cochrane entered the room carrying a surprisingly large, flat metal container resembling a safety deposit box. "I picked up this thing a while back. There's a ledge on the west side of *El Ojo*, just under a coral shelf. I was helping one of the local fishermen who got drunk and managed to run his boat aground on the reef. Long story short, I spotted the box."

Her expression hungry, Rue stood and reached for the box. Cochrane held it out of reach. "I want answers first."

"What's with you navy people?" Rue cried, flouncing back to the sofa and plopping down heavily. "Always with the questions!"

He glanced at Meredith, who shrugged. She'd already tussled with Rue over information several times. Let him win or lose his own fights.

"What's so important about a box full of old papers?" he persisted.

Rue leaped up again, her body rigid with outrage. "What? You opened it?"

"Sweetheart, I found it. I had to open it." Cochrane grinned at the incoherent noises Rue made. He waited until her spluttering died, replaced by a silent glare. "You want the box, you tell me why you risked our lives to find it," he said sternly.

Meredith decided to intervene before Rue blew an artery. "Give her the box, Clay."

He ignored her, still holding the box at arm's length. "Tell me."

"Fuck you." Rue's mismatched eyes gleamed with fury.

Sighing, Meredith relaxed in her chair, intending to wait out the battle of wills. A full minute passed. Two minutes. The fly returned. She ineffectually flapped the magazine. "I'm about ready to knock both your heads together," she warned.

"Just give me the damned box," Rue told Cochrane, "and after I look through the papers, I'll tell you why I want it. Do we have a deal, you big bully?"

"Agreed." Cochrane handed over the box with a flourish.

Rue returned to the sofa, her braid twitching between her shoulders at each step. She didn't smile, but Meredith knew she was pleased.

Cochrane sat down in another chair close by. "Is she always like that?" he asked Meredith mildly, watching Rue while she rooted through the papers making happy noises.

"It's a puzzle she's been waiting to solve."

"A puzzle in German."

"Trust me, you don't want to be involved."

He pointed a finger at her. "You've got Mexican gang-bangers after you. I'm not just the pretty but dumb muscle, you know. I can put two and two together."

"Do you get four every time?" Meredith quipped, instantly sorry when he scowled.

"I'm not joking here, Reid," he said, his voice softening. "If you're in trouble, any kind of trouble, I want to help."

A warm feeling settled in her chest. "I know, Clay. If I need help, I swear you're the first guy I'll call, okay?"

"Fine," he grumped, leaning back in the chair. "Good job on the boat, by the way."

Meredith acknowledged his praise with a grin. "I remember what you taught me, Master Chief. And I've picked up a few self-defense classes along the way."

"You always were a scrapper." His eyes squeezed almost shut in remembered pleasure. "Only the meanest, maddest, baddest motherfucker wins a fight, so…" He paused.

She finished the sentence. "Be the meanest, maddest, baddest motherfucker."

"That's right. Win or lose, there ain't no rules. The graveyard's full of honorable fighters, the bars full of cheaters who survived. Good to know you haven't forgotten."

"No, Clay, not even for a second."

Across the room, Rue frowned at the papers in her hand.

"You okay?" Cochrane called.

"I'm fine," Rue replied absently. She set the papers aside and looked at Meredith. "I'm going to have to study these before I know our next destination."

Our? Meredith was jolted by the single word. She had assumed they'd go on together, of course, regardless of their previous agreement, but to hear Rue's confirmation still surprised her. Realizing Rue was waiting for a reply, she nodded. "Suits me."

"You promised to tell me what's going on," Cochrane reminded them.

"What happened to the ashes?" Rue asked.

He squinted at the non sequitur. "What ashes?"

"The ashes that were in this box with the papers." Rue dusted her hands together. "I found some dust, but no remains."

"Remains." Clay's voice was flat.

Rue glared at him impatiently. "Yes, the human remains. Or the cremains, if you prefer. Guzman was cremated and his ashes were put in this box."

"Oh."

"What's wrong?"

Cochrane swallowed. "I didn't know. I put 'em on my tomato plants out back."

Meredith swallowed a laugh, which turned into a painful lump in her chest, swelling until a hyena-like giggle burst out of her mouth. "Clay! You didn't!"

"How the hell was I supposed to know?" he snarled. Soon his face relaxed and he shrugged. "Good tomatoes that year, though. Can't really complain."

Rue choked. Meredith crossed the room to helpfully slap her on the back. She stayed when Rue clutched at her hand. Feeling self-conscious, she sat down next to her on the sofa.

"Either one of you lovebirds feel like telling me what's going on?" Cochrane asked, putting heavy emphasis on the endearment.

Not sarcasm, Meredith thought, just gentle ribbing. She felt Rue's eyes on her. The hand holding hers seemed to grow cold. "It's your assignment. You tell him."

Despite the interruptions, exclamations, and profanities from Cochrane, Rue managed to tell him the full story of Hugo Krause before dinner.

CHAPTER NINETEEN

Meredith sat at *Lady Vic*'s helm station, waiting for Rue to emerge from belowdecks. They'd gotten away from Clay Cochrane and Isla Mujeres only by promising to keep him updated. A day later, she still had no idea where they were headed. Rue had told her to take a leisurely run around the islands. She hated wasting fuel.

"Where do we go next? 'Cause I'm tired of farting around out here. I assume you've figured out Krause's papers by now, considering you've spent the last twenty-four hours cuddled up to that damned lockbox," she said when Rue came up the ladder.

"Don't be jealous," Rue said, rubbing her eyes. She looked tired, her auburn hair limp. "Sure, Krause kept records, but I'm trying to find out what specific items he took on the U-boat with him and more importantly, the sub's final destination."

Meredith sighed. "Have you found anything useful?"

"Lots of lists." Rue sat in the second helm seat. "Krause took paintings, sculptures, jewels, rare books, objets d'art, relics, artifacts...even what sounds like an Imperial egg."

"A what?"

"You've heard of Peter Carl Fabergé."

"The name sounds familiar."

"From the description, an item on the list sounds like Krause had the Cherub with Chariot egg in his possession. Made in St. Petersburg in 1888, last seen in 1922. Gold, brilliants and sapphires. Worth maybe eight or nine million at auction today."

"And that's on the U-boat?"

Rue pushed her hair away from her face. Her eyes glittered with exhaustion and excitement. "With a lot of other stuff, including a couple of Klimt paintings—I mean, Klimt in his Golden Period, which frankly makes me want to swoon. In 2006, a portrait of Adele Bloch-Bauer sold at auction for $135 million. If the paintings in the U-boat are intact and just as good, my finder's fee is going to be very, very nice indeed. I may retire."

Meredith couldn't muster much enthusiasm for theoretical money. In her opinion, the only dollars that counted were the ones in her hand or in her bank account. "If that U-boat's at the bottom of the ocean, I doubt the contents will be intact," she said in an attempt to inject a note of reality. "Gemstones and gold, but paintings? No way, not if there was a hull breach."

"There are no guarantees in a treasure hunt," Rue said with a sigh, "as I have damned good reason to know. Listen, the U-boat might've been scuttled, torpedoed, destroyed in an accident, or eaten by a giant sperm whale. I hope it's hidden. I hope the hull hasn't got a whacking big hole in it. I hope the contents are intact and I'm not on a wild goose chase. So many hopes, not enough certainties. Sure you still want to tag along?"

Meredith found her gaze wandering to the shadowy hint of cleavage exposed by the scooped neckline of Rue's T-shirt. She dragged her mind away from images of Rue naked, the curves of breasts and hips, the dark red curls guarding the valley between smooth thighs. She lifted her gaze to meet Rue's knowing smirk. "Yes, I'm in."

"Good." Rue cleared her throat and plucked at her shirt, as if suddenly self-conscious. "You know, there's one odd thing. While I was going through Krause's lists, a name kept coming up. A familiar name. I feel like there's more I should be remembering."

"Care to clue me in?" At Rue's skeptical snort, she went on in mock outrage, "Hey, you never know. Try me. I took history classes and everything."

"Okay, smarty-pants. The name's Karl Fuhrman. He was a member of Krause's SS unit, a clerk acting as a secretary. The papers in the box are jumbled up and not in chronological order, but he's mentioned a lot. I found a reference to him making a copy of an inventory list for Krause's private collection. But I know, I just know, somebody recently mentioned Fuhrman's name to me. I can't think who or where."

Stumped, Meredith said nothing.

Rue considered the matter for several minutes. At last, her fist struck her thigh and she bit her lip in frustration. "I wish I could remember! It's important. I feel it."

"Close your eyes."

"What?"

"It's a visualization technique," Meredith explained. "Close your eyes and try to remember where you were when you first heard the name Karl Fuhrman. Try to recall smells, sounds, textures…anything that might take you back to the same place in time. Especially scent. I was once told scent is strongly tied to memory."

"All right." Rue relaxed in the chair, her eyes closed. After a while, she murmured, "Dust and old paper. I remember books."

Meredith nodded, though she knew Rue couldn't see her. "A library?"

Rue frowned. "I don't know, I can't…wait." She hesitated. "Yes, an antiquarian bookstore. In Saint Paul, Minnesota." Her blue eye opened a crack. She focused on Meredith and began speaking more confidentially. "The owner's blond and beefy, but he has a delicate touch when it comes to bookbinding. Hands like a magician."

"Go on," Meredith encouraged.

Rue's eyelid lowered. "He has a file containing service records of SS officers. I didn't ask him where he got them. He told me he was tracing the men."

"He's a Nazi hunter?"

"No, curious about nature vs. nurture." Rue sat up and opened both eyes, looking much more animated. "His grandfather was an officer in the Second SS Panzer Division. His father was a product of the Nazi breeding program, who was adopted after the war by a very nice Midwestern couple and is currently serving a life sentence for murder. My guy wants to know about the descendants of SS officers, whether they inherited their fathers' proclivities, shall we say. I think it's nonsense, but you can't really argue with a man's obsession. He's been tracing the lines of ancestry not only for himself, but all the officers whose papers he's managed to put his hands on. If my memory's correct, Fuhrman was on his list."

"This information helps us how?" Meredith asked.

"It helps us because Fuhrman is still alive." Rue delivered the news with relish. "Or at least, he was last year when I was in Saint Paul following a lead. I didn't connect Fuhrman to Krause then because he isn't mentioned in Krause's journal, but now I think if anybody knows what really happened to U-3019, it's probably Karl Fuhrman."

Meredith felt a tingling in her veins. "Are you sure?"

"Sweetheart, in my line of work, you follow the evidence as far as it takes you and then you deal in possibilities. You find a guy who knows a guy who maybe can point you to yet another guy. The conclusion isn't set in stone. Sometimes the trail dead-ends and you're left with nothing except starting over. But sometimes you hit the jackpot."

"Okay, fine, so the hunt goes on. Where do we find Fuhrman?"

"I don't have the faintest notion." Rue grinned. "But I know somebody who does."

By now, Meredith did too. "The bookstore owner in Saint Paul. I hope you're not expecting me to take *Lady Vic* there."

"Don't be silly." Rue reached into the pocket of her shorts and produced her client's platinum credit card. "We're going to fly. How do you feel about first class?"

Returning Rue's smile, Meredith turned to the marine GPS and began plotting a course to the nearest city with an airport and a marina.

CHAPTER TWENTY

As it turned out, Miami was their only option considering Rue's lack of a passport.

She found herself somewhat reluctant to return to the city because of the restaurant bombing—an illogical fear since the people after Rue had amply demonstrated she wasn't safe anywhere, even in the middle of the ocean. Why should Miami pose a particular threat? Still, her fingers were cold and numb, her belly hollow. She briskly scrubbed her hands together, telling herself not to be silly.

Deciding she should keep busy by packing a bag, after setting a course for Miami, Meredith went belowdecks to the cabin where she found Rue. Not naked, not like before, and not sleeping, but sitting on the bed leafing through a sheaf of papers from the lockbox.

"Hey," said Rue without glancing up.

"Hey," Meredith returned. "Sandwiches okay for dinner?"

"Sure." Rue waited until she'd opened the closet door before adding in a voice an octave lower than usual, "So tell me, Mer... what's for dessert?"

Meredith had only a moment to blink, to process what Rue meant, before a lightning flash of arousal ignited deep inside her. Instant lust closed her throat. She turned around to face the bed, her heart knocking against her rib cage.

Rue knelt up on the bed and tossed the papers on the bedside table. She peeled out of her shirt and bra, dropping the garments on the floor and leaving her naked to the waist. "I think we should eat dessert first," she said, somehow managing to appear positively wicked and wide-eyed with innocence at the same time. "We've got time to kill, right?"

Not trusting herself to speak, Meredith stripped until she wore only the colorful tattoo around her upper arm. She took her time to let Rue admire her from every side. The look of appreciation Rue gave her, a hungry up-and-down appraisal lingering like a caress, did more for her ego than crunches or lunges for her body.

She moved closer until her knees touched the edge of the mattress and she leaned in to kiss Rue. The mouth beneath hers tasted cool like fresh water, but in a few seconds turned hot, so hot every touch seemed to scorch her to the bone. Lightly biting the tempting red bottom lip, she found it as fresh and ripe as promised. She worried the plump flesh with her teeth. The vibration of Rue's moan traveled straight to her sex, touching off a bonfire.

When Rue's lips parted in another moan, she slipped her tongue inside to lick at the unique flavor she identified as belonging to Rue. Their tongues touched. She stiffened and clutched Rue's shoulders, a sweet ache between her legs.

Ending the kiss, she licked Rue's throat and managed to murmur, "My, my, Ms. Stanton, you sure are sweet. I think I'll eat you right up." Moving lower, she laid a series of wet, sucking kisses along the wings of Rue's collarbone, so fragile seeming under the skin.

"Yes," Rue whispered, burying fingers in Meredith's hair.

Meredith ran her hands down the hourglass curves of Rue's body. She hooked her thumbs into the waistband of the woman's shorts.

"I'm working up quite an appetite," Rue said, falling backward on the bed and stretching out her legs. "God, I'm so wet!" She lifted her head to stare at Meredith down the length of her body. With her auburn hair tumbled around her face, her lips swollen and ragged, she looked wild and wanton. Her blue eye gleamed like starlight on snow, but the color of her other eye seemed to deepen from sherry brown to near black with passion.

Meredith felt a thin coat of sweat covering her. Bending forward, she swirled her tongue into Rue's navel, at the same time drawing off the shorts and panties to leave Rue naked on the bed. She touched the scars burned white against Rue's flushed skin. "You're beautiful," she said sincerely. Her fingers glided easily through the delicate folds of Rue's sex. "You're right...you're soaking wet. You're ready, aren't you? How long have you been waiting for me?"

"Please. Please, I need—oh!"

Without waiting for Rue to finish speaking, Meredith slid a couple of fingers inside and drew them out until only the tips remained poised at Rue's entrance, which quivered against the teasing touch as if trying to draw her fingers back in. "What do you need?" she asked, schooling herself to patience despite the desire battering at her self-control.

The moment stretched out, though not in silence. An engine's muted roar seemed overly loud. After a moment's panic cut through her pleasure-drugged haze, Meredith realized the sound was the rush of her pulse in her ears. "Tell me what you need," she said.

At last, Rue focused on her. "You," she replied simply, the single word seeming to expand until it filled the cabin and grew even further to fill an empty, unsuspected space behind Meredith's breastbone. "I want you, Mer. I want you."

Meredith pushed her fingers into Rue's heat as far as they would go, full of satisfaction and triumph when Rue whimpered. She set an almost punishing rhythm, adding a twist of her wrist to each gliding stroke. Rue opened to her like an exotic flower, pink and pouting, growing wetter, slicker, hungrier.

Rue's legs splayed wider apart, the tendons in both thighs straining. Her hips stuttered in little hitching movements of encouragement. When Meredith began licking her, the breath expelled from her mouth in a surprised and delightfully needy, "Oh!"

Meredith flicked the small, firm clitoris with her tongue, delivering velvety blows that wrung groans from Rue. Her fingers worked. She quickened the pace, her mouth filled with pungent musk, her face soaked to the chin. Nothing mattered except pleasing Rue, a thrill as potent, as intoxicating as anything she'd ever known.

Rue's clitoris pulsed once, twice, and she climaxed. Her back arched off the bed. Her slippery, smooth walls tightened on Meredith's fingers with an almost painful grip. The cords stood out on her neck when she shouted her release.

After waiting a few moments, Meredith lowered her mouth to Rue's sex to coax a second orgasm out of her.

"Get your ass over here," Rue finally panted through broken breaths.

The wildfire beneath her skin, banked all this time, suddenly flared to life. Meredith became aware of the heat and the moisture between her legs. Trembling, she crawled farther up on the bed until Rue could reach her.

Rue gestured. "Get up here. I want to taste you."

Understanding dawned. Meredith moved to straddle Rue, her knees planted on the mattress on either side of Rue's head. She straightened her spine and took hold of the headboard. Risking a downward glance, she saw Rue blinking up at her, the beautiful face half-hidden, just as an incredibly soft tongue slipped into her sex.

She threw her head back. A groan came from the pit of her belly. Rue's hands curled over her thighs, the short fingernails digging in slightly. She didn't mind the slight pain, not when Rue lapped at her tender flesh over and over, around and around, deeper and deeper.

Tremors shook her. Glorious sensations drove her higher. She closed her eyes, straining for release. Every nerve she owned seemed to sing under the tension, sparking in Technicolor bursts behind her eyelids.

She had just enough presence of mind not to grind herself against Rue's face when her pleasure peaked. Blind and deaf to everything except the wild throbbing at the center of her body, she seemed to fly apart and come back together in a long, heart-stopping instant that left her sated, sweaty, and breathless at the end.

She rolled off Rue and flopped down on the bed.

Rue made a show of licking her mouth, humming in appreciation. "Delicious," she said, glancing at Meredith from beneath her lashes. "Can I have a second helping of dessert?"

Meredith blushed and shook her head, but her sex clenched on a renewed burst of desire at the greed and the promise in Rue's mismatched eyes.

CHAPTER TWENTY-ONE

To Meredith's guarded relief, nothing dangerous happened in Miami when they arrived. She docked *Lady Vic* in her usual berth and used the marina's Wi-Fi connection and her laptop to book last-minute plane tickets and arrange for a rental car in Saint Paul.

Rue's borrowed credit card smoothed the way at every turn. Meredith marveled at how cooperative people became, no matter the inconvenience, as soon as she told them the price didn't matter. If only all her problems could be solved by throwing a wad of cash at them, she thought with a sigh before calling a taxi service she had used before.

About an hour after completing the arrangements for their travel, her phone rang. She answered the call and found out the taxi driver was waiting in the marina's parking lot. "Come on," she called down to Rue, who had retired to the cabin after breakfast to pack and go over her notes. "Our ride's here. We don't want to miss our flight."

Rue emerged from belowdecks lugging her suitcase. "You don't need to yell," she snapped, her expression sour. "I'm aware when our flight leaves, thanks very much."

Meredith decided fighting with Rue or calling her on her poor attitude would solve nothing and only increase the waiting cab driver's fee. Whatever was wrong, she'd learn about it soon enough. She shrugged and locked up behind herself after Rue left the boat.

The drive to Miami International was accomplished without conversation of any kind. Meredith watched out the window while the driver smoothly negotiated traffic along I-95. By her watch, the trip took twenty minutes, but with a silent Rue simmering like an unwatched pot beside her in the backseat, it seemed like the longest twenty minutes of her life.

After arriving at the overly air-conditioned airport, she and Rue checked their luggage, obtained boarding passes, and submitted to the rest of the security gauntlet. She remembered a time when security measures consisted of a metal detector. The new procedures, while touted as necessary, seemed to nudge over the line into the ridiculous, an impression aided by the sight of helmeted security officers zipping around on Segways. She preferred sea travel to flying, but risking *Lady Vic* on the Mississippi River to Saint Paul wasn't in the cards.

Meredith paused to let a bomb-sniffing dog nose around her shoes.

Afterward, the airline's VIP lounge, located conveniently near their flight's departure gate, proved as quiet and restful as a public library compared to the busy concourses.

After paying for VIP passes, Meredith towed Rue to a table, placed an order, and enjoyed a cold beer and a plate of freshly grilled beef sliders for lunch while her sullen companion refused food and drink, her attention consumed by her cell phone.

"Hey, what the heck's so fascinating on that thing, anyway?" Meredith asked around a mouthful of slider. The chef's signature chipotle ketchup created a pleasant burn in her mouth, instantly cooled by another sip of beer. "Got any good apps?"

"First of all, playing 'see food' with me is kind of juvenile, don't you think?" Rue snapped coldly. "Second, I'm doing my damnedest to get hold of Jacob Olsen, the man we want to see in Saint Paul. If we just show up on his doorstep without warning, he might flip out and refuse to help. So far, he's not answering his phone."

Meredith swallowed. "Maybe he's out of town."

"Maybe he's been abducted by aliens." Rue jabbed a finger at the screen and tossed the cell phone into her carry-on bag. "If Olsen's on vacation or otherwise unavailable, we'll find out where he's gone and, if necessary, track his ass down." She rose from her chair and looped her bag's strap over her shoulder. "Are you done swilling beer and stuffing your face? We have a plane to catch."

"Christ! What's your problem?" Meredith asked under her breath.

She stuffed the last slider in her mouth, snatched the unopened bag of potato chips that had come with her meal and tucked them into her bag. Following Rue out of the lounge, she wondered what had brought on the bout of ill temper.

Earlier that morning had been a slice of domestic bliss, both of them sitting on the deck for breakfast, sharing coffee, toasted bagels, and the last fresh fruit from the Cancún market. Rue had appeared happy, glowing with the smug satisfaction of a well-laid and well-rested woman. What had changed since then to make her so prickly?

Like a porcupine with toothache and piles. Just to mess with her a little, she made Rue wait while she ducked into a newsstand and spent five minutes perusing the bestsellers. On the way to the gate, she stopped at a coffee kiosk to purchase a shot of Cuban espresso, hiding a smile when Rue's face darkened visibly.

"They probably don't have decent caffé cubano in Minnesota," Meredith said, putting on an innocent expression while sampling the sweet, light brown layer of *espumita* floating on top of the cup. The burning hot coffee beneath the foam scalded her tongue.

"Let's go," Rue said when she yelped. "Or I'm leaving you here."

Meredith finished her coffee in time to catch up to Rue, who had already walked away, headed toward the gate. At least they didn't have to wait long before they boarded the plane.

The flight took about three hours. She found herself unable to enjoy the novelty of complimentary champagne due to Rue's seething presence. She took a book out of her carry-on bag—a biography of Horatio Nelson she'd been dipping into for a while, which usually lived on her bedside table—and tried to pass the time by reading, but Rue's fidgeting and muttering kept distracting her. Finally, she had enough.

"Either tell me about the bug up your ass, or I'm popping the emergency exit door and finding out if you can learn to fly before you hit the ground," she said, closing the book and setting it aside to focus on Rue.

"I have a bad feeling about Olsen," Rue said after a few minutes.

"What kind of bad feeling?"

"I don't know. Something's wrong. I feel it in my gut."

"Sure that's not hunger pangs? You haven't eaten anything since breakfast."

"I'm not hungry," Rue huffed. "I'm worried because Olsen isn't picking up my calls."

Meredith tried to feel sympathetic, but she'd had enough of Rue's attitude. "He's probably on vacation, or out shopping, or getting a haircut, or whatever people do for kicks in Minnesota. We won't know for sure until we get there. In the meantime, if you don't quit sulking like a five-year-old, I swear I'm punting your cute butt back to Miami."

Rue scowled and crossed her arms over her chest.

Meredith caught an air hostess's eye. When the uniformed woman came over, she asked for a soda. From her carry-on, she removed the bag of potato chips she'd grabbed on her way out of the VIP lounge. "Drink this," she said to Rue, handing her the can of soda, "and eat this," she continued, passing over the chips, "and if you're a good girl, when we get to Saint Paul, I'll buy you some lutefisk."

"Fuck you," Rue replied with freezing dignity, but she tore open the bag of chips with what appeared to be renewed appetite.

"Ya, sure, you betcha," Meredith intoned, earning a half-hearted glare.

Fortunately, the plane arrived at the Minneapolis-Saint Paul International Airport only twenty minutes late. Meredith herded Rue to Baggage Claim to retrieve their suitcases from the carousel. Declining Rue's offer to help with the luggage, she found the check-in counter for the rental car agency and picked up the keys to their reserved vehicle.

Walking across the open parking lot toward the Toyota Corolla made her itch between her shoulder blades, as though she had a target pinned there. She'd been fine in the airplane, but on the ground, out of view of witnesses, an ambush seemed a distinct possibility.

Rue elected to drive, citing her superior knowledge of the bookstore's location. Meredith agreed without argument, glad the woman's bad humor had passed.

Saint Paul's temperature wasn't appreciably cooler than Miami's, though the air seemed slightly less muggy. She watched the streets, the buildings, and the scenery scroll past the car window, but didn't see much to make the city stand out from every other American urban center she'd visited in the last ten years—just miles of concrete and glass.

Following a forty-five minute drive, Rue pulled the car to a halt at one end of a strip mall. The parking lot was crowded with fire trucks, an ambulance and a couple of police vehicles. Flames licked out from the broken windows of a store in the center of the row of businesses. The firemen were busy plying the blaze with water from a long hose.

"I feel sorry for the poor bastard who owns that store," Meredith remarked.

Rue's face was pale. Even her lips had very little color. In contrast, her hair appeared to burn like the sooty flames. "Jacob Olsen owns the store," she answered in a strained voice.

Meredith could think of nothing else to say, so she sat in the car and watched the bookstore burn, taking with it their hope of finding the lost U-boat.

CHAPTER TWENTY-TWO

Meredith and Rue checked into a room in the historic and luxurious Saint Paul Hotel downtown. Right after they entered, Rue made a call on her cell phone. Clearly wishing for privacy, she retreated to the bathroom and closed the door behind her.

Meredith scowled at the flat-screen television, recalling how her earlier attempt to find out more information from the firemen at the strip mall had resulted in her and Rue being escorted back to the car by a police officer and politely told to mind their own business. She used the remote to turn on the TV to a local news station, adjusting the volume to a murmur.

She crossed the room to the minibar, opened the door, and stared at the contents, trying to decide if a single serving of Jack Daniels would be enough, or if she ought to go ahead and order a whole bottle from room service. Perhaps Rue would prefer vodka to drown her sorrows. She wasn't sure. Unable to make a decision, she hesitated. Finally realizing she'd been standing there several minutes staring into space like an idiot, she closed the minibar and returned to the chair next to the king-sized bed to wait.

Well, this is a crappy end to a crappy day, she said to herself. Gloomy thoughts dominated her mind. Without Olsen's information on Karl Fuhrman, the search for U-3019 seemed virtually at an end. Rue might go on chasing leads, but their association wouldn't continue. Why should it? She'd be no further use if Rue had to follow a paper trail, and she had to return to Miami eventually and pick up where she left off. The notion saddened her.

Apart from the life-threatening situations, she had fun with Rue. They'd made a connection. Contemplating anonymous bar hookups after sharing intimacy with a smart, sexy, playful, beautiful woman depressed the hell out of her.

A bottle of bourbon grew to be more and more of an attractive proposition.

An hour passed. Rue remained inside the bathroom. Lulled by the drone of the TV—hardly a mention of the fire on the news, and the channel now showing a classic black-and-white film starring Bogart and Bacall—she was startled when the bathroom door banged open. Rue emerged smiling, her mismatched eyes bright with glee.

"I'm starving!" Rue cried, spinning across the room over to the bed and falling on the coverlet with a laugh. "I want eggs, Mer. And chicken wings. Do they have chicken wings here? And cheesecake. And some decent wine would be fan-fucking-tastic!"

"What happened?" Meredith asked, puzzled by the change. She got up to fetch the room service menu from the nightstand.

"Jacob Olsen is alive, alive, alive-O," Rue caroled. Her head hung off the edge of the mattress. She made an upside-down grin. "I had a heck of a time tracking down any of his neighbors in the strip mall, but I finally found Mr. Karthusian. He owns the deli next door to the bookstore. Karthusian told me Olsen talked to him yesterday and told him he was taking some time off today to visit his son in Minneapolis."

"When's Olsen coming back to Saint Paul?"

"We're not waiting, we're going to visit him before something else happens."

Giddy with relief—her temporary partnership with Rue would continue, thank God—Meredith produced the room service menu. "To answer your question, they have a breakfast omelet that's served all day, and yes, I see boneless chicken wings here. And cheesecake with seasonal berries. Want me to call?"

Rue made a rude noise and sat up. "Forget room service. I'm too stoked to eat. Let's go talk to Olsen right now. I'll treat you to a nice steak dinner tonight."

"Sounds good to me. Do you know where the son lives?"

"I got J.J. Olsen's name from Karthusian and his phone number from directory assistance. My tablet's still on the boat, but it doesn't matter. The hotel has a business center with computers and high-speed Internet access. We can check an online reverse directory and get the address, then we're all set."

Meredith echoed Rue's smile. "I'll drive, you navigate," she said.

A visit to the hotel's business center provided an address for John Joseph Olsen, whom she assumed must be Jacob Olsen's son, J.J.

"If not, we're back to square one," Rue commented.

"How many other J.J. Olsens can there be in Minnesota?" Meredith asked.

"Not too many, I hope," Rue said, jotting down the GPS coordinates on a piece of paper. "But Olsen's a pretty popular name. We could be here a while."

Outside, the valet brought the Corolla around to the front of the hotel. After sliding into the passenger seat, Rue programmed the navigation system. Meredith sat behind the steering wheel and immediately rolled down the window. The car had been parked in an underground garage, but the interior was still stifling hot.

According to Rue, J.J. Olsen actually lived in Brooklyn Park, a bedroom community of the Twin Cities located on the west bank of the Mississippi River. Meredith followed the navigation system's directions, driving north about a half hour. Traffic was pretty light in the early afternoon, but she'd read on the Internet that at peak rush hour times, congestion would add another twenty to thirty minutes to their return trip.

The single-story ranch home stood in a quiet neighborhood of similar structures. Meredith thought the houses on Rock Cress Drive looked somewhat dated and lacking modern features, the kind of stolid, two- or three-bedroom homes built twenty years ago to appeal to families with small children or a business commuter who spent long hours at work.

A ruler straight driveway bisected the wide expanse of lawn in front of Olsen's house. A brand-new Toyota Prius stood parked outside the closed garage door.

A curtain in the window fluttered.

Meredith parked the car on the other side of the street and timed her exit to avoid being splashed by a pulsating lawn sprinkler spraying water over the pavement. She walked with Rue over to the Olsen house and up the driveway to the front door, rang the doorbell, and waited. From inside the house, she heard clomping footsteps coming closer.

The door opened to reveal a middle-aged blond man whose sunburned face was framed by sideburns. "Yes?" he asked, shuffling from one foot to the other. He kept the door partially closed, forbidding any glimpse into his home.

"Are you J.J. Olsen?" Meredith asked. "Son of Jacob Olsen?"

"That's right." He eyed her and Rue. "You're not Jehovah's Witnesses, are you?"

"No. We're looking for your father," Rue said in a businesslike tone.

"He's not here," J.J. blurted, too quickly to be believed. He began to shut the door, but Rue darted forward and prevented him by jamming her foot and half her body in the crack.

"Look, we just want to talk to Jacob, that's all," she said. "I'd have visited his shop and spoken to him there, but it caught fire today."

"Dad's store was on fire?" J.J. appeared dumbfounded. "When? What happened?"

"I don't know."

"Well, gosh darn it, who are you ladies, anyway?"

Meredith jumped into the conversation. "We hope your father can help us with some information. If we could just speak to him a few minutes—"

"May we see Jacob, please? I want to know about Karl Fuhrman." Rue raised her voice, directing her speech through the doorway. "Can you hear me, Jacob? Karl Fuhrman."

J.J. was thrust aside by an older man, also blond, but clean-shaven. He bared his teeth at Rue and shouted, "Damned Nazi scum! Get out or I'll kill you all!"

Meredith wasn't concerned by the insult or the threat. Her attention was fixed on the sixty-year-old Luger pistol in the older man's hand.

CHAPTER TWENTY-THREE

"Dad! What the heck are you doing?" J.J. cried, reaching for the gun.

Jacob resisted. "Let me handle this, boy." He studied Rue a moment. His gaze turned to Meredith, who tensed. "Go away! Haven't you people done enough?"

"What's been done to you, Mr. Olsen? Who hurt you?" Rue asked, easing a few inches away from the door and spreading her hands apart in a nonthreatening gesture. "I promise, Ms. Reid and myself are only here to talk. Whoever you think we are, we're not them."

"Dad, don't do anything stupid," J.J. pleaded. To Rue, he said, "I'm so sorry. Dad thinks people are after him sometimes. I thought he was over this behavior."

"Damned scum," Jacob muttered.

Rue introduced herself. "We met last year, Mr. Olsen, at your bookstore. Do you remember me? Ms. Stanton. I was asking about a rare book in your catalog, a journal purportedly belonging to Captain Albrecht Weber."

Jacob squinted. "Ya, sure," he said at last. "Last September. No, October."

Taking a chance, Meredith reached out and gently took the Luger from Jacob's lax grasp. She removed the magazine and slipped it into her pocket, then thumbed the toggle joint at the rear to eject the cartridge in the chamber. Once the gun was unloaded, she breathed easier.

J.J. blew out a sigh. "I'm sorry," he repeated. "Ladies, won't you come inside? I could use a glass of pop right about now and I'm sure you could too."

"Do you know who burned down my store?" Jacob asked Rue as she walked inside.

"No, sir, I'm sorry, I have no idea."

Meredith followed while tucking the unloaded Luger into the waistband of her jeans at the small of her back. If Jacob requested its return, she'd turn the vintage weapon over to him. Otherwise, she intended to keep the Luger hidden until she and Rue concluded their business. Out of sight, out of mind, she hoped.

The décor seemed as out-of-date as the house's exterior. The colors in the living room were tan, brown and orange including the wallpaper, carpet, sofa and love seat, reclining chairs, curtains, lamps, and lampshades. All the furnishings appeared to have escaped from the seventies. A macramé owl and a pair of ugly ceramic mushrooms hung on the wall next to an obscenely huge flat-screen television, the most modern piece in the room.

J.J. waved her and Rue toward the sofa. "I'll be right back," he promised.

"Sit down," Jacob said gruffly when his son left the room. He took a seat in a recliner and ran both hands through his thinning blond hair, making it stick up in tufts. "You were asking about Karl Fuhrman. Why?"

"Is Fuhrman still alive?" Rue asked instead of answering his question.

Jacob's glance sharpened, but he relaxed in the chair, tugging the handle on the side to pop up the footrest. "What if he is? What if he's not?" he countered.

"Is he Schrödinger's cat?" Meredith muttered.

"What's it matter to you?" Jacob shot back at her.

The conversation was going nowhere. Meredith leaned forward, her elbows on her knees. "We're looking for U-3019," she said. At Rue's protesting squawk, she added, "Honey, we might as well quit pussyfooting around with Mr. Olsen and just tell him the truth, otherwise we'll be here all day going around in circles."

"And all night, most likely. I'm a stubborn old coot," Jacob said, nodding at Meredith. "I appreciate plain speaking, Ms. Reid."

"Show off," Rue murmured just before her elbow nudged hard into Meredith's ribs.

Meredith covered her wince with a shrug. "We're trying to find Karl Fuhrman," she said to Jacob. "Ms. Stanton believes he may still be alive and he might have information on the missing U-boat. We'd like to speak to him, if that's possible."

Jacob snorted. "Good luck. My son thinks I'm paranoid. Well, I'm a stone-cold sane individual compared to Fuhrman."

"Then he *is* alive?" Rue asked eagerly.

"Not so fast, young lady. Not so fast. First, you tell me what you know," Jacob said. "Then I'll tell you what I know. That's how an exchange of information works."

Rue sat back, frowning. At last, she ventured another question. "Why would anyone burn down your store?"

"I have a lot of enemies," he replied, waving a dismissive hand. "Some people are offended by my work."

"Bookbinding?" Meredith blurted.

"No, I mean my genealogy work. Certain people don't like it when a stranger tracks down a swastika on a branch of their family tree and publishes the findings. I've gotten death threats, had my windows broken, my tires slashed, but I'm not easily intimidated. My work won't stop until I'm dead."

"Don't talk that way, Dad," J.J. said, coming into the living room with a tray containing four glasses filled with ice cubes and four cans of an off-brand soda. He handed a glass and a can to his father, set the tray on the coffee table, and sat down on the love seat.

Jacob shook his head, but didn't answer his son. He spoke to Rue. "I have my suspicions. That's not important right now." "It may be more important than you know," Rue said. In the dimness of the room, her loose auburn hair smoldered darkly, like embers spilling over her shoulders. "We've had attempts made on us too. A bomb in Miami, shooters in Mexico."

"Is that so?" Jacob paused in the act of pouring soda into his glass. "You think it's the same people targeting us both?"

J.J. groaned. "Oh, please, ma'am, don't do this to him," he said to Rue. "Don't feed his craziness, I beg you. He's bad enough."

"If they're really out to get you—" Jacob began heatedly, but Meredith interrupted.

"Someone doesn't want us finding the U-boat or Karl Fuhrman," she said, taking her cue from Rue's attempt to gain his sympathy through mutual paranoia. "Someone wants to keep them hidden. If you can help us thwart them, Mr. Olsen, we'd be grateful."

His faded blue gaze took on a calculating gleam. "Ya, sure, I think I can help. Confusion to the enemy!" He saluted Meredith with his glass of soda and took a drink. "Fuhrman, you say? Nothing easier."

"I recall from our conversation last year that you keep your records in your shop," Rue said. "Weren't they destroyed in the fire?"

"Oh, I tell people the records are in my shop." Jacob's grin looked surprisingly boyish. "I actually keep them in my boy's basement."

"Dad!" J.J. cried, clearly appalled. "You told me those were family papers."

Jacob drank half his soda in a single gulp. "And so they are, my boy," he said around the ice cube he crunched in his teeth. "When I'm gone, those records will be your legacy."

Meredith tried to tune out the spine-chilling sound. "You said the basement?" She rose from the sofa. "I'd love to see it, Mr. Olsen."

"Nothing easier." Jacob dropped the footrest into the recliner and stood, stretching his back. "Let's go, ladies. I don't want to miss the potluck dinner at the bingo hall this afternoon. Mrs. Bergstrom is bringing her famous tater tot hot dish." He lowered his voice to a hoarse whisper. "And Mrs. Bergstrom herself is a hot dish when she's got her teeth in, so I'm hoping to get lucky tonight, if you know what I mean." He winked and leered.

"Uh, okay, good luck with that," Meredith whispered back uncomfortably.

"Be careful, Dad," J.J. called as Jacob left the living room with Meredith and Rue on his heels. "I moved some of those boxes this morning to make room for my weights set."

Jacob grunted an acknowledgment. He led the way to the kitchen, where he opened a door to reveal a somewhat dilapidated, steep wooden staircase. Cool air wafted out of the open doorway, smelling damp and earthy with a hint of mildew. He flipped a switch on the wall to turn on a light at the bottom of the stairs.

"Ladies, my underground kingdom awaits," he said with a dramatic flourish.

Meredith shared a smile of anticipation with Rue.

CHAPTER TWENTY-FOUR

"J.J.'s never understood my work," Jacob said while clomping down the staircase, which creaked and shuddered at every step. "A hobby, he calls it. Hah! My work is a sacred calling. Why, can you imagine the benefits to mankind if the debate between genetic inheritance or personal experience being most responsible for our innate qualities is resolved once and for all? It's why I've been tracking SS officers for thirty-odd years."

Meredith snatched her hand off the railing, cursed softly, and sucked on a splinter lodged in the meat of her palm. Behind her, she heard Rue sigh.

"I publish my findings in the genealogy magazines and on my blog, which I pay a clever college kid to maintain. I'm told the blog's well received by a couple of the national genealogical associations, even if some people don't care for it. I'm doing important work—ah, here we are," Jacob said when they reached the bottom of the stairs.

The basement was concrete block construction and smaller than Meredith had anticipated given the size of the house.

Battered metal filing cabinets lined three of the walls. Cardboard boxes were piled in a heap in the space behind the stairs. A set of weights and a folding bicycle stood by themselves in the center of the room.

"Fuhrman...Fuhrman..." Jacob snapped his fingers. "Over here." He darted to one of the file cabinets and opened a drawer. A small piece of grubby white card taped to the front of the drawer was marked with a capital *B*.

"Excuse me, are you sure you're in the right place?" Rue asked, looking pointedly at the card. "We want Karl Fuhrman. There's no *B* in his name."

Jacob chuckled. "Ya, sure, it's my own filing system. That's *B* for bastard," he said. "I also have classifications like *RB* for real bastard, *CB* for complete bastard, and so on." An anxious expression crossed his face. "Don't tell my son. He's a real churchgoer, like my ex-wife, he wouldn't appreciate the humor."

"Your secret's safe with us," Meredith said, amazed the man could find anything in the jumbled files. She supposed most of the information was stored in his head. "Just out of curiosity, who do you consider real bastards as opposed to complete bastards?"

"A lot of concentration camp commanders are filed under *RB*, and as for *CB*, you'll find Hitler, Göring, Goebbels, Himmler..." Jacob's voice trailed off. He pulled a thick manila file folder from the drawer, opened it, and made a little smile of satisfaction at the sheaf of papers inside. "Fuhrman acted as Hugo Krause's secretary," he continued, removing a page covered with scribbled handwriting and turning it over, "which for sure you know about already. In 1944, he was reassigned to Berlin. Following Germany's surrender, he fled over the Alps into Italy via a ratline."

"Ratline?" Meredith asked.

"An escape route organized by collaborators and supporters to help Nazis escape prosecution by getting them out of Germany after the war," Rue explained.

"Sounds familiar," Meredith said. "Wasn't there a movie with Jon Voight?"

Jacob rolled his eyes.

"The *Organisation der Ehemaligen SS-Angehörigen*," Rue said, pronouncing the German flawlessly as far as Meredith could tell, "or the Organization of Former SS Members, code-named ODESSA, supposedly smuggled Nazis out of Germany, but there's no evidence such a centralized organization existed, although there were enough individuals and agencies assisting war criminals at the time. Including the CIA, believe it or not."

"It's not just a conspiracy theory, you know. It's history," Jacob said. "Where were we? Oh, yes...in 1946, Fuhrman received an entry permit and forged papers under a false name from his helpers and visited the Red Cross headquarters in Geneva, pretending to be a refugee. With the collusion of a pro-Nazi Croatian priest, he was issued a Nansen passport—normally given to stateless victims of the war—which he used to travel out of Europe to Argentina. He landed in Buenos Aires, where he adopted an identity as a Swiss émigré."

"Going to Buenos Aires makes sense," Rue said, nodding thoughtfully. "Argentina under Perón was a friendly place for former Nazis."

"As of six months ago, Karl Fuhrman a.k.a. Carlos Fellman was living at this address." Jacob showed a slip of paper to Rue. "He married a good Catholic girl in 1951 and had six children with her. His descendants include fourteen grandchildren, ten great-grandchildren, and a recently born great-great-grandson."

Rue studied the address. "Fuhrman lives in the Recoleta, one of the best neighborhoods in the city. He must have access to money." She glanced at Jacob.

"His late wife's family, the Graziones, own an international hotel chain, now run by Fuhrman's granddaughter, Sophia Grazione-Fellman," he said. "Karl Fuhrman inherited plenty of money when his wife died. He and his kids have trust funds."

"Do his in-laws know about Fuhrman's past?"

"You bet. Thiago Grazione knows everything. His fascist-leaning older brother sponsored Fuhrman's immigration. Thiago's retired these days."

"Is there anything else?" Rue asked, plucking the slip of paper bearing Fuhrman's address out of Jacob's hand.

Jacob grasped Rue's wrist and looked at her, his expression utterly serious. "Be careful. Thiago Grazione isn't a very nice man. One of my fellow genealogists in Argentina told me he's rumored to have been involved with Triple A."

Meredith had heard of Triple A, the Argentine Anticommunist Alliance—a government death squad in the mid-1970s. Triple A had been held responsible for many "disappearances" and the murders of dissidents and political enemies of the state.

Treasure or no treasure, she didn't like the idea of possibly going against a dangerous man like Grazione in their pursuit of Fuhrman, who may or may not have information about U-3019. For all she knew, the elderly former Nazi had lost his mind to dementia years ago. However, one look at Rue's rapt expression convinced her the woman wouldn't give up. Rue would keep pursuing the lost U-boat come hell or high water.

She had two options. Quit now and return to Miami, go back to her old life and the status quo with every day a cookie-cutter of the last, or continue to follow where Rue led.

Her experiences with Rue so far had been exciting in a chased-by-thugs-shot-at-blown-up-and-harassed kind of way—not what she'd envisioned when she retired from the navy. However, a strong attraction existed, on her part at least. Rue seemed equally willing to invest in some type of relationship, even if only a friendship with benefits. They fit together well, in bed and out. Bottom line? She decided she'd stick around a while longer.

Jacob had been speaking during her reverie. She returned her attention to the matter at hand and heard him say, "— possible, ya, sure, I wouldn't put it past them."

Becoming aware of Rue and Jacob staring at her in anticipation, Meredith had to confess, "Sorry, would you mind repeating that last thing?"

"I told Jacob about the threats, the restaurant bombing in Miami, and the rest of it," Rue said, clearly exasperated, "and he thinks Thiago Grazione's group may be responsible for everything that's happened to us."

Meredith turned to regard Jacob, who nodded and flapped the file folder he held. "Thiago Grazione is a very, very bad man," he said. "A real thug."

"He runs a social club, if you want to call it that," Rue answered. At Jacob's nod, she went on, "I may not know much about Grazione, but I've heard about the group he leads. In my line of recovery work, I deal with a lot of professionals—experts in the field of art theft—and I've been told about a group who sometimes recommissions a particular painting."

"You mean they ask an artist to make a copy?" Meredith asked, confused.

"No. Basically, a representative of the group tells a thief who's been commissioned to steal a painting to turn the work over to them, not his original client. If the thief doesn't comply…well, fatalities tend to happen."

"Why didn't you tell me about this group before?"

"Because it didn't seem relevant. We're not thieves, we haven't stolen anything—"

"Remember the boat, Rue? After the dive into God's Eye." Meredith scrubbed a hand across her mouth. "That Mexican *pistolero* who threatened us, he kept asking, 'Where is it?' Assuming he was hired to do a job, that means we have something his boss wants."

"Don't be—" Rue broke off. In the light of the single stark bulb overheard, she seemed pale and wan, the surgical scars in front of her ears more prominent. "We don't know for sure Grazione's group is behind the attacks on us, Mer."

"But we also don't know they're not," Meredith pointed out, taking not a bit of satisfaction in being right.

Rue stared at her. After a moment, her gaze dropped. "Crap."

Jacob returned the file to the cabinet and slammed the drawer shut.

Meredith thought the loud, echoing sound seemed to carry the weight of finality.

CHAPTER TWENTY-FIVE

After leaving J.J. Olsen's house, Meredith drove the Corolla back to downtown Saint Paul. She let the silence between her and Rue remain undisturbed a while, until the drive ended and they stood together on the sidewalk in front of the hotel, watching the rental car's taillights disappear around the corner as the valet drove the vehicle away.

"What now?" Meredith asked as she and Rue entered the hotel lobby. Suddenly chilled, she crossed her arms over her chest, blaming the sensation on the air-conditioning rather than dismay.

Rue shook her head. "Buenos Aires. I had no idea."

"Any idea what those people might be after?"

"Grazione's group? We don't even know if they're involved."

"Assume they are."

"I don't know. I can guess, but—"

"Just tell me."

"Krause's journal," Rue finally said, her voice calm, but her eyes alight with anger and more than a trace of fear. "Why make unspecified threats? Why try to blow us up or shoot us? It doesn't make sense. Why not just steal the journal?"

"Maybe a couple of reasons. They need to know where the journal is, so they can't afford to kill you. Threats work because you create terror first," Meredith said, taking hold of Rue's upper arm to drag her to the elevator. "You create an atmosphere of fear and uncertainty to soften up the subject's defenses. Then the situation escalates." She lowered her voice when the elevator door opened, but they were alone. She pressed the button for their room's floor and regarded Rue's wavering, distorted reflection in the closed metal doors. "It never occurred to me, but the hostiles weren't trying to kill us." Rue shook her head and opened her mouth to disagree, but Meredith continued with her theory. "No, hear me out. In the restaurant, for example... why set off a bomb inside? We were seated on the terrace."

"The bomb had to have been planted beforehand," Rue said.

"The bomb could have been a chunk of Semtex or C4 with a detonator wired to a cell phone, hidden somewhere in a few seconds," Meredith said into the pause. "Hell, a skilled operative could've disguised himself or herself as a waiter and planted a bomb directly under our table. The place was so busy, we probably wouldn't have noticed."

"You're saying the bomb wasn't meant to kill us."

"Exactly. Just like the 'taxi driver' in Cancún could have shot us both the second we got into that cab, but he was taking us somewhere in the city."

"I heard kidnapping tourists was commonplace in Mexico."

"Cancún's economy is primarily derived from tourism. It's probably the safest city you'll ever walk around in and besides, I'll bet those news stories are exaggerated."

The elevator doors opened. Rue said nothing while they walked along the hall, the carpet muffling their footsteps. Meredith used the access card to open their room door.

Inside, Rue stopped. "Well, if these hostiles, as you call them, wanted my attention, they've got it," she said. For the first time in their acquaintance, Meredith saw her hesitate. "I don't know if we should go on with this job, Mer. I mean, I won't quit, obviously, but you should go home to Miami. The situation's getting way too dangerous."

Meredith felt her mouth settle into a grim line. "I'm not leaving. That's not up for debate. You can't do this alone."

"What do you military types call it? Collateral damage." Rue flushed. "Someone innocent is going to be hurt. I'm afraid that victim might be you. Maybe I should just give these people what they want," she muttered, turning to the window and pulling back the drapes to let the last of the late afternoon sunlight trickle into the room.

Joining her, Meredith looked out the window and said, "That's your call." She wouldn't push Rue in one direction or the other, wouldn't use a lover's influence to nudge a decision either way. For her part, she'd love to continue, but—

She saw a bright glint in the upper-story window of a tall building directly across from their hotel, visible beyond the green geometry of Rice Park on the other side of the street. The building was under construction, swathed in scaffolding.

"I'm probably just being paranoid," Rue said, laughing a little. "We have no proof Grazione's organization has anything to do with our search for U-3019. If Grazione knows Fuhrman, he doesn't need Krause's journal, does he? So I guess—"

The glint winked once, twice, and each time, Meredith's heart thumped.

"—you even listening to me?"

Acting on instinct, Meredith lunged at Rue and pulled her down to the floor a split second before the window shattered, spraying them with broken glass.

"Stay down," she panted into Rue's white, shocked face.

She left Rue there and scuttled on her belly to snatch a pillow off the bed. No second shot answered her daring. Hardly breathing, she reached for the telephone on the bedside table and knocked off the receiver. Nothing happened. She supposed Rue was his primary target and he had no real interest in her, but without being sure, she wouldn't risk standing. Her hand crept up to the telephone. She blindly stabbed at the keypad.

After a moment, she heard the tinny, unintelligible voice of the 911 operator issuing from the receiver on the floor.

"I'm a guest in the Saint Paul Hotel," she said loudly into the mouthpiece, "and there's a shooter in the building across the park. Rice Park. He just shot at our room and broke the window." She recited the floor and room number. Without waiting for a reply, she scooted back to Rue.

"What the hell?" A fine thread of blood slipped down Rue's temple. She seemed partly dazed, partly frightened, and altogether furious.

Meredith shook the pillow out of its cotton case and used a corner of the fabric to apply direct pressure against the shallow, messy cut on Rue's brow. With her other hand, she picked shards of glass out of Rue's hair. "We need to get out of here," she said. "Keep your head below the level of the window. Do not stand. Crawl to the door with me. Okay?"

Rue nodded, so wide-eyed a rim of white showed all around the mismatched irises. At Meredith's direction, she shifted to her hands and knees.

Meredith abandoned the pillowcase. Together, she and Rue moved to the door and crawled into the hall. A few yards away from the room she stood and gave Rue a hand up. The doors lining the quiet hallway remained closed.

"So much for your theory," Rue said, shaking off more bits of glass. "Whoever made that shot meant to kill us."

"No," Meredith said, listening to her gut instinct. "You were standing in the middle of the window, a perfect target without obstructions. The day's almost windless. The sniper was much less than a thousand yards away. Anyone with experience couldn't have missed unless he intended to, especially a professional with a scope." She took hold of Rue's arm and spoke directly to the woman's skepticism, trying her damnedest to make her understand. "That shot was a warning, or most likely a message."

"The people who sent the sniper…what are they trying to tell us?"

"That you'll never be safe anywhere until they get what they want."

The muscles in Rue's jaw bunched under the skin. She touched the cut on her head, which had stopped bleeding, but her probing fingernail broke the delicate crust. The small wound began oozing blood again. She ignored it. "You know, I'm sick of these asshats trying to tell me what to do," she said, pushing away Meredith's reaching hand. "I'm tired of them hurting other people while trying to hurt me."

"Are you…are you going to give them the journal?" Meredith asked.

Rue shook her head. A scattered blood droplet left a red splatter on the elegant golden-cream wall. "Hell, no. I don't know for sure if it's Grazione's group causing us problems, but that doesn't matter. Whoever it is, they can go screw themselves. I'm not a quitter." Her mouth stretched into a ghastly smile. "If I was, I'd never have survived the car accident or all that time in the hospital. You think finding a U-boat is hard? Try learning how to walk again, how to chew your food, how not to scream when a nurse debrides your burns."

With difficulty, Meredith worked up enough saliva for speech. "Jesus."

Rue suddenly turned and marched to their room before Meredith's reflex snatch could stop her. She yanked the door further open and went inside.

Meredith returned to the room, half expecting to find Rue shot through the head. Instead, she found her scribbling something on a legal pad she'd taken from the open suitcase on the chair. At her questioning glance, Rue shrugged and went to the broken window, where she held up the pad.

What's she…oh. Meredith realized Rue wanted the sniper to read whatever she'd written. She went behind Rue, close enough to catch the scent of shampoo, and peered at the legal pad. The message read, *Let's talk. Double your fee. Meet at Grill's bar in half hour.*

So many curses crowded her mouth she couldn't articulate them all.

CHAPTER TWENTY-SIX

"Are you out of your mind?" Meredith asked in a heated undertone for the sixth time since she'd left the room with Rue, following her downstairs to the St. Paul Grill.

"I told you, I'm sick of those guys and their threats. I don't like the rules, so I'm changing them," Rue answered. "Look, if the sniper comes, he isn't going to try anything in the middle of witnesses, is he? We haven't lost anything by opening a dialogue."

"Opening a—damn it, Rue, he's a sniper, a killer for hire."

"And therefore has a price. Let's find out how much. Besides, he might not show up at all, in which case, we can enjoy dinner in peace without worrying about lead poisoning."

After finding a seat at the bar, Rue hid behind the menu while Meredith ordered a double bourbon from the bartender. "Maker's Mark, neat," she said, having a feeling she'd need a healthy dose of alcohol to survive this so-called meeting.

Rue ordered a huckleberry margarita, one of the frillier drinks on the menu, and asked for a sampler of hot appetizers to share.

Meredith shuddered when the bartender slid a pinkish-purple concoction with a salt-crusted rim in front of Rue, who sipped from the straw and made a "yummy" face.

"Do I dare ask what's in there?" Meredith asked, gesturing with her glass of bourbon.

"Huckleberry syrup, tequila, triple sec, agave nectar, sweet and sour, and it's delicious, Mer. Do you want to try it?"

"No, thanks, I'll stick with the classics."

The shared appetizer arrived soon: hot peppered shrimp, crab cakes with citrus tarragon aioli, seared ahi tuna with pickled ginger, fried calamari, and Cajun beef bites.

Despite her nerves insisting she wasn't hungry, Meredith's stomach disagreed. Besides, Rue was right. If the sniper came here, he wouldn't attempt to hurt them, not in such a public place. She might as well eat and enjoy the meal.

Rue saluted her with the margarita and said, "Relax. I do this for a living, remember? Negotiate with criminals. I'm what you might call an expert."

Meredith finished eating the last bite of spicy tenderloin beef. She consulted the menu, considering whether to order a chocolate molten lava cake in lieu of an entrée, when a man dressed in a simple, short-sleeved gray T-shirt and jeans slid onto the stool next to Rue. Was he the sniper? she wondered, studying him surreptitiously.

The newcomer was whippet lean, clean-shaven, brown-eyed, with unremarkable features. His dark hair was cut very short to his scalp. She saw no visible scars, tattoos, or markings of any kind on his face or arms. His skin might have been naturally light brown, or he might be well tanned. His nationality appeared impossible to determine.

From the bartender, the man ordered the Macallan, a fifty-five-year-old scotch costing $750 per shot. He jerked a thumb at Rue. "Put it on her tab," he said.

The bartender turned a mute inquiry on Rue. She swiveled to face the newcomer. "I suppose you're the guy we're waiting for, right? The one who breaks windows from a distance?" When the man nodded, she said to the bartender, "Hook him up."

Once the bartender served his drink and moved down the bar, the man said, "You mentioned double my fee." He picked up the glass and took a slow sip.

"So I did, Mr…?" Rue's voice trailed off suggestively.

He paused. "Mr. Smith."

"Very well, Mr. Smith. If I'm paying you, I have certain conditions."

"And those conditions would be?"

Watching Rue and Smith banter, Meredith wished she had another double bourbon.

"I want to know the name of your employer," Rue said.

"Regrettably, not possible," Smith replied. "My contact is usually through the Internet, no names, electronic money transfer to my bank. Nice and anonymous." His eyes gleamed.

Rue shook her head. "I'm afraid that's a deal breaker."

Meredith lost her patience. She leaned around Rue to snap at Smith, "Anonymous? Bullshit. You know who hired you, to avoid entrapment by Interpol or the FBI, if nothing else. If you weren't careful, you wouldn't be in business very long."

Smith signaled the bartender for a refill. "Call off your dog," he said, giving Meredith a sidelong glance that seemed amused rather than intimidated. "Or should I say, your bitch."

Not the first time an insolent man had called her a bitch and probably not the last, Meredith thought, maintaining a stony expression with the ease of long practice. "Well?" she growled, fixing him with a well-developed naval commander's eye.

The glass halted halfway to his lips. "Suppose you're right," he said, his voice tight. "If you are, my client is probably not someone you want to mess around with—"

Rue interrupted by waving a hand in his face. "What were you hired to do?"

He shrugged. "Warning shots unless otherwise instructed. You figured out I'm not authorized to terminate the target, so no charge for the info…so far."

"Why miss? Why not kill us?"

"Anything else you want to know, I need to see the color of your money."

"How much?"

"For you, doll? A half million US dollars or Euro equivalent."

Meredith involuntarily whistled, but Rue didn't turn a hair. "I need to get in touch with my client," she said, sliding off the tall stool. "Give me ten minutes."

Smith made a show of checking his watch.

Rue walked away, coming to a stop just outside the bar area. She took a cell phone from her pocket and dialed a number. A moment later, she began speaking.

Ignoring Meredith, Smith savored his expensive scotch as if he weren't an assassin for hire—likely wanted by law enforcement agencies around the world, or so she thought.

"Why'd you agree to this meeting?" Meredith finally asked.

He shrugged. "Nothing better to do."

"You've had us under surveillance a while," she guessed. "You know we aren't law enforcement."

"True." He said nothing else, merely continued to sip his drink.

Meredith settled on the stool, watching him out of the corner of her eye.

Rue returned after about five minutes. "All right, Mr. Smith," she said, "where do you want the money transferred?"

He slid two fingers into the front pocket of his jeans and produced a slip of paper with writing on it.

Holding the cell phone to her ear, Rue took the offered paper and reeled off an account number. When she finished, she disconnected the call and sat on her stool. "The transfer's complete. Do you want to verify?" she asked Smith.

Taking out his cell phone, Smith made a call. He spoke in French for several minutes. When he completed the call, his expression showed a newfound respect for Rue. "What can I do for you, boss?" he asked without a hint of sarcasm.

"Who hired you?" Rue asked at once.

He shook his head. "I don't know." At Meredith's impatient growl, he smirked. "I don't know exactly," he amended. "I traced payment to a bank: HSBC, Buenos Aires branch."

Meredith exchanged glances with Rue. The deeper they dug, the more important the Argentinean connection seemed to become.

Rue asked Smith, "Who's the account holder?"

"A trust account in the name of Grazione. That's as far as I went."

"What were your precise instructions regarding me and my friend?"

Smith finished the last of the scotch in his glass, his Adam's apple bobbing when he swallowed. He favored Rue with a direct look. "I was hired to follow you and report on your movements," he admitted frankly. "At my last check-in an hour ago, I reported you and your friend had visited Jacob Olsen. I received instructions to shoot at you, but not to kill. He said something about women breaking easy, whatever that means. Any other questions?"

"Just one," Meredith piped up when he stood. "Why did you betray your client?" She paid no attention when Rue dug a warning elbow into her ribs.

He started to walk away, but paused and said over his shoulder, "Because I'm a professional world-class shooter, not a goddamn babysitter. If that asshole wants a spy, let him hire one. I'm through. Thanks for the bonus, by the way. Toodle-oo, dolls." He disappeared into a crowd of chattering hotel guests entering the restaurant.

After Smith left, Meredith stared at the bar's gleaming surface a long time, thinking over her options. Decision made at last, she glanced at Rue. "Buenos Aires?"

Rue handed her credit card to the hovering bartender. "Buenos Aires," she confirmed.

"My concern?" Meredith blinked. "Grazione might kill us, for one."

"Clearly, we have something he wants. Logic seems to point to the journal. Or the papers we found in Krause's lockbox are also a possibility."

"So he captures us and tortures us to get what he wants. Don't discount the possibility. Thiago Grazione doesn't strike me as the kind of man who uses 'pretty please' a lot."

"I have a plan." At Meredith's impatient gesture, Rue went on, "Velse is hooking us up with more than the jet. When we get to Buenos Aires, we'll be met by bodyguards."

Surprised, Meredith sat up straighter. "Bodyguards?"

"A private security firm," Rue confirmed. "Velse told me he's used them before."

"Sounds like you guys have everything in hand." Meredith closed the journal and passed it back to Rue, who rolled over to lay the book beside her cell phone on the nightstand.

The cell phone's ringing visibly startled Rue. She fumbled the phone to her ear. "Stanton here. What? What happened? What do you want?"

Alarmed by the one-sided conversation, as well as the way Rue sat bolt upright on the edge of the mattress, her spine rigid with distress, Meredith leaned closer and settled a silently supportive hand on the woman's shoulder.

When Rue took the phone away from her ear, her face was drained of color. "Clay's gone," she said woodenly.

At first, Meredith didn't understand. She almost asked, "Clay, who?" until the truth struck her dumb. Retired Master Chief Clay Cochrane, her friend, was gone. Dive accident? Heart attack? Stroke? Angry cuckolded husband? She found her voice with an effort. "What happened? How'd he die?"

"Not dead. Taken." Rue hung her head. "Oh, my God, oh, God." She dropped the cell phone on the bed and dug the heels of her hands into her eyes. "Oh, God."

Desperate for information, Meredith grabbed Rue's upper arms and shook her. "What happened?" she demanded through gritted teeth. "Talk to me!"

CHAPTER TWENTY-EIGHT

The flight from Saint Paul to Buenos Aires, with a brief stop in Miami for passports and Rue's tablet, was fairly long—over ten hours—but Meredith had never been more comfortable on an airplane. Clearly, Elliot Painter Velse spared no expense to make his custom Gulfstream G650 corporate jet as luxurious as possible.

The seats in the large cabin were covered in butter-soft leather, featured heat and massage options, and were fully adjustable. A divan in the rear converted to a double bed. The air smelled fresh, tinged with a sweet floral scent from flower arrangements in vases. Like traveling in an expensive hotel at a cruising speed of Mach 0.85, she thought.

She'd already scrolled through the entertainment options, peeked at the clouds through the windows, and visited the aft lavatory, a marvel of gilt and glossy veneered opulence that wouldn't have looked out of place in a palace. Now she and Rue sat at a conference table eating a five-star meal served by the steward, Harrison—a soft-spoken, middle-aged British man with the polite, impassive demeanor of a guild-trained butler.

Rue said very little through the lobster ravioli in pink sauce, the pear and endive salad, the roasted free-range pork with root vegetable gratin, onion jam, and wine sauce, and the hazelnut cake with cream. She nodded acceptance at the wines offered by the steward with each course, but took only a bare sip of each. She didn't eat much either.

Meredith almost felt bad for stuffing herself—almost. She hadn't eaten a five-star meal in a long time. Had it not been utterly *déclassé*, she'd have asked for a doggie bag.

At the end of the meal, the steward poured coffee into delicate, white porcelain cups rimmed with the thinnest gilt edge and vanished into the galley, leaving them alone.

Meredith cleared her throat, breaking the silence.

"I'm fine," Rue said, toying with a dainty silver spoon. "No, I'm not. I'm just…God, Mer, I've combed through Krause's papers so many times, my eyes are ready to bleed. If there's a clue to the U-boat's location in there, I sure as hell can't find it. And I'm worried sick about Clay."

"Clay will be fine," Meredith said to comfort herself as much as Rue. "He's a tough old son of a bitch. He'll survive." *He'd better*, she added darkly to herself, *or Thiago Grazione is going to have the worst day of his miserable life when I catch up to him.*

"What are we going to do?"

"I don't know. I can't really make any plans till I know the whole situation."

"Well, I talked to Velse and told him what's going on. Remember I told you he hired bodyguards for us? Turns out it's a squad of mercenaries or something like that. He wasn't really clear, just said he'd used the team before and they were good."

"Don't get any ideas about dramatic rescues, Rue. That kind of thing is as dangerous to the hostage as the hostage takers. Last-resort measures have a greatly reduced chance of success. You ought to know. You negotiate with professional criminals all the time."

"That's what scares me. A professional kidnapper is one thing. They just want their money. It's a job. You can negotiate. But Grazione…he's unpredictable."

"We'll get Clay back," Meredith promised. "We'll do what needs to be done."

"Still, it won't hurt to get an informed opinion from these mercenaries Velse hired," Rue told her primly. "If nothing else, we can use them as go-betweens to make sure Grazione holds up his end of the deal."

"Like I said, let's not make plans until we see what's what in Buenos Aires." Meredith reached over to push a lock of auburn hair behind Rue's ear. "We'll get him back."

Rue stood from the table. "I'm going to study those papers some more."

"Would you rather rest? Take a nap?" Meredith asked, moving with her to the front of the cabin. "I can ask Harrison to turn out the bed for you."

"Want to join me? Plenty of room," Rue asked with a sly glance. Her mood seemed to have improved with the change of subject. She snatched a chocolate from a dish on the table and popped the bonbon into her mouth. An expression of bliss crossed her face.

Meredith tried a chocolate. Raspberry. Decadent. Delicious.

"How's your Mile High Club membership?" Rue asked under her breath.

The thought of having sex while Harrison was within eye and earshot made Meredith shudder. She was no exhibitionist. "Thanks, but no thanks," she said. "Gin rummy?"

Rue shrugged and gave her a devilish grin. "Not very adventurous, are we?"

Goaded, Meredith crowded closer, until not a tenth of an inch of space existed between their bodies. "Oh, I'd love to lay you down," she said in a low, thrilling voice, letting the words resonate deep in her chest. She sensed Rue's breath catch and saw her pupils dilate. "Take off all your clothes and lay you down on that bed," she went on. "Watch you spread your legs and play with yourself. You'd like that, wouldn't you, baby? Playing with your pretty little pussy, getting it nice and wet for me."

Rue's lips parted. Color flooded her face. She whimpered.

"Maybe I'll lay down with you," Meredith continued in a hoarse whisper, sliding a hand up Rue's arm. The skin pebbled under her touch. Desire pooled, glowing in the deepest part of her. Waves of arousal beat in time to the pulsating heat and wetness between her legs. Sweat broke out on her forehead. Shivering, she licked her lips, noticing Rue's rapt gaze followed the movements of her tongue. "Maybe I'll let you ride my face," she said, swallowing a sudden flood of saliva filling her mouth. "Maybe I'll—"

Rue's hand shot up to silence her. She looked flushed and wild. "Oh, damn it. Bathroom," she said. "Now," she added as she headed toward the lavatory.

Meredith thought that might be the most brilliant idea she'd ever heard.

Inside the lavatory with the door locked, Rue kissed her fiercely. When she gasped, Rue's tongue, tasting like chocolate and raspberries, pushed deep inside her mouth. She held on to Rue's supple body with both hands while the world dipped and spun.

At last, she broke off the kiss, panting.

The lavatory was a little bigger than the commercial airline standard, but not huge. Nevertheless, Rue spun, trapping her against the sink. Meredith closed her eyes. Her shoulders tensed. The tension traveled to her neck when Rue licked the skin beneath her ear, the caress simultaneously hot and cold.

Rue tucked a hand against her crotch. Meredith took a ragged breath, and another, the clenching ache in her belly intensifying. She scrabbled to unfasten her jeans and push them down her hips. Rue helped, murmuring reassurances, kissing her each time she tried to speak—soft, teasing, fleeting kisses she found frustrating even as they stoked her desire.

Once her jeans were discarded and her panties hung off an ankle, Meredith impatiently sucked Rue's bottom lip into her mouth, held it between her front teeth, and bit lightly, grinning around Rue's rasping moan. She let go when Rue's fingers pushed apart her labia and began moving around inside, spreading her wetness. She felt overripe, dripping juices, open and engorged at the same time.

At Rue's urging, she made a hop to plant her buttocks on the rim of the sink. Her bare flesh flinched at the chilly contact. She spread her thighs apart. Her left foot banged against the door. For a second, she cringed, afraid Harrison had heard and guessed what they were doing, but when Rue touched her, she couldn't bring herself to give a good goddamn.

Without much room to maneuver, Rue managed to sink down into a squat low enough to put her mouth on Meredith's sex.

A burning, impossibly agile tongue found her clitoris. She stiffened at the shock. Her fingers curled around the edge of the sink. The shiny, veneered wood felt as slick under her palms as the place where Rue lapped in long, loving strokes, making obscene slurping noises mixed with hungry groans.

The muscles in her thighs flexed. Her foot banged the door again. The faucet dug into her back, an irritation lost in the growing, sultry rush rocketing upward from her sex to fill her head with static. She needed...she needed just a little more...

She came, writhing as her fingers buried in Rue's hair, a constellation of wild, white stars bursting behind her closed eyelids.

Rue rose and leaned over her, reaching out to grab a guest towel from the holder. She wiped her face and moved into Meredith's embrace. "Feel good?" she murmured.

Meredith nodded. She became aware that at some point, Rue had undone the button and zipper of her linen pants and put her hand inside. Now she saw the movements of busy fingers under the fabric. She imagined what those fingers were doing to the flushed pink folds of Rue's sex, to the swollen clitoris, the creamy glide of flesh on slippery flesh...

Tender emotion swelling her heart, she held Rue while the woman trembled and climaxed, muffling the sharp cries against her neck.

CHAPTER TWENTY-NINE

To Meredith's surprise, the VIP treatment continued at a private airfield in Buenos Aires. A uniformed official met them in the airplane hangar and stamped their passports without more than a cursory glance. When he finished, Harrison, the steward, discreetly passed the official an envelope, which just as discreetly vanished inside the man's jacket.

"Money talks," Rue said under her breath. "All part of the service."

"Lifestyles of the rich and famous," Meredith replied, half-impressed, half-appalled. She avoided looking at Harrison, embarrassed about her and Rue having sex in the lavatory.

A tall woman wearing a sleeveless black T-shirt and khaki cargo pants waited for them at the hangar door. Her skin was like dark chocolate wrapped over hard muscle and bone. Sweat gleamed on her exposed arms like rubbed-in oil. She examined them carefully, her expression neutral. Meredith noticed the holster on the woman's belt. The gun's grip looked well worn, but well cared for.

"*Mma* Stanton?" the woman asked, flicking a glance from Rue to her.

Rue stepped forward. "You're our bodyguard detail?"

The woman inclined her head. "One of them," she said in lightly accented English. "Sadiya Maphane. Please come with me. Everything is ready."

Rue followed Sadiya out of the hangar. Meredith stayed a step behind. Now they were in Buenos Aires—the lion's den, so to speak—her skin seemed too tight. Her nerves jangled with anxious electricity. The hair on the back of her neck prickled. She scanned the airfield and the hangars while she walked toward a parked Land Cruiser.

A woman slightly shorter than Rue stood beside the vehicle. Sunlight added a gilt burnish to her coppery skin and struck blue highlights in her fine black hair. Her dark, almond-shaped eyes and strong features reminded Meredith of Mayan statues.

"Catalina Rivas," the woman said, accepting Rue's hand. A plane roared overhead, angling for a landing on the runway. She waited for the engine noise to subside before continuing. "Mr. Velse hired my team to ensure your security during your stay in Buenos Aires. If you'll step inside, Ms. Stanton, Ms. Reid, we'll take you to your hotel."

Sadiya opened the passenger side door and stepped into the vehicle. In the brief time before the door closed, Meredith caught a glimpse of the female driver, a hard-bitten blonde.

Catalina held open the back door. "Please," she added with a curve to her lips that could only technically be called a smile.

Meredith had a brief moment of concern for their safety then slid into the backseat with Rue on one side, Catalina on the other. *Velse hired the bodyguards,* she thought. *He had compelling reasons to want us protected.* She would trust these women a little and watch them a lot.

The SUV rolled forward, away from the airfield. After a few minutes on the road, she caught her first glimpse of Buenos Aires. The streets were fairly congested, a mix of cars and trucks belching exhaust exactly the same as any other large city. The drivers—including their own—seemed to regard lanes as more of a suggestion than a rule. The cacophony of constant horn honking was nearly muted by the ballistic glass windows.

"You are here to meet with Carlos Fellman, is that correct?" Catalina asked Rue, using Karl Fuhrman's alias. She settled with unconscious grace on the seat.

"In a way. We'd like to ask Mr. Fellman a few questions. We don't have an appointment or anything," Rue answered. "I had hoped to contact him when we arrived."

Catalina looked thoughtful. "Arrangements may be difficult to make. Fellman is closely connected to the Grazione family. You know them?"

When Rue nodded, Meredith felt compelled to say, "There's a complication."

"I was just about to tell her," Rue said with a halfhearted glare in her direction.

"Tell me about this complication," Catalina ordered.

Rue launched into the tale of Clay Cochrane's kidnapping, careful to make no mention of the U-boat or the treasure. She ended on a question. "Do you think you and your team could act as go-betweens for the transaction with Thiago Grazione?"

Catalina studied her, the steady regard bringing a slight flush of color to Rue's cheeks. At last, she asked, "You don't want the police involved?"

"No." Rue's chin rose. "We don't know who to trust."

"And you trust me because Mr. Velse is footing the bill for my services."

"If you care to put it that way, yes."

"You don't consider I might be playing both sides against the middle?" Catalina asked. "Or Mr. Velse might not have you or your friend's best interests at heart?"

Meredith broke in. "Velse has no reason to betray us."

Catalina's sharp brown gaze flashed to her. "As far as you know."

"As far as I know," she conceded the point.

She waited for Catalina to go on, but the woman leaned back in the seat and stared out the window instead. Rue's warning glance wasn't necessary. She recognized the look of a commander weighing the logistics of a mission. Rather than interrupt, she tried to enjoy the sights of the city while the Land Cruiser weaved in and out of traffic.

After a while, the driver parked the SUV in the street outside what appeared to be a nineteenth-century, colonial-style house painted a startlingly sunny yellow in contrast to other, similar buildings in the row, all in shades of mint green, powder blue or white.

Meredith wondered why they'd stopped in a residential neighborhood. Even here, the streets were busy. Pedestrians dominated, not vehicles, but the noise level remained high.

"Wait in the vehicle," Catalina said. Again, the statement sounded like an order. "Do not exit unless Sadiya or myself comes to escort you. Understood?" She opened the door and slid out of the backseat. The door shut behind her.

"Alone at last," Meredith joked. She wiped her damp palms on her jeans.

Rue didn't laugh. "We're in the Boedo *barrio*," she said. "Old and traditional. Not touristy. There's a subway station around here somewhere." She smoothed a hand over her shining, dark auburn hair, which she'd styled in a simple knot secured at the back of her neck. Soft tendrils had already escaped the knot and hung in loose curls around her face. She impatiently blew a curl out of her eye. "It's been a while since I visited the city."

Watching her, Meredith's chest felt tight with more than apprehension.

When the temperature inside the SUV began to edge upward into intolerable, the back door opened, held by Sadiya. "*Tlaa kwano, bo mma.* Please come with me," she said.

Outside, other women stood with Sadiya: the hard-bitten blond driver, a very dark-skinned woman with dreadlocks, and a petite brunette Latina who resembled a ballerina, or so Meredith thought until she saw the HK MP7 compact submachine gun cradled in her hands.

"Sanchez," Sadiya said, nodding at the blonde. She called the Latina, "Carrizo," and the other black woman, "Qwabe."

Meredith and Rue were led into the house with Sadiya taking point, Sanchez and Carrizo in flanking positions. Qwabe brought up the rear.

Was Catalina's team composed entirely of women? Meredith considered asking. She'd always believed female mercenaries were a myth. Like mermaids or the Flying Dutchman, everybody talked about them, but nobody had ever actually seen one. As bodyguards and on security details, yes. Mercenaries? No. Perhaps Rue or Velse got the details wrong.

Her thoughts went to her friend, Clay Cochrane. She couldn't let herself be seduced by hope. She and Rue were on their own despite the bodyguards. She'd do everything possible to rescue him from Grazione, and if her efforts failed...

Well, if she failed, it wouldn't be the first time.

CHAPTER THIRTY

When the group entered the house, Rue's flat-heeled pumps made clicking noises on the tiled floor. Meredith glanced around the tasteful interior, at the eggshell-colored walls, the arched doorways, the wood and iron staircase curving to the second floor. A large mahogany counter took up most of one side of the room, which she quickly realized was a hotel lobby. No clerks, no bellboys, but several armed women stood around the space.

A humid breeze blew through an open archway, carrying with it an abundance of smells: spicy barbequed meat and smoke, the green scent of growing things, a trace of diesel exhaust, coffee. Plenty of noise from outside, too, including a squawking parrot.

Meredith hoped their room had air-conditioning and a shower. The way she sweated, she'd need both before too long or she wouldn't be fit for company.

Sadiya took her and Rue through the archway outside to the back of the hotel.

The hotel had been built around a large central courtyard open to the sky. In a tiled area surrounded by ferns, lime trees, jasmine and hibiscus, Catalina sat in a chair at a white-painted, art nouveau ironwork garden table. She beckoned them to come closer and join her.

Meredith sat. Rue chose a seat next to her, facing Catalina. In the middle of the table stood a tea service with flower-decorated porcelain cups.

"*Mate cocido*, an herbal drink. Very refreshing, very good for you," Catalina said, pouring three cups of a liquid resembling weak tea. "Sugar? Milk?"

Rue waved aside the offered cup. "Can you help us with our problem, Ms. Rivas?" she asked. "I can't conduct my business in the city until our friend is safe."

A jewel-bright hummingbird zipped by Catalina's head on its way to a nearby hibiscus plant. She ignored the bird in favor of sipping her tea, her gaze never wavering from Rue. "To a certain extent, yes, I can help," she said carefully.

"How?"

"I am prepared to assist with negotiations. My team will provide your personal security during the transaction as per our contractual agreement with Mr. Velse. Should the transaction be unsuccessful, my team will escort you and Ms. Reid out of the area."

"What about Clay Cochrane, the hostage?"

"I'm sorry. My brief doesn't extend to hostage extraction."

Rue's hand clenched into a fist.

Meredith bit her lip against the urge to shout. She'd known they would have to rescue Cochrane on their own, damn it, but hearing the fact stated openly made her disappointment keener. She drank the hot, bitter tea and felt more sweat springing out on her body. She resisted the temptation to claw at her itching skin.

"I'm sorry," Catalina repeated. To her credit, she did appear regretful.

"Is it a question of money?" Rue asked.

Catalina's mouth firmed. "No. Not money. As I said, we will help you negotiate with Grazione. That's within our brief. How much does he want?"

"Not money, but I have the article he wants."

"Then my best advice is to give it to him. He and his followers have a certain reputation for ruthlessness, but I've never heard of him going back on his word. He'll make the trade and my people will be there to ensure the exchange goes smoothly."

"There's nothing else you can do?" Rue pleaded.

For a third time, Catalina expressed her regrets. "Qwabe will escort you to your room. Unless it's a problem, I'd prefer you two share quarters so I don't have to split my team guarding two rooms."

"Fine," Rue said through clenched teeth.

"I suggest you rest and freshen up. Take a long siesta. If you wish, we'll take you to see something of the city tonight." Catalina's smooth, soothing tone suggested a governess offering a treat to unruly children as a bribe to make them behave.

"Thank you." Rue rose and marched back inside the hotel, her shoulders set in a line quivering with tension.

Meredith pushed away from the table and followed Rue, the tea roiling uneasily in her stomach. A silent Qwabe showed them to their room—an airy space with dark, heavy, old-fashioned furniture and two queen-sized beds. The quilted coverlets were white with an abstract, almost leafy red and orange pattern echoed by the curtains. A large armchair near the window held their suitcases. Everything looked clean, including the attached bathroom.

Cool air from the window air conditioner washed over her sweaty skin.

Qwabe left, shutting the door behind her.

"I'm tempted to call Velse and see if he'll authorize payment for a rescue," Rue said.

"I don't know if that's the best idea," Meredith said, sitting on the edge of the bed. "Grazione may honor his word and release Clay if we give him what he wants."

"What about Velse? Do you think he'll want a Nazi lover like Thiago Grazione beating us to the U-boat?" Rue began to pace. "Why else would Grazione want Krause's papers? He and his group are after the treasure, I know it."

Meredith grabbed Rue's wrist on her next pass, holding her in place. "You're making me dizzy. Sit down. Let's go through the problem one step at a time."

Rue shook her off, but took a place beside her on the bed. The toe of her shoe impatiently tapped the floor. "First, we have to get Clay back. That's my priority."

"Mine too."

"Then we need to talk to Fuhrman, find out what he knows."

"If he refuses to answer our questions, what then?" Meredith spread her hands apart. "Don't glare a hole in me, Rue. Why should he tell us anything? We have no authority, no means to compel him, and I can't imagine he'd spill the beans of his own free will."

Rue's frown deepened. "We can threaten to expose his past. He's lived a lie all these years, Mer. The Argentine government won't turn a blind eye, not now. He may be arrested, deported back to Germany...he won't get a free ride this time around."

"If Fuhrman runs?"

"We'll follow him. We'll find him."

"You don't think Fuhrman will go to his brother-in-law for protection?" Meredith asked. "If he does, I'm pretty sure Grazione won't risk being exposed as a Nazi sympathizer. Remember what Jacob Olsen told us before we took off? Fuhrman's granddaughter, Sophia, runs the Graziones' hotel business. Maybe she doesn't know about Thiago's past or his strong-arm group. She might cut him off financially if she also controls the family money."

"Or she might not. Or he could tell her to go to hell while he lives off his trust fund. Look, we can't worry about every little thing that might happen—"

"Actually, the more objections we can find at each step, the more potential obstacles we can identify, the better prepared we'll be if something goes wrong. Maybe we need to find out exactly how far Ms. Rivas's offer of help extends."

"I'll ask tonight. She also needs to know when and where Grazione wants to meet. She'll probably want security measures in place beforehand."

"Good idea."

Rue stood and returned to pacing. "All this talk about planning for the worst-case scenario gives me hives. I feel like we're jinxing the whole thing by being too negative."

Meredith joined Rue at the window, where the air conditioner's stream of cool, damp air blew strongest. The upper part of the window was covered with a frosted panel making an outside view impossible. That the obscured view also prevented a sniper from targeting them wasn't lost on her, not after what happened in Saint Paul.

"We can't be prepared for every contingency, but we can try. That way, we're prepared, we don't go in blind, and we have plans in place to deal with surprises. We also have to stay flexible. You're the most flexible woman I know," she said, bumping Rue's shoulder and giving her an exaggerated leer.

Rue chuckled. "I'm tired and it's too hot to play what-if right now. I'm inclined to take a nice, long siesta. Nothing will happen until Grazione contacts us anyway. Want to join me?" She stood up to fold down the bedspread, revealing crisp, white cotton sheets.

Joining Rue on the bed, Meredith closed her eyes and made her mind blank, pushing aside all worries. Rest was good.

When she fell asleep, she dreamed of Clay Cochrane, alive and reaching out to her with his callused hands covered in blood.

CHAPTER THIRTY-ONE

Later that evening, Meredith and Rue were escorted by several members of Catalina's team—but not the leader herself—to a restaurant around the corner from the hotel.

Buenos Aires was a city of walkers, Meredith discovered. Despite the constant stink of gas and exhaust fumes, the steady vehicular traffic, and the ear-shattering din of car horns, passing buses, taxis, sirens, scooters, low-flying planes, and a thousand other sounds, a sea of pedestrians seethed on either side of the street. Surrounded by a half dozen female bodyguards, she felt safe walking down the narrow pavement, if a bit claustrophobic.

The restaurant was small, only twelve tables arranged around a central bar area, but the smell of grass-fed beef on a smoking-hot grill was unmistakable and mouthwatering. She sniffed, grinned, and caught Rue's eye.

"I'm so hungry, I could eat half a cow," Rue told her, sinking into a chair.

Meredith took the other chair. "You and me both."

Sadiya and the other guards took seats at a table directly in front of theirs, in the best position to cover the door. *They must come here often.* The waitstaff didn't spare the group more than a single glance.

A waiter placed dishes of olives, grilled peppers, semidried tomatoes, garlic bread and cheese on the table. Meredith tried an olive and found it stuffed with a whole peeled almond. Neither she nor Rue saw a menu or placed an order. Servers brought chunks of meat off the grill and sliced the marinated rib eye, tenderloin and skirt steak directly onto their plates. Another waiter delivered salads and a bottle of cabernet sauvignon. A third went back and forth carrying little dishes of sausages, empanadas and sautéed sweetbreads.

Meredith almost felt guilty shoveling food down her gullet while the guards had to sit and watch without so much as a shared appetizer, but the beef was too good for regrets. She lifted her wineglass and said, "To absent friends."

Rue repeated the toast and touched their wineglasses together.

The restaurant's subdued lighting almost erased the difference between Rue's brown eye and her blue eye, Meredith thought. She opened her mouth, about to voice a compliment on how the navy, lime green, and white striped sundress flattered Rue's curves, when the subdued clatter of forks on plates was replaced by a sharp, stuttering blast.

Automatic weapons fire.

The empanada fell from Meredith's hand, crushed underfoot when she leaped up from the table and made to grab Rue, but the woman fell on the floor without prompting. In the same instant, Sadiya and the other bodyguards rose from their table and began returning fire.

Terrified customers screamed and scrambled to get away, or cowered together as bullets flew in what seemed like every direction. Meredith squatted down beside Rue. She noticed the staff vanishing through the kitchen door and wondered if she could evacuate Rue that way without either of them getting caught in the crossfire.

Her muscles tensed and flinched, anticipating the pain of a bullet striking flesh.

The rhythmic crashing of her heartbeat inside her head reminded her of a sea whipped to a fury by hurricane winds, the swells slamming into a rocky shore as though determined to chew the land to pieces. She could only wait and hope the storm would pass without loss of life, including her own and Rue's.

As if reading her mind, Rue patted her face and mouthed, "It's okay."

After a few moments, Meredith glanced toward the restaurant's entrance, filled with at least six or seven people wearing dark blue overalls and anonymous, white plastic masks. The attackers crouched on either side of the doorway and played their machine pistols back and forth, spraying bullets into the dining room. She detected something odd. The bullets somehow never came near her, Rue, their bodyguards, or the customers and staff, but pockmarked the central bar, the ceiling, and the walls as though the attackers were deliberately aiming away from people.

Apparently realizing the bodyguards weren't being targeted, Sanchez took three rapid steps forward and to the side while firing her subcompact machine gun in controlled, three-shot bursts with the clear intention of covering Sadiya, who crouched low and moved to a position beside Meredith and Rue.

"Stay with me and do as I say, *mma*," Sadiya said. On her brow, a trickle of blood gleamed wetly from a minor cut near her hairline, almost invisible against her dark skin. "We go out through the kitchen to the rear exit. There's a car waiting in the alley."

Meredith nodded. She took Rue's cold hand in hers and gave it a little squeeze. Rue's slight smile lifted some of the weight of fear off her chest, but only a little. She got to her feet, but at Sadiya's gesture remained hunkered over while bullets chattered overhead. Plaster dust drifted into her nose, tickling her throat and making her cough. Beside her, Rue sneezed.

A gilded light fixture came crashing down near them, spraying bits of glass everywhere. She raised an arm to shield her eyes.

A cry caught her attention.

Sanchez had been shot. Blood darkened the front of the woman's red-checkered shirt. Sanchez's knees buckled. She collapsed facedown, her long length laid out on the floor. She appeared unconscious or dead. Looked like the attackers were no longer sparing the bodyguards, Meredith thought. She and Rue were probably next.

Meredith went to move after Sadiya, but Rue's grip on her hand tightened. She tugged. Rue refused to move. She half turned, impatient words on her lips, but her gaze was instantly snagged by the sight of Qwabe rising from Sanchez's side. The words withered in her throat at the murderous expression on the dreadlocked woman's face.

Qwabe snarled, a flash of white teeth in her dark face. Heedless of the bullets flying around her, she jammed her 9mm pistol into the holster on her belt and lifted the Mossberg 12-gauge pump action shotgun she carried on a shoulder strap. After racking the slide and bracing the stock against her hip, she aimed and fired, repeating the actions twice more.

The full-throated, roaring blasts erupting from the Mossberg made Meredith's ears ring. Heavy slugs tore chunks out of the doorway and the men just outside. One of the attackers shrieked and spun away, his white mask streaked with blood.

The surviving masked attackers continued targeting the bodyguards. Resembling a pint-sized *pistolera* with a Glock in each hand, dainty Carrizo coolly stood in the open firing shot after shot, holding her ground while the other bodyguards overturned tables to use as cover. As soon as she could, she dove for the wounded and unconscious Sanchez and helped Qwabe drag her to safety.

Staying bent over, Meredith held Rue's hand and followed Sadiya to the back of the restaurant and through the swinging kitchen door.

The kitchen was abandoned. Vegetables and herbs were left half-prepared on cutting boards, pots bubbled on the stove, meat turned to charcoal on the grill. The sound of gunfire from the restaurant's dining room was muted.

Meredith straightened and continued after Sadiya, half walking, half running while towing Rue behind her. She headed to the open exit door and the waiting car—a large, dark green, late-model sedan parked in the alley with its engine running. When Sadiya turned to open the back door, a sharp sound echoed off the walls.

Meredith spun around.

A man exited the sedan. Another man stood farther up the alley close to the entrance. He held a pistol with an attached muzzle brake, the source of the sound she'd heard. She risked a brief downward glance. Sadiya had been shot and lay gasping for breath on the filthy street in the middle of overturned containers and reeking trash.

Planting her hands on Rue's upper chest, Meredith shoved her backward toward the kitchen. "Go!" she shouted. She saw Rue catch herself on a stainless steel counter, regain her balance, and run back through the kitchen the way they had come, her voice raised in a shout.

At least she's safe.

A gun muzzle pressed against her temple. The metal felt hot on her skin. Her eyes squeezed shut. *Oh, God…Rue…*

CHAPTER THIRTY-TWO

The car's trunk opened.

Meredith blinked, her eyes watering at the sudden brightness. After spending an unknown amount of time curled up in the claustrophobic, dark confines of the trunk, overwhelmed by exhaust fumes, fear and heat, she could do very little except stare in a semidaze at the men looking down at her.

Rough hands took hold of her shoulders and ankles. She didn't struggle as two of the men lifted her out, but when they put her on her feet, the muscles in her legs and lower back cramped violently. She gasped for air as every part of her body below the waist locked into spasms, making her jerk as helplessly as a hooked fish on a line.

None of the men said or did anything, just watched.

When the spasms passed, she straightened with a groan and spat on the stained concrete floor, just missing someone's shoes. She immediately regretted the impulse. Her mouth was dry, her throat tight with thirst, and she'd sweated enough to soak her shirt. Her head ached and her stomach lurched. Full-blown dehydration wasn't far off.

She tugged on the zip tie securing her wrists, which made the men laugh. A bearded man said something to his companion in Spanish. She comprehended the language, but the almost Italian-sounding intonations these men used required some mental adjustment.

"Water," she said, raising her bound hands to point at her mouth. "*Agua, por favor.*"

The bearded man taunted her, saying she could suck the juice from his banana if she wanted. He gestured at his groin in case she didn't take his meaning.

She pretended not to understand him. Her supposed ignorance of the language might cause them to speak more freely in front of her. Knowledge was power.

"Give her water," creaked an old man who came into the room.

He looked older than dirt. His eyes were almost lost in nests of wrinkles. Liver spots covered his bare scalp and his hands with their swollen knuckles. He wore a tailored Armani suit and shuffled along with a cane. A nasal cannula connected him to a metal oxygen tank wheeled by a blond woman in her thirties wearing nurse's whites.

She had never seen or met Thiago Grazione, but who else could he be?

Grazione's gaze settled on her. He didn't seem triumphant, merely tired. He lifted his cane and waved the tip in the air to emphasize his earlier command. In the overhead fluorescent lights, the diamond pinkie ring he wore flashed sullenly.

Despite his apparent physical frailty, Grazione appeared used to obedience, she observed silently. As if to confirm her impression, the bearded man stopped insulting her and left the room, returning with a glass of water.

She took the glass he thrust at her. It hadn't been washed, but she was too thirsty to care. She drank deeply of the tepid, slightly eggy-tasting water, trying to control the urge to drain the entire glass in a single gulp. After she finished slaking her thirst, she shoved the glass at the bearded man and let it slip through her fingers when he reached for it.

The glass struck the concrete floor and shattered. The bearded man cursed. When he bent over, she bent as well, shoving him off-balance with her shoulder and following up with a double fisted punch high on his inner thigh. Cochrane had taught her not to go for the groin shot right off the bat— too predictable, a blow easily blocked or guarded against.

The bearded man staggered backward, wheezing, while she grabbed the biggest chunk of glass—a long, viciously sharp shard attached to the thicker part of the glass's bottom. She held the makeshift blade, ignoring the burning sting of the edges cutting into her palm.

Grabbing the man by his beard, she set the edge of the shard across his throat. "Let me go or he dies," she said in English, still unwilling to let them know how much Spanish she understood. "Swear to God, I'll cut this pig's neck open if you don't let me go."

Grazione's rheumy eyes were cold and impenetrable. He shrugged, his indifference clear enough not to need translation. "Go ahead. What's one man more or less?" he replied in Spanish, speaking slowly and taking a breath between each word.

Her bluff called, Meredith glanced at the other men in the room. None of them seemed inclined to help their colleague. Disgusted by her tactical error—a move she'd made out of desperation and panic rather than cool-headed planning—she let the bearded man go, giving him a shove and a hearty kick to the backside as he fell forward.

Grazione's laugh sounded like a rusty hinge. He went to a metal chair and sat down. The nurse fussed with the oxygen cylinder and nasal cannula until he waved her away.

Meredith maintained an awareness of the men surrounding her. She let the shard drop. She couldn't risk damaging her hand and the makeshift weapon would likely break off in a significant wound. If it came to an attack or self-defense, she'd have to find alternatives. Glancing around, she realized she'd been taken to a garage. No automobiles in evidence, but the smells of gasoline and oil were unmistakable. A scattering of tools across a workbench in the back caught her eye. She noted heavy wrenches and a small propane or butane torch.

"*Sentar*," Grazione commanded, pointing at another metal folding chair.

Before she could be forced to comply, Meredith sat as indicated.

After glancing at Grazione for permission and being dismissed with a nod, the men drifted to the other side of the garage to sit around a rickety table and play cards. Even the bearded man limped off after giving her a glare promising future pain and death.

The nurse pointed a Glock at her with rock-solid aim.

She kept her bound hands in sight, on her lap with her fingers laced together.

His eyes closed, Grazione simply breathed for several long moments. At last, he waved his hand a second time.

The nurse began to speak. Her English was lightly accented with the peculiar singsong rhythm she'd heard other Argentineans use. "Señor Grazione knows Señora Stanton has the inventory papers belonging to Hugo Krause. He will have the papers from her, or you will die and your friend will die. Señora Stanton will die too, then he will have the papers anyway. Do you understand?"

Meredith didn't reply. Putting aside the flesh-crawling realization he'd had her and Rue under surveillance a while, she watched Grazione. The old man didn't show much expression at all. He reminded her of a captain she'd served under during her assignment as a junior officer aboard an *Avenger*-class minesweeper in the Persian Gulf.

Like Captain Matthews, Grazione appeared to possess an absolute, unshakable confidence that things would go exactly the way he'd planned, admitting no room for error, twist of fate, or act of God. Such lack of doubt was powerful, but also left him peculiarly vulnerable. His ego would suffer a massive blow if his plan failed. Thwarted and taken aback, he might make mistakes, leaving her an opening for escape.

These thoughts flashed through her mind in a few brief moments. She decided to wait for an opportunity to poke a stick in Grazione's wheel. "I understand," she replied, waiting while the nurse made a Spanish translation.

Grazione grunted an acknowledgment. He folded his liver-spotted hands over his cane's silver handle and continued to wheeze breath after breath.

The nurse lowered the Glock, took a cell phone from her pocket and dialed a number. She spoke in rapid Spanish, the flow of words too quick for Meredith to follow.

About twenty minutes after the nurse ended the call, an old, withered man in an electric wheelchair came rolling into the garage. A patch covered his left eye behind thick glasses. His right eye, somewhat magnified, was a chilling blue. Reaching Grazione, he exchanged a few words in Spanish, once glancing at Meredith over his shoulder and asking a question she translated as, "Is this the one?" When Grazione answered in an undertone, the newcomer pivoted the wheelchair to face her directly.

"In English, yes?" he asked in a husky voice.

His accent was different than the nurse's. A definite Teutonic flavor, she decided, his pronunciation sharp and precise. She nodded.

"Your friend, she has the inventory belonging to *Standartenführer* Krause." The German military rank rolled off his tongue easily, no hesitation.

She didn't feel a need to answer. *Must be Fuhrman. Christ, all these old men positively pickled in evil. Karma's falling down on the job.*

He went on. "You found Krause's lockbox. The papers were inside. This is known to us. And now we will have them."

She nodded at Grazione. "He already told me as much," she said to Fuhrman. "What about Clay Cochrane, is he okay?" At Fuhrman's blank look, she added, "The man you kidnapped from Mexico. Let him go."

The nurse muttered a translation to Grazione, whose eyes remained closed.

"Bah." Fuhrman's mouth worked. His visible eye glittered. "It doesn't matter." He waved dismissively. "As soon as we have the papers, you will all be executed."

The nurse drew out the Glock from its hiding place and aimed the weapon at her again.

CHAPTER THIRTY-THREE

At Fuhrman's words, the pit of Meredith's stomach dropped out. For a moment, she found it hard to breathe, swallow, or make a sound as fury and fear swept through her in alternating waves of hot and cold. Her muscles trembled. She wanted to howl, to rend, to destroy. The anger abruptly crystallized and sharpened, leaving her able to think.

She felt the muscles in her face draw tight, as though she wore a mask. *Never let an opponent know they're cornered,* she thought. *Always leave an exit, even if it's only imaginary. People who have nothing to lose are the most dangerous animals on the planet.*

Grazione's eyes popped open, as if he sensed the taint of violence in the air. "Do nothing that cannot be undone, Señora Reid," he cautioned in his breathless Spanish. The nurse translated a heartbeat behind. "My brother-in-law, he does not speak for me."

Fuhrman shot Grazione a venomous glare.

Meredith didn't trust either of them. She decided Grazione had to die. Somehow, to end the threat against Rue, she had to kill him, even at the cost of her life. His death would throw his tightly controlled organization into chaos.

"You have my word," Grazione went on in his laborious manner. "You and Señor Cochrane will be free when I have the papers. Why would I kill you? It's not good business." His smile attempted to be reassuring, but to her, the curve of his lips and the gleam of his dentures seemed more like the shining edge of a blade aimed at her heart.

Lowering the Glock at Grazione's order, the blond nurse made another call on her cell phone. She handed the phone to Meredith, who held it to her ear a little awkwardly because of the zip tie binding her wrists together.

"Hello? Mer? Are you there? Are you okay?" she heard Rue ask.

The shock of Rue's voice almost undid her. She blinked fiercely, fighting sudden tears. "I'm here," she answered, somehow managing to speak through the press of emotions gathered into a lump in her throat.

"Thank God! Oh, Mer, I'm so sorry—"

"Don't believe him," Meredith warned, interrupting Rue. "He'll kill everyone, don't meet him, don't give him what he wants, me and Clay are dead already, just get out of this goddamn country, baby, get out and—"

The nurse tore the phone out of her grasp, wrenching her thumb. "You have your proof of life," the woman said into the phone in English. "Follow our instructions if you want your friends to live." She ended the call.

Grazione called Fuhrman a fool. "You shouldn't provoke her!"

Fuhrman sneered. "You've killed for less reason, Thiago. Why stop now?"

Meredith struggled not to yell out her frustration when Fuhrman spun his wheelchair around, essentially putting himself between her and Grazione. Her fingers spasmed. Would she get a chance to take out Grazione before it was too late? Had she said enough to keep Rue safe? Tasting blood, she realized she'd split her lower lip between her teeth.

"Señora Reid, I have given you my word," Grazione said wearily.

The nurse translated the old man's lie into English.

"You are a fool if you take the word of a thief," Fuhrman told her in English.

Grazione heaved a few breaths. "Karl, you're tired," he said as the frowning nurse took his wrist to check his pulse. "You should rest."

Fuhrman took a long time to answer. "It is not my fault," he murmured resentfully.

Meredith saw mixed emotions replace Grazione's usual stony expression. She identified sadness, irritation, guilt…the rest of the complicated tangle flew across his face too quickly to analyze before his mask dropped into place.

"It is not my fault," Fuhrman repeated. "The terrible things they did in the war. I was only a clerk. I kept the records. I had no choice."

She thought the mantra sounded like something Fuhrman had been telling himself for more than sixty-five years. She understood the truth, a painful lesson learned as a navy officer: no matter how bleak the situation, there was *always* a choice. Absolute dead ends didn't exist. When people said they had no choice, they meant circumstances had left them with shitty, deadly, or distasteful options.

"I should have gone with Krause under the ice," Fuhrman went on. Memories gathered like shadows in his visible eye. "I should have gone with him to drowning maudlin—" He broke off when Grazione began to cough.

The nurse said something, drowned out by Grazione's harsh coughing echoing off the garage's concrete block walls. A thick, jelly-like thread of mucus dangled from the corner of his mouth. He pressed a hand to his chest. The nurse made a phone call. Within a minute, a male nurse arrived with a wheelchair. Together, they transferred the gagging and breathless Grazione and whisked him out of the garage.

Meredith slid slightly forward, toward the edge of the chair. She made an effort to pull herself together and reassess the situation. Grazione was out of reach. Shooting a glance at the men playing cards in the corner, she decided to remain cautious and focus on gathering information in case she managed to escape later. What Fuhrman said lingered in her mind. She had no idea what he'd meant by "drowning maudlin." Mere rambling, perhaps? The man had to be in his mid- to late eighties. Perhaps he'd begun to experience bouts of dementia.

"Why the hell do you want those papers anyway?" she asked Fuhrman, who gave no indication he heard her. "They're useless lists for the most part—so many silver rings, so many brass keys, so many carpets, so many candlesticks...so many dentures, for God's sake!" She laughed derisively. "Who the hell catalogs dead men's false teeth?"

Fuhrman's fist thumped the wheelchair's arm. "We did what we were told to do." He focused on her. "I was a clerk. I did not question my superiors."

"Because you were a good soldier."

"What I did was necessary."

"I doubt it. Compulsively writing down the details of every single item, valuable or not, stolen from people far better than you'll ever be—I call that insanity."

"You do not understand. *Standartenführer* Krause's code depended on the numbers."

Meredith's breath caught. Was Fuhrman about to reveal a crucial piece of information? She attempted to keep her tone cool. "Sounds like a bullshit excuse to me."

"He told me," Fuhrman insisted. Once again, his gaze turned inward, looking at the ghosts in his past. "I made a duplicate inventory list just for him, but the numbers weren't the same. He gave the real numbers to me. I wrote them exactly as he wished. Exactly!"

"Why would he do that, Karl? Why change the numbers?"

"Ah, not all, but enough. Just different enough for Krause and his code. He didn't want to forget, you see, and the numbers were the key. His nephew's key." He chuckled. His expression cleared as the present appeared to reassert itself. He mumbled a guttural string of unintelligible words, what sounded like mixed German and Argentinean-flavored Spanish to her. Raising his voice, he called in Spanish to the men playing cards. "Sosa! *Ven aquí.*"

The bearded man threw down his cards on the table, rose from his chair, and obeyed the summons. "*Sí*, señor?"

"Give me a gun," Fuhrman ordered, still speaking Spanish.

Shrugging, Sosa pulled a .45 pistol from his belt holster and handed it to him.

Meredith remained on her guard, uncertain what the old man wanted with a gun.

Fuhrman flicked off the safety and pointed the pistol at Meredith. "Keeping you alive serves no purpose," he said to her in English. She'd seen dead fish on ice with warmer demeanors. "Thiago is too ill to see that now, so I will take care of the matter for him."

Sosa gave her an anticipatory smile.

The way Fuhrman handled the pistol made it clear he was no novice, though she doubted he'd used a firearm since the war. She curled her fingers over the edge of the chair seat. At point-blank range, he couldn't miss, and ducking bullets only worked in movies.

She inhaled deeply. Her nerves steadied. The tremors in her limbs ceased. Her vision narrowed. She readied herself to act.

A low rumble vibrated through the floor under her feet a heartbeat before the muffled thunder of an explosion took her by surprise.

CHAPTER THIRTY-FOUR

The far wall crumbled. A rapidly expanding cloud of concrete dust billowed through the garage. Figures poured through a hole in the wall, skirting the broken blocks and rubble scattered over the floor. Meredith blinked. Catalina Rivas's team looked like well-armed apparitions with their weapons, clothes, hair and skin daubed with whitish gray powder.

Grazione's men abandoned their game. Before the last playing card fluttered to the floor, they began shooting at the women, who returned fire.

Meredith got out of the chair while Fuhrman was distracted. Holding her breath and squinting against the gritty particles still lingering in the air, she went across the garage, headed for the worktable she'd spotted earlier.

She snatched up the butane torch, pushed the air control lever back, and clicked the ignition button. A small jet of intense blue flame burst from the end of the nozzle. She returned the torch to the table and used the flame to melt part of the plastic zip tie securing her wrists, careful not to singe herself. The strip parted after a moment, leaving her hands free. Deciding the torch wouldn't make a very effective defensive weapon unless she was attacked by a rogue crème brûlée, she turned off the flame.

The nape of her neck began to warm. Instinct insisted someone was near her position. She picked up the biggest, heaviest wrench on the worktable and whirled around ready to strike, only to halt abruptly when she recognized Sadiya.

Runnels of sweat cut through the dust coating Sadiya's dark face, creating a terrifying striped war mask. A blood-spotted bandage was wrapped around her head. "Let's go, *mma*," she said shortly, turning and firing a three-shot burst from her automatic weapon. A man screamed and fell facedown on the garage floor.

Meredith started to follow Sadiya and realized Fuhrman had been caught in the crossfire. Apparently unable to escape, he'd managed to back his wheelchair into a corner and sat at bay, his borrowed gun raised in both hands. The muzzle trembled.

She gave in to a spur-of-the-moment impulse. "We need Fuhrman...I mean, Fellman," she said to Sadiya, catching the woman by the arm. The triceps felt as hard as tile under the skin. She let go. "We need what he knows. We'll have to—"

Sadiya shook her head. "No time."

A gunshot cracked. The bullet whizzed so close to her head, Meredith could've sworn the shot parted her hair. "Shit!"

"Move!" Taking her by the elbow, Sadiya hauled her toward the hole in the wall.

Meredith resisted. "What about Clay? They still have him."

"I said move!" Sadiya insisted, pulling harder.

The bearded man, Sosa, barreled into Sadiya, almost knocking her over.

When Sosa turned his gun on the bodyguard, Meredith took a two-handed grip on the oversized wrench, cocked it over her shoulder like a softball bat, and slammed the tool forward into his kidney. "*La concha de tu madre,*" she spat at him when he toppled over, howling in pain. "Enjoy pissing blood, asshole."

Sadiya kicked his gun away and nodded at her.

Once she'd stumbled past the concrete fragments littering the floor, Meredith found herself in the street outside a large building. Dawn painted the neighborhood in soft grays and yellows. Behind a row of houses, the hidden sun left bloody streaks across the sky. She was bundled into a large SUV by Sadiya, who left her in the backseat. The door slammed shut. Through the bullet-resistant tinted glass, she heard the muffled sounds of the continuing firefight. She laid down the wrench on the seat beside her.

After a moment, Sadiya returned, sliding into the driver's seat. She started the engine as six other women piled into the vehicle, all of them in a hurry.

Meredith found out why when one of Grazione's men exited the garage with a grenade launcher. "Haul ass, goddamn it!" she cried, slapping the back of the driver's seat.

Sadiya needed no urging. Wrenching the steering around, she sent the SUV peeling away from the house. The smells of sweat, gun oil and scorched rubber filled the cab. The SUV reached the street and accelerated faster, fishtailing slightly on the corner.

"How are you?" asked Catalina Rivas, turning around in the front passenger seat. Like the others, she wore US Army camouflage fatigues. Her gaze shifted. "Any injuries, Tricia?" she asked the woman in the seat on Meredith's left side.

"Shallow cut on her palm, no stitches needed," Tricia replied with a faint Irish accent. She opened a first aid kit. After donning nitrile gloves, she quickly removed a few fragments of glass from Meredith's palm with a pair of tweezers, disinfected the wound, and applied a gauze bandage. "Keep it clean and dry. Any redness or swelling, you come find me."

"Sure thing." The disinfectant stung, but Meredith began to relax a little. Or as much as she could relax, crammed inside a recklessly speeding vehicle with a bunch of adrenaline-hyped women carrying enough weaponry to start a minor war. "Are you a doctor?"

"Nurse," Tricia replied, snapping off the gloves. She was very pretty, with dark blue eyes and dark hair hanging past her shoulders. Unlike the others, she didn't appear armed.

Noncombatant, Meredith decided. *Nice to have a medical assist on tap.*

"How you holding up, Reid?" The familiar voice of Clay Cochrane came from the second row of seats behind her.

Relieved, she turned around. "Son of a bitch! Are you okay?" she asked, her relief turning to worry when she got a good look at him.

A scabbed cut ran from his temple, cutting diagonally past his eye to his cheekbone. An ugly, purple bruise spread over the other side of his face. He frankly stank and appeared rough, unshaven, unwashed and somewhat thinner since she'd last seen him in Mexico.

"Nothing I can't handle," Cochrane replied with a grin crinkling the corners of his eyes. He winced and touched his bruised cheek, but his smile didn't fade a bit. "Sweetheart, you know I've been beat up worse by shore patrol in a Tokyo Soapland."

Meredith wished she'd killed Grazione when she had the chance. He was a sick old man, but still ruthless and powerful. He'd given the order to kidnap and hurt her friend. He'd had her and Rue hunted and harassed. She recalled his unblinking stare.

After her retirement from the navy, as a treat she'd gone deep-water diving in the Azores off Pico Island. The blue sharks had been as curious as puppies, but a much more aggressive mako shark—an eleven footer—had cruised around her and the rest of the dive group. A flick of its tail and the mako had disappeared in the distance only to arrow back a few seconds later, a sleek, sharp-nosed, deadly predator on the hunt.

The mako's eyes had been flat and stark black. She'd gotten the impression those eyes hadn't belonged to a living creature. More than the bristling teeth designed to shred flesh, the shark's soulless, lifeless gaze had terrified her. For much the same reason, so did Grazione. A man so lacking in humanity was capable of any atrocity.

A touch on her shoulder brought her back to the present. "What did that guy want, anyway?" Cochrane asked.

"The papers from Krause's lockbox."

"What the hell for?"

Meredith shrugged. "I'm not sure. Did he want any information from you?"

"Nope." Cochrane imitated her shrug. "Asked me not a single question."

"Then why the—" She gestured at his bruised face.

"Because I wasn't about to sit on my ass and hope for rescue," he said. His chuckle helped ease the pain and guilt she felt. If not for his association with her, he'd never have been in danger. "I tried to escape. Twice. The guards didn't mess me up too bad, just enough to clue me in on how much they didn't enjoy chasing me down. Would've been three escape attempts—God knows I'm a stubborn SOB—but the cavalry sprung me." He flashed a devilish smile at the brunette woman seated next to him. "I really appreciate a lady who knows how to handle the big boys' toys," he said, flirting despite his injuries.

Meredith rolled her eyes in disbelief and embarrassment. Clearly, getting knocked around by Grazione's goons hadn't really damaged him. "Clay, you do know that's a Desert Eagle in her hand, right?" she asked, despite experience having taught her she'd be ignored.

"A fifty caliber's got quite some recoil for a girl," Cochrane said to the brunette. His leer was somewhat lopsided given the extent of the bruising and swelling on his cheek. He went on while the woman stared at him in disbelief, "I mean, you must have strong wrists—"

"Buckle up," Qwabe interrupted in a startling, working-class British accent. She'd been watching something over her left shoulder.

"What's going on?" Meredith asked, risking a glance and seeing nothing significant.

Qwabe shifted to kneel on the seat so she faced backward. "Trouble."

The Citroën behind their vehicle suddenly veered into the next lane and accelerated, quickly closing the gap and maintaining speed to come alongside. Three AK-47s nosed out the open windows—one hostile in the passenger seat, Meredith noted, two in the backseat.

"Incoming!" shouted Catalina.

Meredith had just enough time to think, *Oh, shit* before the first volley of bullets hammered into the SUV.

CHAPTER THIRTY-FIVE

"Unfasten your seat belt," Tricia said to Meredith after tucking the first aid kit under her seat. "We need to move."

More shots thumped into the SUV's armored sides and rattled against the windows, now covered in a lacework of cracks. Meredith knew "bullet resistant" didn't mean bulletproof. Eventually, if their pursuers kept up the barrage, the glass would shatter. Or those macho morons would set their AK-47s on fire if they continued shooting on full auto.

With some awkward maneuvering, she and Tricia shifted over to allow Qwabe to sit next to the window, which put the woman behind the driver's seat and in direct line of sight with the shooters in the Citroën keeping pace with their SUV.

At some unspoken signal, the driver and passenger side windows on the SUV's right side lowered. Instantly, Qwabe thrust her shotgun's muzzle outside and fired at the Citroën. Blood erupted over the face of the man nearest the window in the backseat.

Catalina wedged her slender body sideways between Sadiya and the steering wheel. From the awkward position, she also shot at the Citroën.

Sadiya stomped hard on the gas. The SUV's engine caught for a heart-stopping instant then roared as the tires bit into the asphalt. The vehicle hurtled forward into traffic.

Meredith clung to her seat, watching Tricia's calm expression with envy. Behind her, she heard Cochrane yelling, but whatever he said was whipped away by the wind rushing inside the SUV through the open windows. She turned her head, both to watch the unfolding action and to let the wind blow her hair backward, out of her eyes.

The Citroën fell behind. Sadiya increased speed and swerved the SUV around a slower-moving pickup truck. From the manic horn blowing that greeted the maneuver, the SUV must have missed causing an accident by a hair.

Catalina squirmed out of Sadiya's lap and sat up in the passenger seat. She slapped a hand on the dashboard to avoid slamming headfirst into the windshield when Sadiya sent the SUV careening through traffic, weaving in and out of busy lanes. After a while, the wild ride calmed. The SUV eventually entered a familiar part of the Boedo district.

One by one, Meredith peeled her aching fingertips from her seat. Looking outside, she recognized the sunny yellow hotel. Rue waited in the street.

As soon as the SUV parked and she exited the vehicle, Rue ran toward her crying, "Oh, my God! I thought you were dead!"

"Rumors of my demise have been greatly exagg—oof!" Meredith grunted when Rue's solid body impacted against hers.

"No jokes," Rue muttered, desperation and heartfelt relief coloring her voice. Her embrace tightened. "Damn it, Mer, I was worried sick."

"Sorry." Meredith trembled at the sudden flood of emotion putting her on the knife-edge of tears. "Jesus, I'm so, so sorry." To gain time to pull herself together, she released Rue and jerked her chin at Cochrane. "Look who hitched a ride."

Rue gave her a pointed look, as if she wasn't fooled a whit by the attempted distraction. She greeted Cochrane with a smile that faded when she saw his swollen face. She whistled. "Ooh, that's a heck of a shiner. How'd the other guy come out of the fight?"

"In keeping with the immemorial custom of the US Navy: fucked up beyond all recognition." Cochrane accepted Rue's careful hug. His hand wandered down to cup her buttock. "Did you miss me, sweetheart?" he asked over her surprised squeak.

"Like a thundering dose of the clap," she replied, giving him a shove, but her twinkling eyes belied her scowl.

Catalina led the group into the hotel, where most of the bodyguards trooped upstairs. Tricia remained behind, taking Cochrane aside to evaluate his injuries.

Meredith and Rue followed Catalina out to the courtyard garden. This time, instead of tea, the table had been set with a bottle of liquor, cans of ginger ale sweating in a bucket of ice, three tumblers and three shot glasses. The label on the bottle read Fernet Branca.

After sitting down, Catalina added ice to the tumblers and emptied a can of ginger ale over the ice. She poured Fernet Branca into the shot glasses. "The national beverage of Argentina. You should try it," she said, offering the drinks without further explanation.

Meredith picked up her shot glass and held it to the light. The dark brown sludge inside took on a hint of green. She sniffed. The fumes didn't just sting her nose—they tried to crawl up her nostrils and strangle her brain. The stuff in the glass seemed to pack a punch.

Well, she'd been brave enough to drink the rotgut brewed out of ersatz Kool-Aid and raisins by a cook's assistant in an illicit still aboard the *Prescott*. She'd even let Clay talk her into getting drunk on home-brewed cobra wine and scorpion vodka at an awful hoochie-coochie bar during liberty in Pattaya. In comparison, Fernet Branca couldn't be that bad.

She took a healthy swig, recoiling when a horrible, biting, medicinal, astringent bitterness filled her mouth. The actual taste hit her a second later: a confusing jumble of licorice, mouthwash and unidentifiable spices. Her eyes stung with unshed tears. Her throat felt like she'd swallowed red-hot barbed wire. If she was dying, she hoped she didn't linger.

Catalina chuckled. "They drink a shot with ginger ale in San Francisco. Try it."

Meredith took a swig of ginger ale. The tooth achingly cold, bubbly stuff soothed her throat. When she finished, she gasped out a breath, inhaled, and managed to whisper, "Wow."

Rue tipped her shot glass and drank the Fernet Branca without turning a hair. Finished, she set the tumbler on the table and licked her lips as if she'd enjoyed the deadly sludge. "Not bad, if a little weak," she said to Catalina. "You have something with more kick to it?"

"What, like drain cleaner or battery acid?" Meredith muttered sarcastically. Her lips were still somewhat numb and her nose ached as if she'd been punched.

"I think Tricia has rubbing alcohol in her kit," Catalina offered.

Rue shook her head and reached for the bottle. "I'd rather not spend all day tomorrow paralyzed from the neck up, so I'd better stick to this herbal paint stripper."

Remembering the blonde who'd been shot during the firefight in the restaurant, Meredith took the opportunity to ask, "How is Sanchez doing?"

"She'll be fine in a few weeks," Catalina replied. "The bullet grazed her…" She hesitated. "*Arteria subclavia*. You understand?"

Meredith nodded. Catalina seemed calm, but a deep vertical line appeared between her brows and her jaw muscles were tensed. *She keeps grinding her teeth like that and her dentist will think he's hit the jackpot.* "What changed your mind about hostage extraction?" she asked. "You were against a rescue operation when Clay was taken."

Catalina fished an ice cube from the bucket, dropped it in her tumbler, and poured another shot of liqueur. "My risk assessment changed when Grazione altered the parameters. The bullet in the alley missed spilling Sadiya's brains by centimeters," she said. "Another bullet could have killed Sanchez. Two good reasons to change my mind, yes?"

"I won't argue and I'm grateful for your help," Meredith said. "By the way," she added, reaching for a second can of ginger ale, "for what it's worth, I don't know if Grazione's alive or dead at this point. Last time I saw him, he wasn't looking very chipper." Catalina's proud features sharpened. Her almond-shaped eyes narrowed. "Explain."

Meredith complied, telling Catalina and Rue what she'd observed of Grazione's condition. "Don't get me wrong," she concluded, "he's in control, his people still obey him, but he looks and sounds like his health's real fragile. He's on oxygen and can barely breathe. After a few minutes, the nurses had to carry him away in a wheelchair."

"Grazione's been dying for years, he's lived far longer than he deserves," Catalina said thoughtfully, "but perhaps this time he won't cheat death."

"Fuhrman's lived past his sell-by date, too, but he was healthier physically than Grazione. Mentally, not so much," Meredith said, jerking when Rue kicked her in the shin.

"I'm sorry, Ms. Rivas," Rue said to Catalina, ignoring Meredith's pained grunt, "but Ms. Reid has suffered quite an ordeal and needs to rest. I'm sure you understand. If you don't mind, I'll take her upstairs for a little siesta."

Catalina seemed amused, or at least that's how Meredith interpreted the slight quirk on the right side of her mouth. "Of course," she said. "I'll see you at dinner tonight. When you're ready for lunch, or if you need anything, let one of my team know your requirements."

Meredith could take a hint. Two things were clear: Rue wanted a private talk, and she was displeased about something. Her shin twinged when she rose from the table to follow Rue into the hotel and up the staircase to their room.

CHAPTER THIRTY-SIX

"I can't believe you said that!" Rue exclaimed as soon as the door shut behind them.

Meredith flicked on the window air-conditioning unit to help cool the stuffy room and prevent accidental eavesdropping. "What did I do wrong?"

"You used Fuhrman's real name. He's called Carlos Fellman here, remember?"

"So?"

Rue frowned. "So…I don't know. What if Rivas checks him out?"

"Is it likely she'd find out anything useful in an Internet search?"

"Well, no, but—"

"Then there's no reason to panic." Meredith rubbed her bruised shin meaningfully.

"You're so reasonable, you make me sick." Rue sat on the armchair. Sweat had darkened her auburn hair and blotched her turquoise sleeveless top. "Sorry I'm such a bitch."

Meredith resisted temptation and didn't offer an embrace. At the current temperature, they'd both spontaneously combust if they got too close to each other.

She went to the bathroom to splash water on her face. The water was heavily chlorinated and not very cold, but still refreshing. She wet a washcloth in the sink. Returning to the room, she handed the washcloth to Rue. "Ready to tell me what's on your mind?"

"Thanks," Rue murmured. She ran the washcloth over her bare arms and neck, sighing in pleasure. Finished, she folded the cloth in half and held the pad to the back of her neck. "Okay," she said, "out there you mentioned Fuhrman's mind is starting to go."

"That's the impression I got, yes," Meredith replied. "He's not completely gaga, but he's starting to live more in the past than the present, I think."

Rue nibbled her bottom lip. "Give me an example."

"Out of nowhere, he started reminiscing about the war, how he was just a clerk, he followed orders, nothing was his fault— the usual Nazi apologia—and how he should have gone in the U-boat with Krause." She tried to recall Fuhrman's exact words. "He was talking about Krause and said, 'drowning maudlin.' Does that mean anything to you?"

Rue shrugged and shook her head.

"Fuhrman said he made a duplicate inventory list, but Krause told him to change some of the numbers from the original record as part of a code." Meredith wished she had better news. She'd been in a prime position for getting information out of Fuhrman, but all she had to report were an old man's senile ravings.

"Is that all he said?"

"We were interrupted when Rivas's Amazons made their grand entrance."

Rue didn't acknowledge her smile. She stared at nothing in particular. Whatever inner thought held the woman's attention, Meredith thought, must be a doozy.

She opened the door. As expected, a member of Catalina's team stood right outside the room smoking a cigarette. A tattered veil of smoke hung in the air. From farther down the hall came the sound of laughter, like the rest of the team enjoying well-deserved downtime.

The guard squinted at Meredith through the smoke. She didn't look pleased to be there, but her tone was friendly when she asked in English, "You need something, señora?"

I know how much it sucks to be stuck on watch while your buddies take liberty after a mission. "Just lunch, if that's okay," Meredith replied.

The guard took a drag off her cigarette. "Sure," she said on a gust of smoke. She went down the hall to a closed door and banged on it with her fist.

"What's your hurry, Otero?" asked Sadiya when she answered the door. Behind her, Meredith glimpsed Qwabe having her dreadlocks groomed by another woman.

"Food run," Otero replied.

Sadiya glanced over her shoulder. "Carrizo, your turn."

Carrizo protested as she came out of the room, "Damn, 'Diya, I had aces in the hole and Smitty just raised me twenty *verdes*. She's bluffing. She can't have more than a pair of twos. Do you know how much I can get for American dollars on the black market?" Despite her grumbling, she flashed a grin at Otero and took up a position in the hall.

Otero trooped downstairs. Sadiya shut the door.

Meredith followed Sadiya's example. She turned around to find Rue rummaging through her suitcase. Most of the contents were now strewn over the bed. At last, Rue found the object of her search: the same tablet PC she'd brought aboard *Lady Vic*.

Focused solely on the tablet, Rue stumbled her way back to the chair and sat down. Her stylus danced over the touch screen. "Krause's code has to contain information on the U-boat," she said "Otherwise, why devise a code in the first place?"

"I don't see why it matters," Meredith said, retrieving some articles of Rue's clothing and folding them neatly. Disorder made her uncomfortable, like an itch she couldn't scratch. "We have the list Fuhrman made for Krause, but without the original inventory to compare it to…" Her voice trailed off when Rue's eyes rose to meet hers. The smugness in the woman's mismatched gaze made her pulse quicken. "You have the original list!"

"During the war, the complete official catalog of Krause's operation in Antwerp was copied in an album compiled by the *Einsatzstab Reichsleiter Rosenberg*. A lot of the albums the ERR produced went missing after Germany's surrender," Rue said, tapping her tablet with the stylus again. "An American soldier took an album from Hitler's home—you know, the Eagle's Nest in the Alps—in 1945. A couple of years ago, the grandson found the album in the late soldier's effects and donated it to the German National Archives, which is where I found and copied it shortly after Velse hired me for the job."

"We can compare the numbers, find the discrepancies, and then what? I don't mean to rain on your parade, but I'm not a cryptographer. Are you?"

"I'm sure it's a simple code meant to hide his secret from casual view."

A knock at the door signaled the arrival of lunch, delivered by Otero: *parrillada*, a mixed grill of ribs, sausages, other meats and offal. The scent of charred meat was mouthwatering, if becoming a little too familiar.

Meredith took the tray and set it on the bed. At least the cook had included potatoes and a salad, though the vegetables looked rather lonely in the midst of all that protein.

Rue glanced at the food and groaned. "Good thing I'm not a vegetarian."

"They're real carnivores in Argentina, aren't they? I think this is cow's udder," Meredith said, poking at the item in question. "Apart from the ribs and a steak, we've got kidney, blood sausage, chorizo, and…" She squinted. "Large intestine, I think."

"I've learned not to ask. Just eat." Rue put aside her tablet and stylus. "I need a printer and a copy machine," she said, taking an empty plate from the tray and serving herself from the platter. "I want to make a print copy of the ERR list—I have it backed up on a flash drive—and the inventory papers we found in the lockbox. Makes it easier to compare the two lists side by side and find out which numbers Fuhrman changed."

Meredith agreed. "I'll help you once we have physical copies of the documents. If we split the pages of each list we'll finish quicker. Now eat your udder before it gets cold." She smirked when Rue snorted and smacked her thigh.

After lunch, she went out of the room to find Otero standing in the hall, propped up against the wall. The guard had another cigarette hanging from the corner of her mouth. A liberal scattering of ash and a few crushed butts littered the floor under her combat boots.

"Ms. Otero, can you tell me where we can find a copy machine? And a printer?" Meredith asked, waving smoke away from her face.

Otero shook her head, scattering cigarette ash. "Nobody leaves the hotel," she said in her careful English. "Orders."

"Okay, is there a printer in the hotel? Or a copier?"

Otero shrugged. Turning, she led the way downstairs.

Meredith hastily fetched Rue and followed the guard into the hotel's office—a cramped space furnished with a desk, a set of bookshelves, and an ancient copy machine approximately the size of a VW Bug. The clunky-looking computer on the desk was also a dinosaur, at least twenty years old. *Probably still used MS-DOS*, she thought.

Rue examined the computer and confirmed her suspicions. "No USB port, no DVD drive…this thing still uses floppy discs, for God's sake," she whispered in horrified awe.

"It's urgent we get these copies made as soon as we can," Meredith explained to Otero. "Is there an Internet café anywhere close?"

Otero repeated her earlier statement, "Nobody leaves the hotel." No arguments swayed her. She'd been given orders by Catalina Rivas, she said stubbornly. Persuasion, bribery and begging didn't make a dent in her stoic resolve.

The argument ended when footsteps sounded on the tiled lobby floor outside the office. Otero's spine snapped straight.

The cigarette dropped from her mouth. Her eyes narrowed. She trained her subcompact machine gun at the office doorway. Meredith felt Rue's hand creep into hers.

CHAPTER THIRTY-SEVEN

A man in his fifties or early sixties entered the office, followed by Catalina.

Otero lowered her weapon, stood aside, and surreptitiously ground the toe of her boot on the smoldering cigarette on the floor to crush it out.

Rue released Meredith and took a few quick steps forward, her hand extended. "Mr. Velse," she said with a strained smile. "May I ask, sir, what brings you to Buenos Aires?"

Ah, this is the money man. Meredith studied him, deciding his blue eyes were set too close to his nose and gave his face an unsettling, secretive feline cast. She got the impression he held himself still, kept his thoughts private, and gave very little away.

Elliot Painter Velse accepted Rue's hand, giving her fingers the lightest touch. "Your last report intrigued me," he replied. "I wanted to hear about your progress in person. And this is Ms. Reid." He turned to regard Meredith with a shuttered gaze.

"Mr. Velse, welcome to Buenos Aires," she said, giving him the same neutral expression she'd had to plaster on for superior officers during her career. The navy had taught her the art of smiling to a bastard's face while concealing her true feelings. Velse returned his attention to Rue. "Do you have anything new to report? I understand from Ms. Rivas that you had some trouble. Yes?"

"Perhaps we should have our discussion in a more private setting," Catalina interrupted smoothly, looping her arm through Velse's as though they were old friends.

Meredith caught Rue before she followed Catalina and Velse out of the office. "What's he doing here?" she asked quietly.

"I have no idea," Rue replied. She ran her hands over her dark auburn hair in a nervous gesture. "I wish Rivas had told us he was coming. I'm not exactly dressed for a business meeting." Another gesture indicated her baggy pants, tank top and sandals.

"You're fine." Meredith took hold of the fluttering hands. "Why didn't Rivas warn us?" she asked. "Out of courtesy, if nothing else. Unless Velse told her not to." The possibility didn't sit well with her.

Clearly still fretting, Rue pulled free and continued to the courtyard, stopping in front of the table where Velse and Catalina had taken seats. She remained standing. "Is something wrong, sir?" she asked Velse.

He shook his head. "How can I speak against progress? You've come such a long way, Ms. Stanton, further than I dreamed when we began this venture. But I think—"

"Excuse me, Mr. Velse, we're very close, incredibly close, to finding the last known location of U-3019," Rue interrupted. "Some new information has come to light from Karl Fuhrman. I recommend you not pull out—"

This time, Velse interrupted. "Pull out? No, Ms. Stanton. I have no intention of giving up until I've found my family's property. However, considering the threats you and Ms. Reid have faced, the danger you've put yourselves in on my behalf, I decided it was time you had some extra assistance in your endeavor."

Meredith edged closer to Rue, who appeared nonplussed.

"Your reports make it plain: Thiago Grazione has no intention of stopping until he succeeds in taking the U-boat for himself," Velse added, his gaze burning yet cold. "For decades, the Graziones have sheltered a man responsible for destroying my maternal ancestors, the Schilders. Only one young girl survived the camps. The rest, all the aunts, uncles, nieces, nephews, daughters, sons, wives, husbands, died because they were Jewish, they were rich, and the Third Reich let filthy scavengers like Krause and Fuhrman do as they pleased as long as the quotas and coffers were filled. Understand me—I will *not* allow a Nazi worshipper like Grazione to take the treasure. Not while I breathe." His hands trembled with the force of his emotions. He accepted a glass of water poured by Catalina.

Meredith privately admitted a degree of sympathy for Velse. No matter how great his net worth, money couldn't bring back his murdered family. He may not have known any of his Belgian relatives who suffered and died in concentration camps, but he obviously felt their loss, no doubt due to his grandmother's influence.

Once Velse had been seen to, Catalina said to Rue, "Señor Velse has come to renegotiate his contract with me. My team and I will accompany you wherever you go and provide transport and support in any capacity necessary for the success of the mission."

Rue nodded. Her gaze moved to Velse. "Thank you," she said sincerely. "I'm chasing a lead, and Ms. Rivas's assistance will come in handy, I'm sure."

Velse swallowed a mouthful of water and set down the glass. "A lead?"

"Yes, sir. I hope to gain access to a printer and a copier to help me analyze some information we obtained from Fuhrman," Rue told him.

"You didn't tell me you interviewed Fuhrman."

"My partner, Ms. Reid, spoke to Fuhrman after Grazione's men kidnapped her. The details were to be in my next report."

Catalina assured Rue she would arrange for immediate access to the needed equipment. She rose from the table and returned to the hotel.

"Sit down," Velse invited her and Rue, folding his hands together on the tabletop.

A simple gold wedding ring glinted on his left ring finger, at odds with the impressive platinum Vacheron watch encircling his bony right wrist. Meredith thought the watch looked complicated enough to solve differential calculus problems while simultaneously presenting true solar time, lunar time, and mean time.

Velse stared down his long nose at her, cat like and almost cross-eyed in his intense study. The effect was chilling rather than humorous. "What did Karl Fuhrman say to you?"

As near as she could recall, she told Velse what had transpired in the garage between herself and Fuhrman. When she finished, he nodded and turned to Rue with raised eyebrows.

"I haven't connected all the facts," Rue admitted, folding her hands together as if emulating Velse's posture. "The new information seems to indicate Krause kept the U-boat's destination in his private papers. As you know, we've recently obtained them. Fuhrman talked about a code. Comparing the official inventory list with the private list should give us the numbers. After that, it's a question of breaking the code, if one exists."

"Whatever it takes," Velse said, picking up the glass and taking a sip of water.

Catalina returned. She gave Velse a nod and beckoned at Rue, who excused herself and followed the woman into the hotel.

Since Rue didn't seem to want her, Meredith stayed at the table. She'd noticed when Velse reached for the water glass, the cuff of his shirtsleeve rode up, exposing the beginnings of a tattoo on the underside of his wrist: a line of digits in faded black ink.

He noticed her interest. "My grandmother was held at Breendonk a while before being transferred to Auschwitz with other Jewish prisoners," he said, brushing the tattoo with a fingertip. "She had one just like it. I had this tattoo done on my twenty-first birthday, a reminder of what my family lost in the war and what can never be regained." He glanced at her. "I suppose you believe I want the treasure out of greed, yes?"

"No," Meredith answered forthrightly. "It's a matter of honor."

"More than that," he said. "Money is nothing to me. True wealth is family. My relatives are gone, killed with no regard because they were Jews and therefore unworthy to live. Unworthy to be human. Men like Krause, men like Fuhrman, were part of the machine that snatched them up, starved them, tortured them, killed them, and laid their poor, shattered bones in the cold earth of Breendonk, Treblinka and Auschwitz."

The starkness in his expression kept Meredith silent.

He sighed and leaned back in the chair. "The Führer and the Third Reich stole more than our family's legacy, Ms. Reid. It stole their lives. All my money won't resurrect the dead. So I seek to discover what is left of them, those aunts and uncles, those cousins, those nieces and nephews, who lived decades ago in a country I've never visited, only heard about in my grandmother's stories. I want to put my hands on a necklace and say, 'These are the diamonds given to Great-aunt Rebekkah when she married Great-uncle Moishe.' I will have my family's stolen history under my roof and perhaps…" His voice trailed off. When he spoke again, his tone softened. "Perhaps my *bubbe*'s spirit will find peace at last."

Stricken by his sadness, Meredith didn't know what to say.

Fortunately, Rue returned with a sheaf of papers. "I have the copies," she said. "If you'll excuse us, Mr. Velse? We'd like to get started right away."

He waved a hand in dismissal, his gaze far away.

Meredith left Velse in the courtyard with his memories and his ghosts. For the first time since leaving Miami, she wasn't excited at the prospect of finding the lost U-boat. Instead, she felt a chill, as if she planned to rob a grave.

CHAPTER THIRTY-EIGHT

In the cramped hotel office, Meredith laid aside her pencil with a sigh and wiped her burning eyes. Several hours of tedious, repetitive work had been needed to tease out the altered numbers from Krause's private inventory papers. She and Rue hadn't stopped to do anything more elaborate than visit the little señoritas' room and drink lots of strong, black coffee. Her bladder was full, her stomach empty, and her stiff back reminded her she wasn't a twenty-year-old midshipman anymore, cramming for a leadership ethics exam.

She stood up from her chair, put her hands on her hips, and bent and twisted until her vertebrae cracked like popping corn. "God, I've sat so long I'm fossilized."

Rue huffed. "That's a horrible sound. Why don't you scrape your fingernails on a chalkboard next?" she asked, tapping the printouts on the desk to neatly corner the stack.

Ignoring the complaint, Meredith lifted the sheet containing the numeric code she and Rue had learned by comparing the two sets of papers. "What does it mean?" she asked, examining the rows of digits covering half the sheet. The numbers appeared random. If a pattern existed, she couldn't discern it, but she'd never been good with puzzles anyway.

"I have no idea. God, nothing's ever easy, is it?" Rue wearily scrubbed her face with a palm, turning her pale cheeks pink. Despite the air-conditioning, her mascara and eyeliner had melted, leaving soft, dark smudges beneath her mismatched eyes. "We need a cryptographer. Does Clay have any talents in that direction?"

Meredith snorted. "Clay can do a lot of things, but code breaking isn't one of them."

"Damn." Rue tucked her tablet PC into its brushed aluminum case and came around the desk. "I hoped we wouldn't have to use outside help."

"We can't do everything ourselves."

"You're right. But if I tell Velse, he'll hire the world's greatest cryptologist to analyze the cipher. That's one more person involved and with Grazione still in the picture, I'm not sure who we can trust. I'd rather limit our operation as much as I can."

"Well, Ms. Rivas doesn't strike me as the kind of person who'd betray her employer or his representatives," Meredith pointed out.

"Her professional ethics aren't in question, true." Rue picked up the sheet of code. "Come on. Let's go find her."

Leaving the cramped office, Meredith felt like she'd been liberated from a prison cell. She nodded at Tricia on her way through the lobby. The nurse had proved invaluable in providing cold packs to treat her bruises and acetaminophen to alleviate pain from the cut on her palm, which throbbed every time she forgot and used her hand.

Rue led her to a large room just off the lobby—the hotel's dining area. Modern paintings hung on the primrose-painted walls. A monstrous mahogany sideboard held a coffee urn, cups, and plates of fruit and pastries on its wide marbled top.

Ready to prowl through the pastry selection, Meredith paused when she spotted Cochrane standing by the urn. He looked much better. Tricia had worked miracles on his battered face. The early morning sunlight streaming through the windows revealed much less swelling in his cheek, though the bruise remained dark. He waved at her. Should she go over? The coffee smelled good. *Damn it, looks like Rue has other plans.* Rue made a beeline toward a table in the corner. She hurried to catch up after casting a final, longing glance at the urn and the sugar-sparkling pastries.

Catalina sat by herself, working on a laptop. She glanced up at their approach. "If the *facturas* from Flores Porteñas aren't to your taste—"

"No pastries, thank you." Rue sat in the seat next to Catalina. "We've got the numeric code," she went on, handing over the sheet of paper, "but I can't make any sense of it. You?"

After studying the code for several minutes, Catalina confessed her ignorance and returned the paper. "You need a specialist. I'm sorry, Señora Stanton, I don't know anyone offhand. If you give me a few hours, I may find a name for you."

"No, that's okay. No need to go to all that trouble," Rue said. "I just need to contact a man in Minnesota. His name's Jacob Olsen. I have his number."

"Do you trust this man?"

"Absolutely. He's not a cryptographer, but I'm sure he can put me in touch with someone who is, and I trust his judgment."

"Then please use my phone," Catalina said, pushing a satellite phone across the table.

While Rue made her call, Meredith seized the excuse to wander to the sideboard and get a cup of coffee. She sampled a syrupy, flaky, freshly baked pastry and took a swig of coffee that tasted more bitter because of the sweetness in her mouth.

"I'm headed back home to Mexico in about an hour," Cochrane said, reaching across her for a bun. "Velse is putting me on a private jet. I plan on finding out how much really expensive liquor I can drink before I pass out or expire from alcohol poisoning."

"You have a cast-iron liver, old man."

"You think they have honey roasted peanuts? I miss those things. Nowadays, the stewardesses chuck a bag of pretzels at your head. And speaking of the oh-so-friendly skies…" He beamed, forming a buxom female shape in the air with his hands, and waggled his eyebrows. "Maybe I'll get lucky more ways than one."

"Behave yourself," she admonished halfheartedly, already missing him.

She studied the lines of his face, the familiar geometry of experience and age. Cochrane had been friend, co-worker, even father figure for half her life. Deliberately cutting herself off from him when she'd retired from the navy had felt as wretched as losing a limb.

"Do you need anything? Money-wise, I mean," she said. Cochrane could be damnably stiff-backed about accepting help, but he wouldn't appreciate her beating around the bush either. "You've been away from your shop and there could be expenses—"

He halted her speech with a laser-like glare, which softened almost instantly. "Nah, Velse said he'd compensate me for lost time, inconvenience, emotional distress, yadda, yadda, and all that other bullshit provided I don't report my kidnapping to the local *botons*."

"What?" Meredith bristled with suspicion. "If you want to report Grazione to the police, you go right ahead. Velse can't tell you what to do."

"He sure can when he's paying me a roll of money big enough to choke a porn star," Cochrane retorted. "The cash transfusion he put in my account will make my bank manager weep in envy. It's like winning the damned lottery, Reid."

"Okay, fine. Long as you're happy." She understood how the need for money could overrule common sense. She just didn't appreciate people like Velse who thought they could buy anything or anyone they pleased and have everything their own way.

Cochrane shook his head. "Look, don't be a stranger. Pick up the phone. Pay a visit. I'll slay the fatted calf, show you the sights, break out the less dangerous hooch. Maybe I'll introduce you to my lady friends if you promise not to recruit them to your team."

"What, and leave my toaster oven collection unfinished?" She mirrored his smirk. "You didn't tell me you'd found a woman who actually fell for your line of BS."

"Women, Reid. Plural. Hell, I'll have to whack the girls off with a stick when word gets out about my new financial status."

"Letcher."

"Nag."

Meredith hugged him, careful not to jar the coffee cup in his hand. "Don't do anything stupid, old man," she whispered in a voice like gravel on concrete. No tears, no genuine sadness, just warmth and a twinge of regret. Noticing Rue waving at her, she added, "Fair winds and following seas, Master Chief Cochrane," before releasing him.

"Fair winds and following seas, Captain Reid," he answered with a grin. "And if any son of a bitch stirs up trouble for you and Ms. Hot Stuff, give him a kick in the ass from me."

"Will do." Her spirits lifted a little. Knowing she wouldn't lose touch with Cochrane again, she chuckled and crossed the room to find out what Rue wanted.

CHAPTER THIRTY-NINE

"I talked to Jacob," Rue said, indicating Meredith should take a seat at the table with her and Catalina, "and he says he knows someone in Buenos Aires who's really into ciphers."

"Where does that leave us?" Meredith asked.

"The expert lives in the Palermo *barrio*. We're headed out there in a couple of hours." Rue squinted when a shaft of strong sunlight poured through the windowpanes, turning the old scars in front of her ears to burning silver streaks. "His name's Sam Lee. Jacob says he's a bit odd, but apparently he knows his stuff. A real code breaker."

"You think he can figure out Krause's code?"

"I don't know, but he's all I've got at the moment."

"And if Lee doesn't pan out?"

Catalina broke in. "I know someone, ex-GRU," she said. "But we will try Mr. Lee first. He's local. My contact is in Mumbai and he is not entirely reliable."

Rue agreed. "You're okay with it, Mer?"

"No problem here," Meredith said, keeping her voice neutral despite the desire to hear the story of how Catalina Rivas became acquainted with an ex-Soviet military intelligence agent. Perhaps one day, she'd know the woman well enough to ask.

A shy teenaged boy came around with cups of café *con leche* and a platter of croissants stuffed with ham and cheese. Meredith took a sandwich and a second one for Rue.

Catalina stepped away from the table to arrange transport and other necessities. "I know this man's address," she said to Rue when she returned about ten minutes later. "Palermo Soho. Lots of foreigners and tourists. There is a hippie market today. That's good for us. If we're careful, we won't stand out too much." She went on to detail the plan. "Two SUVs will leave the front of the hotel in twenty minutes. They'll drive around the city to draw possible surveillance away," she said. "The two of you will leave the hotel by the side entrance with Sadiya and I. A full security team will meet us in Palermo Soho. Lee lives on the top floor of a building called Las Hermanas. You won't go inside until the team has secured the building and Lee's residence. Do you have any questions?"

"I'd like a weapon, if possible," Meredith said, pushing aside her empty coffee cup. She'd considered the pros and cons last night, and decided she'd rather have to hire a defense attorney and deal with a manslaughter trial than have her or Rue end up in a coffin.

Catalina nodded. "That can be arranged. Do you have a preference?"

"Sig P226, if you have it."

"Would a Glock 19 do?"

Rue broke in. "You aren't serious!" she exclaimed.

"As a heart attack," Meredith replied, taking Rue's cold hands in hers. "I'm not walking helpless into another ambush. Don't worry. I have good judgment and I know how and when to use a weapon."

"That's what scares me." But Rue didn't pull her hands away, not even when Catalina made a call on her cell phone and Sadiya arrived at the table carrying a Glock 19, an extra magazine and a pancake holster.

Meredith fastened the holster to her belt so the Glock would stay secured snugly in the small of her back. She performed a quick field strip of the semiautomatic weapon, aware of Catalina and Sadiya watching her with professional interest. "Nice," she commented while putting the gun back together. "Someone took good care of it."

"Do you have any experience with firearms?" Catalina asked Rue.

"No. I'm more likely to shoot an ally than an enemy." Rue paused and frowned thoughtfully. "But I wouldn't mind a taser if you have an extra one."

Catalina's bright, white crescent of a smile lightened her severe features. "Would a five million volt stun gun suit you, Ms. Stanton?"

Fifteen minutes later, after the decoy SUVs pulled out from the front of the building, Meredith and Rue followed Catalina and Sadiya to the hotel's side entrance.

Meredith slid a hand to the pancake holster and checked the Glock's draw a final time. Satisfied, she slipped outside and into the backseat of a waiting Ford Focus. Rue got in beside her, while the two mercenaries took the front.

Traffic was thick on the roads from the Boedo *barrio* to Palermo. The longest delay came from a street closed by protestors—the *cacerolazo*, Catalina explained from the front passenger seat, who banged pots to signal their frustration with government policies. Many other drivers slowed their vehicles to blow horns in support or shout abuse at the large group.

At last, after bouncing over a cobblestoned street, the Ford arrived at an old neighborhood called Palermo Soho.

Meredith exited the vehicle and stood on the sidewalk across the street from Las Hermanas watching five women led by Qwabe pile out of a parked Jeep and troop inside the building while she, Rue, Catalina and Sadiya waited for the all-clear.

She glanced around. Down the street, she glimpsed a colorful art fair in progress. The "hippie market" Catalina mentioned, she supposed. Her gaze drifted to the building opposite, a three-story house in the Spanish style sandwiched in a row with chichi boutiques, small eateries and an ethnic grocery store. Oak trees spread welcome shade everywhere.

A loud scream snapped her attention back to Las Hermanas. Smoke poured from a broken window on the upper floor. Her first instinct was to help the coughing people beginning to run outside, but Sadiya's grip stopped her before she'd gone more than a step.

"Wait," Catalina commanded, her gaze fixed on the building. Judging by the tight set of her shoulders, she seemed worried.

A murmuring crowd gathered to gawk. The volume of smoke reduced to a trickle, and finally stopped. Qwabe appeared in the window, waving her shotgun.

Catalina led the way across the street, her gun drawn.

The windowless ground floor was tiny and gloomy, dominated by an ornate wooden staircase. A pair of red-painted doors on either side were firmly shut. Six rusty metal mailboxes hung in a row on the wall. None were marked with names, only numbers.

Qwabe waited for them, almost a silhouette in the dim light. She jerked her head, her dreadlocks bouncing on her shoulders. Catalina's nod sent her upstairs ahead of the group. Her long legs easily took two steps at a time.

Meredith tried to keep up and maintain an anxious eye on Rue at the same time. The air smelled more like smoke than fire. The acrid odor caught in the back of her throat and stung her eyes. She coughed. Where was the fire department? What or who had started the fire? A coincidental accident? An attack? Was Catalina's team responsible? She hoped not. They were supposed to meet with Sam Lee, not burn out him and his neighbors.

On the second-floor landing, both apartment doors stood wide open, evidence of the occupants' haste to evacuate. From the uppermost floor, she caught the faint sound of a television program's laugh track carrying down the staircase.

Qwabe leaned in to whisper in Catalina's ear.

"What happened?" Meredith asked, noticing the rest of the security team's absence.

The question went unanswered. Qwabe continued leading the group to the third floor where three team members had taken strategic positions on the landing. The origin of the television noise became apparent—one of the two doors was open.

Meredith glanced inside the apartment. The visible window was covered in an opaque film admitting some light, but not much for such a sunny day. A feeble blue-white light flickered, probably from a television set. She smelled smoke strongest here, and the landing's walls and ceiling were soot stained. No sign of charring on the floor or anywhere else. *Not fire. Smoke grenade.*

A sixtyish woman with pale blond, almost white hair came to the doorway. "I suppose I have you to thank for this mess," she stated flatly in a Midwestern American accent, waving a thin hand to indicate the landing. Her sharp, unfriendly gaze shifted to Rue. "What the hell do you people want? You the ringmaster of this circus, Red?"

"We're looking for Mr. Sam Lee," Rue replied, clearly trying to mask her unease. "Do you know him?"

"Honey, you've got to get your facts straight," the woman bit out. "I'm Samantha Lee. Sam to my friends. And you definitely don't fit into that category."

Meredith flinched.

CHAPTER FORTY

Inside the apartment, Sam Lee sat on a sofa and continued to bristle with hostility. "I really wasn't expecting an armed invasion," she said tartly to Rue.

"I'm very sorry," Rue replied, taking a seat on the opposite end of the sofa.

Meredith remained standing, sensing fury hovering in the air like ozone from distant lightning. She edged a little closer to Rue, just in case Sam made her displeasure more tangible. "Jacob Olsen told us you might be able to help with a problem."

A cold, glittering glance swept her way. "If I refuse?" Sam asked.

"We'll leave at once," Rue promised. "I'm happy to pay for any damages, Ms. Lee. And of course, I'll compensate you for your time either way."

Sam snorted and leaned forward to snag a cigarette from a crumpled pack on the coffee table. She eyed the security team crammed into the small apartment. "You don't need the muscle, Red," she said to Rue. "Tell 'em to wait outside and we'll talk.

Otherwise, you can go to hell." She lit her cigarette with a lighter, leaned back against the sofa cushion, took a drag, and blew out a lungful of smoke that blurred her features.

Rue nodded at Catalina, who gestured at Qwabe. The team filed out of the apartment, but not, Meredith noticed, off the landing. They remained just outside, weapons at the ready.

"I'm sorry we got off on the wrong foot," Rue said, her nose wrinkling slightly when cigarette smoke drifted her way.

"Wrong foot…is that what you call it?" Sam crossed her skinny legs and regarded Rue with what appeared to be amusement. "A half-dozen mercenaries armed to the teeth come pounding on my door. What am I supposed to think? They set off my first line of defense. I was getting ready to bug out when one of them made it into the apartment and held me at gunpoint." She clucked her tongue. "Should've been a bit faster, but age is getting the better of me, I suppose."

"First line of defense?"

"Smoke grenade."

Rue nodded as if booby traps in a residential building were a normal, expected part of everyday life. "Again, I apologize. It wasn't my intention to strong-arm my way in here and make demands. Like my partner told you, we're here to ask a favor."

"Jacob Olsen sent you." Sam pursed her lips. Her coral-colored lipstick had been applied a little crookedly. "He's a good man. Kind of a nut, but no malice in him." She leaned forward, resting an elbow on her thigh, and stabbed the cigarette in Rue's direction. "Look, Red, I don't know you. I don't know your friend. I sure as hell don't know that party of gun-happy *amazonas* you've got out there. I do know your people broke my door, scared the ever-lovin' shit out of my neighbors, and interrupted my favorite *telenovela*. So unless you've got something better than, 'Jacob sent me,' I'd like you to fuck off back to Fairyland or wherever you came from, pronto."

Meredith caught a subtle gleam close to Sam's leg— something peeping out from under the sofa cushion. A gun, she thought. Should she tell Catalina? No. She was closer. Securing the weapon herself made more sense.

Before she had the chance to suit deed to words, Sam whipped the gun out of hiding and pointed the muzzle at Rue. "Tell your people to stay where they are," the white-haired woman warned. "I can squeeze off at least three or four shots before they get through the door and every bullet's aimed at your heart."

Rue stared, her brown eye cold, her blue eye colder, seemingly unmoved by the threat. "Ms. Lee, my only intention is to transact some business today. If you'll let me explain—"

Sam cut her off. "You," she said to Meredith. "Tall, dark and handsome. I want you to drop the *pistola* you've got in that pancake holster. Be careful and do it slow. In case you haven't guessed, I'm feeling nervous for some reason."

From the doorway came movement. Catalina appeared on the threshold. "Ms. Lee, we want no trouble," she called. "Please don't make me have to shoot you."

"Nobody's getting shot as long as everybody does what they're told," Sam countered. She stood while Meredith complied with her order. "Put the gun on the coffee table. Good girl. Now go sit next to the redhead. As for you, Ms. Rivas, stay where you are and your clients won't come to any grief. Push me, though, and I'm liable to do anything. I'm unpredictable that way." Her mouth stretched in a nasty grin. She flicked her cigarette out the broken window. The gun's muzzle remained steady.

Meredith sat next to Rue on the sofa. What-ifs peppered her thoughts like grains of unexploded gunpowder, ready to blow up in her face. So many things could go wrong here, she couldn't bring herself to list them. Best-case scenario—everybody lived, she told herself, making an effort to be patient, be watchful, and be ready.

"Jacob said he'd send you an email," Rue said, sounding calmer than Meredith felt.

Sam moved to a computer in a corner of the room. "Don't even think about rushing me," she snapped at Catalina. "If what Red says pans out, this'll all be over without shedding a drop of blood or a single tear." She tapped the keyboard, keeping the bulk of her attention on the situation in the room rather than the monitor. After a few moments, she relaxed. "Okay, so Jacob sent an email vetting you and asking me for a favor," she said, setting the gun down and leaning a hip against the computer desk. "What do you want?"

Meredith sighed. "May I?" she asked, waving a hand at the Glock on the coffee table.

"Knock yourself out, sweetie pie," Sam said breezily. She shifted an expectant gaze to Rue, who pulled a piece of paper out of her cargo pants pocket.

"I hope you can tell us what these numbers mean," Rue said, passing over the paper. "We think it's a World War Two code used by a Nazi SS officer. Jacob said you were the only person he knew who might break it. He said—"

"Jacob's sweet," Sam interrupted dryly. She held the paper to the light from the window, which had the added effect of throwing her wrinkles into relief. Her skin resembled aged parchment. "What's the context? Why do you think this code dates from the war?" When Rue hesitated, she added, "*You* came to *me*, Red. If you want to know what this code says, you need to trust me with the truth and give me as much information as possible."

Rue pressed her lips together tightly, but soon answered, "I believe the code contains a clue to a location. It was devised by an SS officer. I don't know many other details except the message was created either at the tail end of the war or just after Germany surrendered."

"Not a lot to go on. Do you have anything else? Another part of the code?"

"No. That's it."

Sam tapped the edge of the paper against her bottom lip, leaving a little orange lipstick smear on the white surface. "With such a small sample, I can't promise anything, but I'll do my best. The fee's $7,500, nonnegotiable, payable in cash, US dollars or Euros only. As soon as the money's transferred to my bank account, I'll start working on the code."

"How long will you need to decipher the message?" Meredith asked, picking up the Glock and returning it to her holster.

"As long as it takes," Sam answered, setting the paper on her desk and resting her fingertips on it. "Code breaking isn't easy. I can think of a half dozen ciphers your SS officer could have used, including machine-based cryptographic systems. Or an Ottendorf cipher—book ciphers are a bitch if you don't have the key."

The word "key" resonated in Meredith's memory. "There's one other thing…sorry, Rue, I almost forgot. I don't know if this is important or not, but I heard the writer's nephew was a U-boat commander and this nephew was the key to the cipher, whatever that means."

Sam stared at her until she fidgeted. "Hmm, that makes things a little easier," she said slowly. "Not much, mind you, but it's a place to start."

"Can you really figure out the message?" Rue asked. "I can't waste time here—"

"Hush." Sam held up a skinny finger, the nail painted deep red to match her blouse. "If the cipher can be cracked, Red, I'll crack it."

"Are you that good?" Meredith asked. Samantha Lee didn't strike her as a typical code breaker. She'd always envisioned such people as weedy math nerds or eccentric, absentminded geniuses. On the other hand, anyone who rigged smoke grenades to protect their living space *was* eccentric, if not downright paranoid.

"I'm that good. I used to do this kind of thing for a living."

"Where'd you work?"

Sam lit another cigarette and peered at her through the smoke. "Langley."

CHAPTER FORTY-ONE

"I had no idea a retired CIA code breaker lived in Buenos Aires. Hope we hear from her soon." Rue sipped from a bottle of beer and leaned back in her chair.

"Let's hope so," Meredith replied. She and Rue sat alone in the courtyard garden enjoying a couple of ice-cold beers liberated from the kitchen. Not a brand she recognized and a little too hoppy for her taste, but she took another swallow anyway. "Any idea how long before Ms. Lee deciphers the code?" she asked. "It's been a couple of days already."

Rue shrugged. "I don't know. Not too much longer, I hope. Every day we spend in the city, I feel like I'm walking around with a target on my back. I keep waiting for Thiago Grazione and his thugs to make another move."

Meredith made a noncommittal noise. The beer left a dry taste in her mouth, but somehow also quenched her thirst. She checked the level in the green-tinted bottle. Time for another? With a sigh, she decided she felt too relaxed to get up yet. The sunlight, the heat and the occasional smell of flowers reminded her of Miami. "How's Velse?"

"Holed up with his cell phone," Rue said. "I swear that thing's surgically implanted in his ear. I haven't seen him without it since the day he arrived." She glanced toward the hotel and sat up straighter. "Catalina," she called, getting to her feet. "Any news?"

"Not good news," Catalina replied, coming to the table to sit in a third chair.

"What happened?" Meredith asked, realizing she'd scooted to the edge of her seat. Her insides seemed to vibrate with tension. She forced herself to wait.

Catalina looked tired, but her dark eyes gleamed with some strong, unreadable emotion. "Ms. Lee went missing this morning. Please, Ms. Stanton, do not shout at me," she added in response to Rue's immediate barrage of questions. "I will tell you what I know. Please." She gestured at Rue's abandoned chair.

Rue sat down warily.

Meredith bit the inside of her cheek in frustration. She wasn't superstitious, but she'd swear their venture was cursed. "What happened?" she repeated.

"We've kept surveillance on Ms. Lee's apartment in shifts around the clock. You recall we were very careful not to be followed to the apartment, yes? I believed we were successful, that if Grazione's men were watching the hotel, they were misled by our decoy cars, but I would be a fool not to take precautions. Covering my ass, I believe you Americans say." Catalina sighed. "My guards had nothing to report until this morning. Just after shift change at eight o'clock, one of them entered the apartment and found Ms. Lee gone."

"Do you think she's dead?"

"No blood, no bullet holes, no signs of a struggle, but Ms. Lee is not a young woman. How difficult would it be to overpower her?"

Rue murmured, "Sam got the drop on your people, didn't she?"

Catalina grimaced, but acknowledged the hit with a nod. "What do we do now? Where do we start looking?" Meredith wanted to know. She stood, unable to sit still any longer. Rue's touch on her leg made her sit down again.

"We wait, Ms. Reid," Catalina said. "First, we must know where to begin looking." A breeze blew strands of her fine black hair across her mouth when she spoke. She pulled them free with an impatient gesture. "Only then will we know what to do."

Like searching for a very small needle in a very big haystack. Meredith repeated the thought aloud.

"A human-sized needle mixed with almost three million other needles in a seventy-eight square mile haystack," Rue commented. She turned a thoughtful gaze on Catalina. "Are we sure Sam didn't leave of her own accord? I mean, we think the worst because of Grazione, but Sam's ex-CIA. I know she's a code breaker, not a field agent, but still—the woman is nobody's fool. Maybe she had a dentist's appointment."

Meredith snorted. "Maybe she went out for a mani-pedi or a bikini wax."

"Maybe I didn't care much for the Amazon escort and gave 'em the slip," Sam said, walking into the courtyard with a smirk on her face. The breeze ruffled her white hair, lifting strands from her shoulders like dandelion fluff. She stood hipshot by the table, staring first at Catalina, then Meredith, and finally Rue. "Got another one of those beers, Red?"

Catalina half turned in her seat and waved at the hotel. She said to Sam, "A moment, *por favor*. Join us."

Sam folded into the remaining chair next to Rue and plunked a worn leather purse on her lap. "I guess you'd like to hear about the code," she said, crossing her denim-clad legs. Her bright orange sneakers matched her lipstick color.

"You think?" Meredith muttered.

"Now, now, don't be that way. I have news. Good or bad, that's up to you." Sam dug a pack of cigarettes out of her purse. She spent a few minutes lighting a cigarette and taking several puffs. Smoke carried into the hibiscus trees, blotting out the scent of flowers. "Do you ladies want the gory details or the short 'n' sweet version?"

"Did you break the code?" Rue asked.

Sam nodded. "Yep. A variation of *Doppelkastenschlüssel*—a Double Playfair cipher." The cigarette bobbled in the corner of her mouth while she spoke. She produced a brown envelope from her purse. "Your original and a copy of my decipherment."

Catalina accepted the envelope. "Are there any other copies?" she asked.

The casual tone didn't fool Meredith. Judging by the woman's narrowed eyes, the pseudo indifference didn't fool Sam either.

"When I'm bought, I stay bought," Sam said flatly, dropping her lipstick-stained cigarette on the grass. "You came to me, remember?"

"I forget nothing," Catalina replied with cool aplomb. She slid the papers out of the envelope. Her gaze flicked over a page. She took a smartphone from her jacket pocket and performed an Internet search. The result caused her eyebrows to rise. "Interesting," she commented, passing papers, envelope and smartphone to Rue.

Meredith leaned over to look at the typewritten page in Rue's hand. What she read struck her as utterly implausible, not to mention ridiculous. She looked at the smartphone's screen and at the women seated around the table, expecting someone to laugh or point out the hidden camera. No one did.

"You've got to be kidding," she said at last to Sam.

"Sorry, sweetie, it's the real deal. No bullshit," Sam said. She paused while Qwabe slapped a beer bottle on the table in front of her and stalked back to the hotel. "You don't like what you see," she continued to Meredith, "hire another cryptographer."

"The Antarctic," Meredith scoffed.

Rue set the papers aside and glanced at the top sheet. Her mismatched gaze shifted to Catalina. "Will you have one of your people double-check these coordinates?" She gave Sam an apologetic smile. "Not that I don't believe you, Ms. Lee."

"Aw, hell, Red, I sure wouldn't believe me if I were you," Sam said, saluting Rue with the upraised bottle and taking a swallow of beer.

Catalina rose and walked through the courtyard to the hotel. "Goddamn it." Meredith thumped her fist on the table. "She has to be wrong, right? I mean..." Her voice trailed off when her brain finally caught up to her astonishment. "We have to go to Antarctica?" she squeaked in dismay.

"Looks that way," Rue said. She regarded Sam. Her mouth thinned. "I have a hard time understanding why an entire page of numbers yielded only a set of coordinates."

Sam lit another cigarette. "Sorry, Red, didn't I make our deal clear? I guess maybe the invasion force beating down my door rattled me. The fee you paid—thanks for your generosity, by the way—gets you coordinates. Nothing else. You want the entire message, it'll cost you another thirty grand. Don't bother searching me or my place. The message is in here." She tapped the side of her head.

Meredith pushed her chair back and stood, letting her expression settle into granite hardness. She stared down at Sam long enough for the slightest tinge of pink to color the woman's cheeks before she spoke in a clipped tone. "Ms. Lee, I never took you for a liar and a cheat, but I suppose my judgment was off the day we met."

Sam rose suddenly. "Fool you once, shame on me," she said, putting a hand in her purse. "I think I'll just be going, if you don't mind."

Meredith moved to block Sam from leaving the courtyard. In the corner of her eye, she saw Catalina stand and step to a similar position, flanking the former CIA analyst.

"Ganging up on an old woman?" Sam asked, starting to draw a gun from her purse.

Catalina pulled a Beretta from a concealed holster somewhere on her person, beating Sam to the punch. "Have you ever been interrogated by an expert, Ms. Lee?" she asked softly, her almond-shaped eyes half-lidded and glittering. "The art of extracting information from an unwilling subject has come a long way in recent years—"

"No," Rue interrupted. She remained seated, staring up at Sam. A moment passed in silence, and another, and finally she said, "I'm confident we can work this disagreement out to our mutual satisfaction. Please, sit down, Ms. Rivas, Ms. Lee."

Cautiously, bristling and staring at each other like a pair of hostile cats, Catalina and Sam put away their weapons and resumed their seats.

Meredith followed suit. She noticed Qwabe and Carrizo arrived to linger near the courtyard. Both guards were conspicuously armed. *How did they know we needed help?*

A light breeze lifted some of Catalina's feathery black hair away from the side of her head, revealing a micro transceiver in her ear and answering Meredith's question. Someone inside the house was monitoring the meeting.

Rue didn't look at the guards. She maintained a steady gaze on Sam. "Thirty thousand dollars is out of the question," she said calmly. "I could see my way to paying an extra five thousand as a bonus for your quick decipherment."

Meredith folded her arms across her chest and bit her tongue, keeping her opinion to herself with difficulty.

"Ten thousand," Sam countered.

"Six."

"Another seventy-five hundred and I'm out of your hair."

Rue waited, a faint smile tweaking the corners of her mouth. When Sam began to shift uneasily in her chair, she said, "Done."

Relaxing by degrees, Meredith hoped the bargain would stick this time.

CHAPTER FORTY-TWO

Antarctica...Meredith wished she had another beer.

Catalina set a very small video recorder on the table in front of Sam. The device was matte black, about the size of a C-cell battery.

For a moment, Meredith wondered why Elliot Velse hadn't been invited to join them. She realized a second later that by revealing his presence to Sam Lee, who had proved somewhat untrustworthy, Velse's security would be compromised.

Sam eyed the recorder with distaste, but nodded. From her purse she withdrew another large brown envelope. "For you," she said to Rue, who accepted the envelope while still talking on her cell phone to a bank clerk about the transfer of funds.

Once Rue ended her call, Sam's manner turned brisk and businesslike. "I'll summarize my findings, if you don't mind. I've included the full, original German message and an English translation in the package."

Rue gestured for the woman to proceed.

"Excuse me if I repeat anything you already know," Sam said, tapping ash off the end of her cigarette. "In 1939, before war broke out in Europe, the German government sent a scientific and military expedition by steamship to Dronning—or Queen—Maud Land in Antarctica with a twofold objective: annex a piece of the continent for Germany to construct a base of operations for their whaling fleet, and scientific study. Officially, of course."

Drowning maudlin. No wonder old Fuhrman's out-of-context ramblings had been gibberish to her, Meredith thought.

"Unofficially," Sam went on, "the chaos as the war started gave ideal cover for a top secret building project: a discreet U-boat base housed in a natural ice cave."

Rue frowned and placed her hands flat on the table, on top of the brown envelope. "That's a myth. Historians working with the German archives have disproved—"

"Sweetie, I don't really give a rat's ass about bureaucratic paperwork. I'm just adding a side order of context to your coded message." Sam put the beer bottle to her lips, tipped back her head, and gulped half the contents. She kept the sweating bottle in her hand while she spoke. "The British and Americans discovered the existence of the U-boat base in 1942. Then in '47, the US Navy ran a covert operation in the Antarctic."

Meredith snapped her fingers as Sam's narrative began to make sense. "Operation Highjump. I remember from a history class." She frowned. "That particular op wasn't covert and had nothing to do with Nazis. The navy was tasked with establishing a scientific research outpost. And assessing strategic sites of military significance, of course."

"Highjump provided cover for a much more covert navy intelligence operation: locate the Nazi base and recover hidden gold. They found out about the gold when a couple of U-boats were picked up in Argentina right at the end of the war, supposedly following a final Antarctica run. I imagine the captains and crew spilled everything they knew once the interrogations started. Despite the intel, the navy operatives failed," Sam said.

"I'm still not buying it."

"Believe me or not, I don't care. But consider I used to be a senior cryptanalyst for the CIA. Don't you think I might have given myself access to deeply buried, highly classified documents that would otherwise never see the light of day?"

"Why would you?"

"Boredom. Curiosity. For the hell of it. Take your pick."

"I suppose you're going to tell me next that Hitler didn't commit suicide," Meredith said sarcastically, folding her arms across her chest. "He and his best buds hid out in Antarctica in their awesome man cave and plotted world domination."

Sam gave her a flat stare. "Let's not bring mythology into the discussion."

"I've heard enough." Rue lifted her head. "Thank you, Ms. Lee. I'm sure you have other business today, so I think we shouldn't keep you any longer."

"Before I go, I'll give you a piece of advice free of charge: stay out of this one, Red." Sam stood, a breeze blowing white hair into her eyes. "No matter what you think you'll find on that base, it's not worth the risk."

Catalina rose from her chair. "What do you know?" she asked, her voice low.

"I'm retired, not out of the loop. I hear things. That's all I'm going to say." Sam looked at Rue. "Take care of yourself, Red. Why don't you get out of town for a while? Avoid Santiago. If you and your people can't handle a little wisdom, take my advice and go home." She finished the beer, left the empty bottle on the table, and walked away through the garden and out of sight.

Rue didn't sit in her chair very long. "I need to talk to Velse." She picked up the brown envelope. "Mer, you coming?"

Meredith shook her head.

"Suit yourself." Rue headed into the hotel, followed closely by Catalina.

Meredith stayed put. Her input wasn't necessary and frankly, she wanted to be alone a while to consider Samantha Lee's parting words. Several things about the stilted-sounding statements struck her as odd.

Noticing Catalina had abandoned the mini video camera on the table, she figured out how to watch the recording of Sam on the diminutive screen. When she finished, she leaned back to consider the message piece by piece.

Why don't you get out of town for a while? No meaning other than the obvious, she assumed. The next sentence held more promise. *Avoid Santiago.*

She picked up Catalina's smartphone—also left behind in the rush to tell Velse the news—and did an Internet search. Santiago was the capital of Chile. So far, so good. But instinct told her to dig deeper. What did the name Santiago mean? Saint Iago, which reminded her of Thiago Grazione. In Catholic countries, many children were given saints' names.

Her interpretation would do for the moment. On to the next sentence: *if you and your people can't handle a little wisdom, take my advice and go home.*

If she took the words at face value, Sam had made a dig at their group for not having the sense to quit. She knew the ex-analyst believed them foolish for going after the U-boat base. The part about "a little wisdom" sounded like pure hubris, though, as if Sam were bragging about her intelligence—which could mean IQ or collected strategic information. That kind of boast didn't jibe with what little she knew of the secretive woman.

She went online, squinting at the smartphone's display screen, and performed several searches, finding and discarding various results for "wise." Finally, she checked "wisdom" and eventually learned a startling fact: the name Sophia meant "wisdom."

A connection fell into place. Sophia Fellman-Grazione, granddaughter of Carlos Fellman a.k.a. Karl Fuhrman, and CEO of the Grazione family's hotel chain. If Sam wasn't leading them astray for some reason of her own, Sophia was involved.

"Mr. Velse is consulting some expert or another on the feasibility of an Antarctic expedition at this time of year," Rue said, breaking into her thoughts and dropping down into the chair next to hers. "What's got you so wrapped up?"

Meredith explained her findings.

Rue shrugged. "Well, that's not cryptic at all. Are you sure that woman wasn't just messing with you for kicks?"

"I'm sure. Well, almost positive. Sam was a cryptanalyst. Maybe that's why she didn't tell us straight out. Too used to thinking like a corkscrew." Meredith sighed and raised her arm to blot sweat from her forehead with her shirtsleeve. "According to the message, we need to be careful of Thiago Grazione and his grandniece. We already knew about Thiago. Sophia's a new player." She recalled a conversation in a basement in Minnesota, when she and Rue had learned about Fuhrman's current family situation courtesy of Jacob Olsen. "You said Grazione belonged to a group of people who basically steal art from art thieves."

"Yes, but to be honest, what I'm working from are rumors." Rue sounded exasperated. "I mean, if you're in the recovery business, you're exposed to whispers in corners, hinted allegations—nothing concrete. I heard about an underground group. I heard they threatened art thieves. I heard Thiago Grazione was in charge. Would I swear any of it was true? No. Plausible, sure. Grazione's a thug. Just don't assume I know more than you because I don't, and my ignorance is probably going to get us all killed," she ended on a distressed note.

Meredith reached over to Rue's hand where it rested on the table and stroked a thumb down the soft, pale inner wrist, tracing the blue vein just beneath the skin's surface. "We'll figure it out," she said. "Nobody's going to die. Not on my watch."

"Promise?"

"Cross my heart."

CHAPTER FORTY-THREE

Two weeks later, Meredith sat in a pressurized cargo bay with Rue, Catalina Rivas, and a number of bodyguards in a hired Lockheed C130 Hercules transport plane. They'd taken off from Punta Arenas, Chile and were an hour into a nearly five-hour flight to their Antarctic destination. Her ass already hurt.

The webbing seats lining both sides of the bay were as uncomfortable as hell and the engine noise made hearing protection necessary. The constant vibration churned her stomach worse than a storm with gale force winds and cross-swells. She recalled Velse's luxurious private jet with a sigh. No gourmet dinner on this flight. Not even pretzels or a lukewarm cola. Probably a good thing, she thought, since the "toilet" on the plane was designed for men only: a hose attached to the bulkhead and sporting a funnel on the end.

Unable to talk to anyone without shouting, she reflected on the last couple of weeks in Buenos Aires. She had kept busy helping Rue and Catalina make the complex arrangements required to continue their search for U-3019.

Rue nudged her. She leaned over and slipped out an earplug to hear the woman's bellow through the turboprop racket, "Wish we had Wi-Fi!"

She nodded. When Rue didn't say anything else, she replaced the earplug and tried to find a position on the seat that didn't make her thighs go numb.

Grazione's organization remained a threat. Three days ago, one of Catalina's support personnel—a cybersecurity expert called Padma Gupta—returned from an assignment and discovered well concealed spyware planted in the group's server. Meredith figured the hacker had to be a member of the opposition, leaving her to further believe Grazione knew precisely where they were headed and why.

The hunt to locate the missing German U-boat had turned into a full-fledged chase against a mostly unknown group, which appeared to own resources sufficient to be a significant threat. At Velse's suggestion—actually a thinly veiled order—Catalina had recalled most of her mercenaries from other jobs. She'd prepared her team as much as possible given the environment, but anything could happen at the bottom of the world.

They would be on their own, far from reinforcements or rescue. Hours passed while Meredith held Rue's hand, simultaneously looking forward to and dreading the expedition.

Following a rough landing on the airstrip in Antarctica, she pulled on her extreme cold weather gear: thermal underwear, wool shirt, moleskin pants, fleece jacket, waterproof polar parka, waterproof nylon trousers, mittens over gloves, hat, scarf, three pairs of thick socks and boots. For the brief trip to the field camp, the clothing seemed excessive, but she didn't argue.

When everyone was ready, the pilot lowered the rear cargo door.

Instantly, a blast of shockingly frigid air whipped into the transport plane. Even through the multiple layers she wore, the cold struck her like a fist made of razor-sharp shards of ice, driving the breath from her lungs. Beyond the open cargo door lay the darkness of a perpetual winter night. The continent wouldn't see sunlight until the seasons turned.

She waited with the others while the transport plane's crew unloaded a big Tucker Sno-Cat vehicle capable of holding eight to fifteen people in the oversized cab. Instead of tires, four individually mounted track and rubber tread systems ensured navigating the icy, rocky terrain wouldn't be a problem.

Sadiya walked over and pushed a very light, very compact Heckler & Koch MP7 submachine gun into her mittened hands. "In case of emergency," she said, helping her pull the strap over her head and settle it across her body.

Meredith nodded her thanks, hoping she wouldn't have to use the weapon.

The team left the cargo bay in pairs. Meredith found herself with a pale-eyed female mercenary she hadn't met in the past. The woman proved curt but professional, escorting her through the dark to the Sno-Cat and ensuring she didn't break her neck over any bumps or ruts in the ice. Once at the vehicle, the woman disappeared back toward the plane.

Inside the Sno-Cat, the temperature remained cool despite the engine running and the heating system presumably doing its best. Someone sat in the driver's seat—another of Catalina's mercenaries made anonymous by a hooded parka.

Meredith took a seat next to Rue and settled the MP7 in her lap, the muzzle pointed at the floor. "Hope it warms up soon."

"Me too." Rue paused when Qwabe shuffled up the aisle to the rear, leaving clumps of snow in her wake. "I had no idea Antarctica would be so cold. I mean, I've been to Russia in winter, but this place…it's like another planet."

"Why couldn't the Nazis have built a secret base in Miami?" Meredith mock whined.

"Rio de Janeiro."

"Alexandria."

"Paris." Rue laughed, her eyes sparkling. "Have you ever been to the City of Love?"

Meredith shook her head, strangely muted by the sight of Rue's beautiful face framed by the synthetic fur trimming the hood. A few strands of her hair had spilled out, the auburn color darkened by melting snow. She suddenly felt an overwhelming desire to kiss the woman's rosy mouth, her eyelids, her brow, the silver scars in front of her ears.

"Paris is beautiful in springtime. Maybe it's a cliché, but it's true." Rue put out a hand to cup Meredith's cheek. "I'd love to show you Paris one day."

"I...I'd like that," Meredith managed to say. Turning her head, she kissed Rue's palm. "When we're done, when everything's over—" She broke off, unsure if she had the courage to continue. She knew Rue's body very well. The woman's heart was another matter.

The moment for confession passed when more mercenaries swarmed into the Sno-Cat. Rue removed her hand and turned to gaze out the window, leaving Meredith to mourn the loss of contact and the spark of warmth Rue's touch kindled inside her.

Once everyone found a place to sit, the trip from the airstrip to the field camp began. Little could be glimpsed of the scenery outside except pale, vague blobs she supposed were snowdrifts or ice. Thin, pale green and rosy veils of light shimmered across the sky, dancing over the bright stars—the famed *aurora australis*. She'd never seen anything so beautiful in her life except the woman sitting next to her.

In less than thirty minutes, the Sno-Cat arrived at their field camp, an abandoned research station the advance team had repaired and renovated for their use. Meredith hustled inside the well-lighted building with the rest, glad to get out of the biting cold.

She left the MP7 with a bunch of other firearms shed by most of the mercenaries and followed Rue to the large central common room. Apart from several gas stoves pumping out heat, the room contained computers and communications equipment, long picnic-style tables with attached benches, coffee and tea urns, and storage boxes and bins lined along a wall.

"Shift schedule over there," Catalina announced loudly in English as Meredith, Rue and the other women came into the room. "Permission is required to swap shifts. No one is authorized to leave the building unless you have prior clearance."

Curious, Meredith checked the printed schedule pinned to a corkboard on the wall. She and Rue hadn't been assigned guard duty or scut work, but they'd been allocated a five-minute shower every third day. Thank God for extra-strength deodorant.

She elbowed her way out of the crowd around the schedule and scanned the room for Rue, finding her standing near a computer, speaking on a satellite phone. As she came closer, Rue ended the call, turned, and smiled at her.

"Mr. Velse," Rue explained, setting down the phone on the table. "I let him know we arrived safely. As you can imagine, he's a bit anxious."

Meredith leaned a hip on the table. "No kidding. So am I, to be honest." She glanced down at the tips of the sheepskin-lined suede slippers she'd been given to wear after she shed her boots. "Do you still think it's a good idea to go after the U-boat?"

"Good idea? No. We're facing a lot of challenges, a lot of dangers, a lot of unknowns. But I believe the U-boat's out there, Mer. Just waiting all these years for someone to find her." Rue's gaze drifted inward. "A ghost ship haunted by the evils of the past." She shook her head. "Sorry, didn't mean to dip into melodrama."

"That's okay." Meredith took a breath to calm her fluttering stomach. She'd been a navy captain, goddamn it. She could manage a simple question without feeling like an awkward teenager asking a crush to the prom. "When we're finished here, would you…I mean, I know you're busy and all, but I thought… well, maybe if you and me—"

Her halting speech was interrupted by Catalina. "We have a situation."

"What's happened?" Rue asked, stiffening to attention.

Meredith felt her spine snap straight in reflex.

"A blizzard's coming in fast. Snow with winds up to eighty knots." Catalina spread her hands apart. "*Lo siento*, Ms. Stanton, looks like we have to wait it out."

"How long?"

"Two or three days."

Rue shrugged. "So be it. I'm sure your people will find enough to do." She paused. "I've waited longer in worse conditions," she remarked when Catalina walked away.

Same here, but seldom with so much to say and so little courage to actually say it, Meredith thought, but kept her mouth sealed tight against rash declarations.

CHAPTER FORTY-FOUR

The storm lasted three days.

Toward the end, Meredith could almost taste the eagerness in the air. The camp was secure, the food decent for canned and freeze-dried supplies, but nobody wanted to linger a moment longer than necessary. The mercenaries were like hounds straining at a leash and Rue wasn't far behind. The woman's impatience to get out and get going was an almost tangible thing, seeming to manifest most visibly in her bristling, flyaway, static-charged auburn hair.

Finally, the blizzard blew itself out.

Exiting the building at eight o'clock the next morning was like stepping into midnight, just darkness and shadows beyond small pools of illumination cast by the security lights. The wind cut through her uncovered face with vicious, razor blade insistence. Each breath scoured her nose, throat and lungs like frozen steel wool.

She hastily climbed into the waiting Sno-Cat. Rue, Catalina and Sadiya sat huddled together, bent over a grid map on a tablet, so she chose another seat and settled in for the trip.

Their field camp stood in Argentinean territory near Belgrano II base on the eastern shore of the Weddell Sea. Catalina's plan involved a brief journey overland to the coast, then switching to Zodiac boats to enter the waters off Queen Maud's Land, the area claimed by Norway. Somewhere in the natural ice caves lay the U-boat's coordinates.

At Elliot Velse's order, they hadn't asked the Norwegian government for permission. Meredith supposed he wanted to confirm the U-boat's existence before unraveling the necessary red tape. Or perhaps he intended to keep the operation hush-hush and sneak out U-3019's contents under the Norwegians' collective noses. She wasn't sure of much except this was a reconnaissance mission to determine the sub's location and condition.

The Sno-Cat rumbled off, bumping over snowy hillocks. She gripped the back of the seat ahead of her and held on, hoping like hell the vehicle didn't lumber into a crevasse.

Never had she felt more like a third wheel, she thought, staring at the nonview outside the window and mulling over the last few days. Since the group entered Antarctica, Rue and Catalina stayed busy running the show. She'd managed to snatch the odd hour or two of Rue's company, but not enough. Not nearly enough to satisfy her need for the woman.

When had she gone from a roll in the hay to contemplating her grandmother's engagement ring, tucked away in a safety deposit box in a Miami bank? The last seventy-two hours, she'd had little to do except navel gaze and she still didn't understand when and how Rue got so deep under her skin. She only knew at some indefinable moment, Rue had marked her as surely as a long-ago tattooist's needle had etched her upper arm.

Brooding wasn't like her, but she allowed herself to indulge until the Sno-Cat reached their destination and she put aside her personal problems for another day.

Traveling by the ten-passenger, inflatable rubber Zodiac boats was bracing, to say the least. She pulled up her thick scarf to protect the lower half of her face. In the darkness, the sea appeared placid, the surface peppered with fields of broken ice and icebergs—some big, some small, some looking jagged, as if violently torn from a glacier, others as smooth as glass, sculpted by who knew how many decades or centuries of wind.

An anonymous parka-clad woman manned a searchlight at the bow. The circle of light aided navigation, but quickly grayed ahead into twilight. "Ice!" she suddenly shouted.

Instantly, the Zodiac swerved to avoid a chunk of ice the size and shape of a refrigerator. Meredith kept a strong grip on one side of the boat and wound her other hand into the hem of Rue's parka. Near misses and a few minor impacts happened several times. She realized ice could be damned difficult to see in the dark, even with a searchlight.

The current was deceptive, too, sending slabs and blocks of ice swirling toward them at about one or two knots, she estimated. An almost clear piece floated close to the boat. She dared take off her glove, put out a hand and brush her fingertips over the ice. Numbing cold registered first, then pain. She snatched her hand away, cursing. The edge was sharper than she'd anticipated. A shallow cut ran across all four fingers in a stinging, sluggishly bleeding line. She tugged on her glove, hoping no one saw her make such a dumb mistake.

Movement stirred, a ripple appeared in the water next to the Zodiac. Her mouth dried when a killer whale's sleek, black dorsal fin broke the surface. The orca shadowed their boat a few minutes, keeping an easy, gliding pace before finally diving under the surface.

"Christ," she murmured, willing her heart to start beating again. She'd seen dolphins and whales during her navy career, but never close enough to touch.

Not long afterward, the motor stopped and the rubber boat slipped onto shore at the foot of two massive glacial peaks. Several mercenaries sprang out to pull the boat higher. The second Zodiac landed nearby. Meredith accepted someone's help clambering over the side, feeling ungainly and out of breath for no apparent reason.

The small brown, white and gold pebbles crunching under her boots were smooth and water worn. A wordless exclamation jerked her head around. A searchlight swung over to illuminate a slope where a group of penguins slid down like black toboggans, hit the bottom, and leaped into the sea. The searchlight flicked away and cut off.

Meredith blinked at the renewed darkness. She saw darker shadows moving around—the other women in extreme weather gear—but still felt like she'd been abandoned alone on an ice floe. The sky overhead, the vastness on every side, were simultaneously too immense and too claustrophobic. She started when someone touched her arm.

"There's chocolate in your coat," Rue said, her warm breath smoking out of her mouth in plumes of vapor. "Eat something."

"I will." Meredith brushed her mouth over the corner of Rue's eye, getting an amused crinkle in response.

Smaller lights sparked, blue-white beams slashing through the gloom. She recalled the headlamp in her pocket and lowered her hood to fumble the strap over her head.

Rue took off her glove, dug in her parka pocket, produced a chocolate bar, and tore off part of the wrapper. She gnawed a corner of the frozen candy and swallowed. "The coordinates are about five hundred yards east. A team's headed out to scout the location and mark a trail in case a snowstorm. The rest of us will wait here."

"Hope we don't freeze solid. Hey, I'm a daughter of the tropics with suntan oil in my veins," Meredith protested when Rue scoffed. "Miami native. First time I saw snow was my cadet year in Annapolis and I thought I'd die from frostbite."

"I'll keep you warm, don't you worry," Rue purred, pushing the chocolate bar in her pocket. In profile, her brown eye was hidden in the shadow of her hood, but her blue eye twinkled like a crystalline star in the headlamp's pure white light.

Meredith moved closer, expecting a kiss.

Instead, Rue laughed. "We're setting up a temporary shelter behind those rocks. Staying busy will warm you up in no time. Let's go, lover girl." Still laughing, she quickly kissed Meredith's mouth—a shock of sweetness and heat—before moving away.

By the time the scouting party returned, Meredith swore she'd rather wrestle a greased pig than put up another aluminum-framed tent. However, the privilege of sitting in the large kitchen shelter, warmed by propane space heaters, was worth the trouble of helping erect the structure and drag the rest of the supplies from the boats.

Pots of water simmered on the camp stoves. She jockeyed with the rest of the group for space to enjoy a cup of strong, heavily sweetened tea and a slice of well-buttered sourdough bread as a reward for her labors. When someone passed around foil bags filled with the guilty pleasure of instant macaroni and cheese, she didn't refuse.

Sadiya entered the kitchen tent, throwing back her hood. Her dark face gleamed wet with melting snow. She accepted a cup of tea and blew over the surface before sipping.

Meredith accompanied Rue to the front.

Catalina worked her way past the women seated on the floor. "Situation report."

"Good, *mma*, very good," Sadiya answered in her accented English. She drank more tea and continued, "I left Jones and Ruiz at the site—"

"Did you find anything?" Rue interrupted, bouncing a little in her impatience.

Sadiya stared down at her. Meredith feared the woman might take offense. Suddenly, she smiled—a beautiful, wide grin showing white teeth and pink gums. "*Ee, mma.*" She finished the cup of tea in a gulp and turned her smile on Catalina. "We found a door."

CHAPTER FORTY-FIVE

The door found by Sadiya's team was more like a steel hatch, frozen shut under a solid layer of ice several inches thick. Meredith noticed Catalina engaged in a long discussion with another woman, a Nordic blonde, and nudged Rue. "Who's that?"

Rue glanced up from her contemplation of the icebound hatch. "Viveka Forsberg, a specialist in cold weather operations. We brought her in at Mr. Velse's suggestion."

Viveka broke off her conversation with Catalina and went to the hatch where she squatted and probed and chipped at the ice with a hand ax, looking thoughtful. She returned for a longer talk. At the end, Catalina issued a flurry of orders, sending a number of her women moving at a trot down the marked path toward the temporary camp.

"No easy fix," Catalina explained when Rue and Meredith approached. "Boiling water will melt the ice, but in this cold, the water will freeze again too rapidly, making the problem worse. So we must first chip several channels in the ice."

"To carry the water away," Meredith said, envisioning the labor ahead. She whistled. Under the floodlight brought up from the camp, the ice had the hard sheen of diamonds and probably hadn't been disturbed in seventy years.

Rue frowned. "Why not just blow the hatch? You must have brought explosives."

"Yes, but that is not an option." Catalina shifted to put her back to the freezing wind. "We're illegally trespassing in Norwegian territory, Ms. Stanton. I want to avoid doing anything to attract attention."

"We're in Antarctica, hardly the most populated place on Earth."

"There are research stations, scientific expeditions, tourist camps, sightseeing flyovers...perhaps not so many in the winter season, but an explosion would be seen for miles, even by ships at sea. Someone will be sent to investigate."

"How long for the brute force option?"

Shrouded in the heavy parka, Catalina's shrug was barely perceptible. "We have fifteen pairs of hands. Five teams of three working in shifts...perhaps two or three days." At Rue's impatient protest, she added, "In these conditions, my women can only work so long. I won't risk their health or their lives. In combat, yes. To uncover a hatch, no. Not for you, not for Mr. Velse, not for money, not even for God," she concluded, her expression fierce.

"Look, you know Grazione found out about the base. He has people coming here," Rue said, her voice low, her gaze intense. "They're getting closer by the minute. People with orders to take what's under that hatch and believe me, they won't be asking nicely. Our only chance is to gain access as quickly as possible before the other team shows up."

Meredith decided to step in before Rue angered the mercenary captain further. "The job takes as long as it takes," she said flatly to Rue. Turning to Catalina, she went on, "No one's asking your soldiers to risk themselves needlessly. You're the boss, period. You make the decisions on how you want to complete the mission objective."

Clearly mollified, Catalina nodded.

"Is there anything you need, anything we can get here in the way of equipment or manpower or both that'll speed up freeing the hatch?" Meredith asked, speaking over Rue's annoyed grunt.

"Bringing in other soldiers or hired workers would take too long," Catalina said, slanting a glance at Rue. "As I said, two or three days. We have enough supplies."

"Then we'll leave you to it." Meredith practically dragged a red-faced Rue to a secluded spot near a snow-covered boulder. "Not even an admiral argues with a captain on her deck," she said before Rue could do more than open her mouth. "And only a fool picks a fight over something they know nothing about. Stand down, sweetheart. You won't win this one."

Rue seemed to struggle with her temper. At last, she deflated, looking sheepish. "You're right. I'm just—we're so close, Mer. So goddamned close."

"If the U-boat's there, it isn't going anywhere."

"Yeah."

"Are you good now?"

"I'm fine. I will be fine." Rue's statement sounded like a mantra.

Meredith waited.

At last, Rue shook herself. "I won't push, but I don't have to like it."

Meredith embraced the woman somewhat awkwardly due to their muffling layers of clothing. *Like hugging the world's biggest, plushest teddy bear, not that I'd ever tell her that.* "Come on. You need to call Velse and give him the latest news."

She escorted Rue along the slippery path to their camp.

* * *

Following a little more than forty-eight hours of backbreaking labor in round-the-clock shifts, Meredith stood next to Rue and Catalina while Viveka Forsberg supervised the first attempt to open the hatch.

A portable space heater had been borrowed from the kitchen and set up to direct warmth at the hatch and prevent ice from forming. Qwabe knelt and took the wheel in a two-handed grip. Her dark face was set in a rictus, her teeth clenched as she struggled, but the wheel remained locked in place.

Viveka dribbled a polar-rated antifreeze lubricant around the seal and liberally doused the hinges before kneeling down and taking a grip on the wheel herself. Together, she and Qwabe heaved.

Meredith held her breath. Metal squealed on metal, the sound like fingernails on a chalkboard. She winced.

Qwabe shifted to her feet and squatted to put her weight into the next pull.

At last, the wheel jerked a half turn, almost spilling both women over. Viveka rolled over, butter yellow hair spilling from her parka's furred hood, and grabbed the lubricant, smearing the viscous stuff on the shaft. She worked the wheel a few times and nodded at Qwabe. Their next heave turned the creaking wheel further. Viveka continued adding lubricant until the wheel spun stiffly under Qwabe's hands.

The hatch cracked open.

Meredith took a step backward as freezing air rushed out of the pitch-black hole carved into the ice. She wrinkled her nose in anticipation of staleness or rancid odors. Instead, the smell of the sea came to her in a faint, salty wave.

Viveka shone a flashlight inside the hole. "There's a ladder," she reported.

"How far down does it go?" Catalina gestured for two mercenaries to drag the floodlight closer.

"I don't...wait." Viveka lay on her belly, her head and shoulders inside the hole. Her voice floated out, eerily hollow. "I see something."

"What is it?"

Viveka shimmied backward until she was clear of the hole. "A submarine."

Rue practically hurled herself on the frozen ground to shine a flashlight into the hole. She hung so far inside, Meredith feared she'd overbalance and fall. "Yes, I see it," she confirmed, the echo not diminishing her excitement in the least. She backed out and let Meredith help her stand. "When can we go inside?" she asked Catalina.

"After a meal and a few hours' rest," Catalina answered. "I'll leave guards posted here, but my women are tired and so are you, Ms. Stanton."

Recognizing the thundercloud gathering on Rue's brow, Meredith plucked her sleeve. "Hey, remember what I told you?" she asked sotto voce.

"Yeah, yeah, yeah. The sub's not going anywhere." Rue glared at Catalina. "Two hours. Make the most of it." She stalked off toward the camp, muttering about bullies.

Catalina shot Meredith an amused glance, but didn't comment on the display of ill temper. "I'll send someone to rig for lights below. I doubt any of the old generators work after all this time, even given German engineering."

Meredith left Catalina to organize the next phase of the expedition and returned to the camp, anticipating a hot meal. Rehydrated, freeze-dried beef stroganoff with noodles or chili mac with beef? She'd always had a good appetite, but working in below-zero temperatures made her want to eat the world some days. Especially fat and sugar. If she split a stick of butter and put a Hershey bar in the middle, that would be the ideal sandwich.

She considered further disgusting food combinations and cravings as she rounded the last corner of the path and stopped, momentarily taken aback by the people in bright red parkas walking around the kitchen shelter and poking through the two-person sleeping tents.

Realizing two important facts—she didn't know these strangers and they appeared well armed with automatic weapons—she ducked behind a boulder to hide. Something else occurred to her, the question raising her hackles.

Where was Rue?

CHAPTER FORTY-SIX

Meredith hustled to the hatch, keeping as low as possible. "We've got company," she said, keeping her voice level despite the impulse to shout. No time to let fear or frustration get the better of her. "Twenty hostiles armed with AK-47s." She'd spent several precious minutes near the camp gathering intelligence. "I spotted a ship lying offshore too."

Catalina stared, her gaze calculating. "Ms. Stanton and the others?"

"No sign. Probably under guard in the kitchen shelter."

After a moment, Catalina whirled around and called for Sadiya.

The flat crack of a bullet split the night. Meredith ducked instinctively. A split-second later, she realized the floodlights made her and the rest of the women excellent targets. One of Catalina's mercenaries clearly had the same idea. The floodlights switched off, plunging the area into a darkness brightened only a little by faint gray light from the moon and stars.

She scrabbled for cover, banging her face painfully against an unseen rock, and crouched there, waiting for her eyes to adjust. The chill breathed from the permafrost beneath her body crept into her clothes. Her breath steamed into vapor. She covered her mouth with a gloved hand to prevent any telltale clouds from giving away her position.

Gunshots crackled, the hostiles and the mercenaries exchanging fire. She tucked her head down, wishing she had accepted an assault rifle from Qwabe that morning. She also wished she'd killed Thiago Grazione when she had a chance in Buenos Aires.

Her hand curled into a fist. Whoever led the assault team wouldn't miss the advantage given them by possessing hostages. Helpless anger tightened in her gut. *Rue!*

She forced herself to reach for composure, for focus, for the calm and considered reasoning she'd learned to command. The heat of her fury cooled, replaced by a glacial cold more profound than the icebound land around her.

The gunfire slowed and finally ceased.

A woman's voice rang out, speaking English with a familiar singsong rhythm. "I am Sophia Fellman-Grazione. We have your people. Reinforcements are on the way. You cannot win. Surrender, Ms. Rivas, and your soldiers may leave. We only want the U-boat."

Meredith knew the owner of that voice: the blond nurse she'd seen in the garage with Grazione during her kidnapping. Sam Lee had warned them about Sophia, Karl Fuhrman's granddaughter and Grazione's grandniece. If Sophia led the attackers, she clearly took a hands-on role in her family's business, be it hotels or matters far more sinister.

Catalina shouted back, "What are your terms?"

The conversation continued back and forth, exchanges of demands and guarantees. Meredith wondered why Catalina wasted time negotiating. She felt certain the woman wouldn't betray Velse, or her and Rue by extension. A possible answer came to her: Catalina might have sent rescuers to the camp to retrieve their people and counterattack the enemy from behind. A good tactic, provided the team wasn't exposed.

"Very well," Sophia said at last from her concealed spot. "Are we agreed? You have the word of a Grazione, I speak for the family and—"

From the direction of the camp, a man's alarmed shout ended on a gurgle. Immediately, Catalina shouted an insult in Spanish and the mercenaries began firing.

Meredith began calculating the odds of reaching the camp if she crawled on her belly, angling behind the hostiles. The threats of friendly and unfriendly fire aside, the need to see Rue was like a living thing in her chest, threatening to gnaw her apart.

She felt the sting on her face a split second before she heard the bullet ricochet. Gritting her teeth against the burning pain, she pulled off a glove to touch the wound. The skin above her eyebrow had split, probably cut by a rock fragment. She replaced her glove. Nothing she could do right now and the cold would soon stop the bleeding.

Meredith brought her stiff legs under her, preparing to rise. A touch on her shoulder brought her around swinging. Fortunately, she missed.

"We go, *mma*," said the squatting, shadowy figure with Sadiya's voice.

A hand guided her around the rock and into the open. Her flesh crawled, but she trusted Sadiya and kept moving in a hunched scurry. To her dismay, the woman led her in the direction of the hatch, not the camp. She resisted, her boots skidding on the ice.

"Come," Sadiya insisted, tugging her sleeve.

A bullet whizzed by Meredith's head, too close for comfort. She abandoned her protest, hunkered down as much as possible and hurried after Sadiya, passing a long boulder where a couple of mercenaries continued to fire three-shot bursts at the hostiles.

She found Catalina and a few others standing by the hatch. The hole glowed. Someone had gotten portable lights running below. Ambient light shone on grim expressions.

"You go in," Catalina said. "We'll follow."

"What are you—" Meredith clenched her jaw.

"We're going to ground inside the base. The hatch bolts from the inside. We'll be safe." Catalina shook her head. "Ms. Stanton is already inside. Go." She lowered her voice. "None of the women covering our retreat need to die because of your stubbornness."

Put that way, Meredith hesitated no longer. She crouched to find the ladder's rungs and lowered herself through the hatch. A continuous *putt-putt-putt* sound and the odor of diesel fuel drifted from below, signaling a portable generator.

"Mer!" Rue called.

She continued climbing until she reached the bottom to accept Rue's embrace. "Are you okay?" she murmured, pressing her cheek against the woman's temple.

"I'm fine, but your face is covered in blood." Rue held her at arm's length. "No holes except the ones you were born with, I hope."

Meredith snorted a laugh and drew Rue away from the ladder as mercenaries began making rapid descents. "What happened at the camp?"

Rue started down a corridor big enough for them to walk side by side. The smooth ice walls, carved millennia ago by nature, amplified her voice. "We didn't see them coming. One minute, we're drinking tea. The next, those thugs show up."

"Was anybody hurt?"

"I don't think so. Carrizo was with us in the shelter. You remember her—the Latina ballerina with the Glocks. She thought the enemy had taken Zodiacs from their ship offshore and landed them farther up the beach so our lookouts didn't spot them."

"Did you see Sophia Fellman-Grazione?"

"I saw a blond woman giving orders. Was that her?"

"The same woman played nurse to old man Grazione when he had me as his 'guest.'"

Rue blinked. "She must be a member of Thiago Grazione's group."

"That's what I thought." Meredith followed Rue to an area where the corridor widened into a good-sized room crowded with women.

The mercenaries were busy picking through a small supply of freeze-dried food and munitions—clearly whatever they'd managed to carry from camp during the retreat. She didn't see Sadiya or Viveka, but recognized a few faces from Buenos Aires. Rue called over someone with a first aid kit.

Meredith stood still while the cut on her eyebrow was cleaned and taped shut with butterfly bandages. She glanced around. "This is it? Hitler's secret base is kind of a letdown."

"Oh, honey…just you wait," Rue replied, grinning.

Once Meredith finished having her wound dressed, Rue prodded her farther down the long corridor. The room where the women congregated had been slightly warmer due to body heat, but when the corridor opened into an immense cavern, the temperature plummeted.

Meredith's steps stuttered to a stop.

Portable lamps reflected light on the stark white walls, bringing out hints of blue and green in the ice. Cables snaked over the floor to a generator in the corner. The mercenaries had done a lot of work in a short time.

Her gaze lifted and locked on an impossibility that shouldn't exist.

U-3019.

CHAPTER FORTY-SEVEN

Meredith sat on a plastic crate with a mug of tea warming her hands, still having difficulty processing the U-boat locked into the ice right in front of her. "Son of a bitch," she said for the third time, shaking her head in mingled admiration and disbelief.

"Isn't it amazing?" Rue sat next to her and proffered a peanut butter energy bar. "Catalina won't let me enter yet. She says she wants the sub safety-checked first."

"Good for her." Meredith unwrapped the bar and took a bite. Rue must have been holding it close to her body to prevent freezing. She glanced around while she chewed and swallowed. "Our only escape route is blocked. How long until Sophia and her people blast open the hatch? When they do, we're trapped."

Rue leaned against her. Although their heavy parkas prevented actual touch, Meredith set her mug on the floor to brace an arm behind the woman.

"I'm pretty sure they won't use explosives up top," Rue said. "Not until they're certain they won't damage the sub. Catalina has a contingency plan in mind."

"Okay. Shoot."

"Her mercenaries managed to salvage some explosives during the retreat—C4, I think she said. Anyway, there's enough C4 that if Sophia The-Apple-Didn't-Fall-Far-From-the-Tree Grazione decides to blast her way inside, we'll threaten to destroy the U-boat."

"And ourselves with it," Meredith pointed out dryly.

"Well, yes," Rue admitted, flushing a little, "but we'd have the advantage and she'd be in just as much danger."

Meredith nodded and chewed another bite of energy bar. She understood the value of mutually assured destruction. She also understood the limitations, but there weren't any other options. "Is there another way to the surface?"

"Catalina sent a team to investigate some tunnels branching off this chamber."

"I can't imagine anybody with a military mindset not including at least two emergency exits in the design of an operations base."

Rue straightened when Carrizo emerged from the U-boat's conning tower and waved. "That's the go-ahead. Are you coming?"

Meredith brushed off crumbs and stowed the energy bar wrapper in her pocket. She stood, her booted foot hitting the mug, which fell over with a clang. The tea inside had frozen, making her grateful for three pairs of thick woolen socks. "Sweetheart, just try to stop me."

The submarine had been secured to a dock, where a layer of transparent ice made footing uncertain. Meredith followed Rue up a ramp to a set of steps. She paused at the sight of a large crack in the U-boat's hull. Frost sparkled like diamond dust on the edges of the gaping wound. Likely decades of constant pressure from grinding ice had ruptured the outer hull, but from what she could see, the inner pressure hull remained intact, at least in this spot.

Rust streaked the steel plates, flowering thickly on rivets and welds, and trickling down the sides like running sores.

"I'm surprised she's still afloat," Meredith commented.

Rue trudged onto the foredeck. "Me too."

Walking carefully on the wooden deck planks, once flat but now rucked up or sunken in, Meredith sidled past the raised "cigarette deck" or *wintergarten* with its mounted antiaircraft gun. From there, she reached the conning tower amidships and climbed to the top and the open-air bridge. She lowered herself through a hatch into the darkened control room compartment, swearing under her breath when the aluminum ladder shifted and groaned each time her boots landed on a rung.

Inside, the U-boat was pitch-black and the air smelled stale. A light shone directly in her face. She raised a hand to block the dazzle.

"Sorry," Carrizo said, lowering her flashlight.

Meredith was jostled from the side by Rue, who had preceded her on the ladder.

"Where's the cargo?" Rue asked Carrizo, producing a small LED penlight from her parka and clicking it on.

"Torpedo room, this way," Carrizo replied. "*Ten ciudado*, señoras. Sometimes the floor is..." The petite woman made a wobbly gesture with her free hand.

Carrizo led them aft from the control room. Her flashlight's beam made shadows jump and elongate weirdly in the narrow spaces packed with electronics, dials, gauges, switches and pipes. The low ceiling and close quarters left very little breathing room.

Meredith sidled through the engine compartment behind Rue. The complicated machinery, including battery-driven electric motors, bristled with valves, tubes, indicators, hoses, cylinders, instruments and more ductwork. Catching sight in the corner of her eye of something anomalous, organic rather than mechanical, she paused. "Wait a second."

Carrizo obligingly shone her flashlight at the mass huddled on the floor near a box-like compressor: a preserved dead man, his body frozen half on its side. He wore a German uniform and a dark blue greatcoat. His shirt collar was torn open. The bloody, vertical gouges on his throat had gone black, as had the tongue protruding from his mouth. Frost coated his staring eyes and matted hair. The exposed skin on his face and hands was pale and waxy.

"Are there others?" Meredith asked Carrizo, who shook her head.

Rue drew a breath, visibly steadying herself. "That must be Krause's nephew, the U-boat's captain. I wondered what had happened to him after the war."

"How'd he die?"

"If I had to guess, I'd say he was gassed. At some point after the U-boat docked here, seawater must have gotten into the batteries. The chemical reaction created chlorine gas. Not an unknown hazard...these subs leaked like sieves. Krause escaped. His nephew didn't and died of asphyxiation. Not a very pleasant way to go."

"Remember the old woman we talked to on Los Dolores? Señora de Perez. She said Krause had lung problems, so he didn't get out unscathed."

"He was exposed to the gas, but not as badly as his nephew. Okay, that explains why he didn't unload the U-boat and take everything with him when he left. He couldn't. He had to abandon the sub or risk dying." Rue suddenly grinned. "Krause probably just grabbed whatever valuables he could shove in his pockets before he beat feet."

Meredith nodded. They'd never know the truth, but Rue's theory seemed to fit the facts. "Then the cargo must be mostly intact." She felt a smile stretch her cold-stiffened face.

"Come," Carrizo interrupted, giving the dead man a sidelong glance and making the sign of the cross. "We go now."

Reaching the aft torpedo room, anticipation curled in Meredith's gut. She almost ran into Rue's back when the woman abruptly halted in the passageway.

"Oh, no," Rue moaned. "Oh, God, no."

Meredith moved for a better view. Her buoyant mood turned leaden in an instant.

A visible crack ran the length of the port bulkhead. From the evidence, the pressure hull had been breached too, letting seawater flood the compartment. Solid ice rose almost to the hatchway's bottom lip. In some places, wood splinters and bits of canvas poked from the surface. Irregular patches of ice were as translucent as glass, giving her glimpses of colors and shapes in the depths—priceless paintings and jewels beyond reach.

Rue babbled under her breath, staring wide-eyed at the trapped treasures. "We need picks, pry bars, blow torches...no, hot air blowers. Or maybe we can lift out the whole block of ice. That might be better. Keep the paintings frozen until we get them to a restorer—"

A shrill whistle reverberated through the U-boat.

Carrizo's head snapped up. "We must go," she said urgently.

"No, I can't, not yet, I have to figure this out," Rue protested, but Carrizo paid no attention and began herding her back down the passageway.

Rue broke free and snatched at a wooden box about half the length of her forearm, sitting with a few others on a starboard side bunk where crewmen would have slept when U-3019 prowled the deep Atlantic waters, a sea wolf hunting Allied prey.

"I need something for Mr. Velse, to prove we found the U-boat," she said, stuffing the box down the front of her parka before Carrizo came to prod her away a second time.

Meredith lingered briefly in the passageway.

From the moment Rue's improbable quest for the U-boat and its stolen cargo entered her life, things had changed. She had changed. She'd faced threats and challenges as a navy captain, but Rue brought a brightness, a vitality, an enthusiasm for life she had believed she'd lost years ago. Each step on their journey together had brought her into danger, but also into joy. Somehow, without quite knowing when or where, Rue had become her North Star, the compass point of her heart that meant home.

Now the quest was over, would Rue still want her?

She shook her head. She'd been indulgent long enough. Too long, perhaps. Mindful of time passing, she turned to follow Carrizo and Rue out of the submarine.

CHAPTER FORTY-EIGHT

"There's another exit," Catalina said, rushing over to the dock. "We must go. The others have had time to plan, to bring reinforcements and equipment from their ship. They will be here as soon as they open the hatch and this is not a place I'd choose to take a stand."

"No, there must be another way," Rue protested. "The paintings…everything's in there. Damaged, yes, but salvageable."

"Listen to me, señora—six of my women are injured. We are running out of ammunition." The proud bones in Catalina's face stood out starkly and her dark eyes glittered. "You can come with us or we'll leave you here. There's no other choice."

Rue opened her mouth, but an explosion drowned out her words.

The *boom* burst against and through Meredith's skull. She fell against Rue as chunks of ice rained from the cavern's ceiling. One of the larger pieces hit the floor near her and shattered, spraying her with needle-like fragments and snowy powder.

"Go!" Carrizo shouted, pushing her and Rue toward the back of the cavern.

Four ropes fell through the hole where the hatch used to be. A handful of hostiles wearing Arctic camouflage quickly rappelled down to the floor, shooting assault rifles as they descended. Automatic gunfire tore through the room, chewing into the ice. Catalina's mercenaries scrambled for cover, returning haphazard fire.

Soldiers continued dropping into the cavern.

Meredith stumbled when more icy shrapnel hit her face. She recovered her balance and took off as fast as she could, aware of Rue keeping pace next to her.

She heard Sophia Fellman-Grazione. "The U-boat is ours," the woman said in Spanish, her words carrying clearly by some quirk of acoustics.

Rue halted and refused to budge another step. "That bitch," she growled. "That thief. I swear to God, I'll kill her with my bare hands."

"Bring the explosives," Sophia went on. "We'll crack the submarine from the surrounding ice and tow it home—a great victory for the family."

"And for you, but are you certain that's wise?" asked a strange male voice. "The cavern may be unstable. We should bring experts. Perhaps Señor Grazione—"

"I won't leave here without the treasure. Great-uncle Thiago expects us to return with the paintings and he's the head of the family...for now."

"Sí, señora."

Meredith didn't wait to hear more. She forced Rue to move.

The cavern's rear wall was obscured by shadows, but she managed to detect a darker patch that turned out to be a tunnel. She rested her gloved hand on the wall to feel her way. A few steps in, an eye-wateringly bright, reddish light bloomed ahead: a safety flare held at arm's length by the pale-haired specialist, Viveka Forsberg.

Meredith crouched and dragged Rue with her along the tunnel, following Viveka and a group of mercenaries. Although the ceiling seemed to have sufficient clearance, she didn't need to whack her head if it dipped unexpectedly.

She ran, hearing shouts, screams, scuffling footsteps and her own harsh panting in her ears. A shrill, agonized wail wavered up into the higher registers before cutting off. She ran in near total darkness, in a suffocating nightmare relieved only by the flare bobbing far ahead, a baleful light as crimson as a demon's eye. She ran as more bodies crowded into the tunnel at her back, hot on her heels, pushing her forward and threatening to roll over her.

The flare winked out, leaving her blind, her eyes open wide and straining to see anything in the surrounding unrelieved black.

Finally, she collided with someone and halted. She tried to catch her breath, a task made difficult because of the mercenaries squeezing around her.

Gunshots coming closer. Meredith steeled herself against despair. Whatever the mercenary group's rear guard had done to fend off the hostiles during the flight down the tunnel, a new wave was on the way. They were trapped unless they found a way out.

"We'll be okay, right?" Rue whispered.

"We'll be fine," Meredith lied when a bare hand touched her cheek.

A face came close to hers. Not Rue. "*Mma* Rivas is hurt. Bullet in the shoulder," Sadiya said, her breath warm despite the chilling words. "She is alive, but has lost much blood and isn't awake now."

A couple of glow sticks snapped on, shedding a neon green luminescence on a dozen women in the small space, all armed, all appearing angry or grim.

"Put those out unless you want to make it easier for the enemy to target you," Meredith snapped. The glow vanished, probably stuck into a pocket or up a parka sleeve. "What's the butcher's bill?" she asked.

"Six injured, two seriously," Sadiya told her. "They'll have to be carried out, *mma*. There is a ladder here. The condition is not good, but—"

Meredith felt the woman's shrug. "Will the ladder bear weight?"

"*Ee, mma*, but for how many, for how long, I do not know." Sadiya gave her a serious look that said she needed to make a decision.

Getting to the outside was only the first of their problems, Meredith knew. Distance could be deceptive in the dark, but she had a feeling they'd run pretty far, maybe as much as a half-mile. Normally, reaching the beach and the boats wouldn't be a problem. In the Antarctic winter, over rough terrain, navigating an enduring night with temperatures at -77 degrees, when even the smallest error might mean death…she didn't favor their chances. But staying here meant certain death, either when Sophia's planned explosion went off or the soldiers found them. Braving the surface gave them a slim chance.

The gunshots were even closer. Time had run out.

"Give me a weapon," Meredith ordered Sadiya, her tone falling into command as easily as breathing. The familiar old quarterdeck feeling settled on her as if she'd never relinquished her ship. "You take Ms. Stanton up top with the first group. The walking wounded next, then whoever needs help. I'll stay here with a team to cover your retreat."

"No!" Rue exclaimed. "Mer, you can't—"

"I'll be right behind you, don't worry." Meredith stripped off her gloves, took Rue's face between her hands and pressed their foreheads together. "And don't cry, please don't cry. Tears will freeze your eyes shut."

"Goddamn it, I'm not upset," Rue gritted, "I'm furious!"

"No arguing." Meredith aimed a kiss at Rue's mouth and grunted in pain when sharp teeth sank into her bottom lip. She pulled back, grinning and tasting blood. "Just go."

"If you say 'I love you' right now, I swear to God, I'll kill you myself," Rue muttered.

Meredith grunted again when Rue's lips caught hers in a kiss. She closed her eyes despite the darkness and poured everything into the joining. She kissed Rue as if they'd die in the next few minutes. As if the world—her world—would come to a shuddering end if she didn't crawl into this woman's skin and curl up inside her, warm and safe.

She gave the very last piece of herself to Rue in the kiss, a part she hadn't known she held back, and in the giving, she was freed.

Rue suddenly pulled away, pushed through the crowd, and disappeared.

Meredith missed Rue already. She accepted a 9mm pistol from Sadiya, checked the magazine, racked the slide to load a bullet into the chamber, and flicked off the safety.

Behind her, she caught the sound of rattling, shifting metal, and soft cursing as one by one women climbed the shaky ladder. She didn't hear any more gunshots. The hostiles were smart enough not to give away their positions yet.

She grabbed the nearest mercenary. "How many more glow sticks do we have?"

The answer came a moment later. "Eight, señora."

"When the enemies close in, activate the sticks and throw them ahead as far as possible to give us something to shoot at. Who are your best knife workers?"

Two women were thrust closer.

"Go find a hiding place down the tunnel, I felt some crevices when we were running," Meredith instructed. "When we engage the enemy, eliminate targets at will, but don't expose yourselves if you can help it. And get back here before we bug out. Clear?"

She couldn't tell if her orders were well received or not, but she felt them move away.

The yellow starburst of a gunshot flashed in the blackness of the tunnel. The bullet plowed into the wall. Someone on the enemy side had grown impatient.

She barked, "Now!" and readied her pistol.

Sickly green glow sticks activated and tumbled end over end through the air. Meredith picked a target and began firing before the sticks landed on the floor, illuminating some members of the hostile force jammed into a narrow bottleneck. *Luck is on our side for a change.* More gunshots erupted on both sides as the mercenaries poured fire on their enemies.

Hands grabbed her and pushed her toward the back of the group. Someone shoved her onto the first ladder rung.

She climbed, clinging as the ladder swayed and bits of wall crumbled, up and up until the fresh air met her face and other hands reached out of the dark to draw her to safety.

CHAPTER FORTY-NINE

Meredith found herself scrambling after Rue. "What's going on?" she managed to gasp, trying and failing to get a hold on the woman's hood.

"Hurry." Rue didn't pause for breath.

Fearing Rue had bolted in a blind panic, Meredith was about to dig in her heels when she felt someone else move to her other side. A shimmering curtain of light danced from horizon to horizon, the *aurora australis* reflecting blue and sea-foam green on the ice and giving her a glimpse of Sadiya's stony expression.

"We must hurry, señora," Sadiya said, passing over a pistol magazine. The pale glow cast shadows over her face, hollowing her cheeks. "To the beach."

Meredith ejected the spent magazine from her pistol and popped the new magazine in place without breaking stride. The pistol went into her pocket.

Women in parkas jogged closer and fanned out around her and Rue. The group loped over the frozen terrain like wolves. Several carried wounded comrades on their backs.

Behind her, Meredith heard gunshots and cries. She hoped all the mercenaries had escaped the tunnel.

She continued at a half trot, her sense of time gone with the minutes bleeding together into an endless struggle to force her limbs to move. Under her layers of clothing, she sweated profusely. Cold stung the inside of her nose and throat. Dry air blowing strong off the sea ice leached the moisture from her skin until she thought her forehead or cheeks might crack.

Flakes of snow as hard as miniature pellets suddenly battered her face. She blinked. Winds blasted from the northeast, almost knocking her off her feet. She leaned into the storm, grabbing her hood with one hand and reaching for Rue with the other, her grip anchoring them together while she trudged after the toiling shapes ahead of her in the swirling snow.

As quickly as it began, the storm ended on a final flurry of snow. The wind died. Quiet fell over the barren, icy landscape. Meredith glanced up at the black dome of the sky, where what seemed like millions of stars glittered in scattered diamond pinpricks.

Rue panted in her ear, "Almost there."

Meredith summoned her remaining energy and pushed on, her legs burning with the effort. She shivered even as she sweltered in her wools and fleeces. Seductive madness crept around the edges of her resolve, whispering she ought to ditch the parka, lose some layers before heat exhaustion took her down—a real danger in Miami during the hottest weather. But she'd listened to the lectures on polar survival at base camp. Knowledge overrode instinct. The extreme cold weather gear was the only thing between her and deadly hypothermia.

She kept slogging through the powdery snow that shifted under her boot soles like sand. *Soon*, she told herself, *soon, we'll stop.* She imagined hot tea, slices of salami, cookies, chocolate bars and oatmeal with dried fruit. The taste of raisins bloomed in her mouth. A break to eat and warm up wasn't possible, she knew, but the dream was nice.

Rue took her arm to guide her over rattling pebbles. They'd reached the beach.

So had their enemies.

Bullets whined past, fired from the glaciers at the back of the beach. The night exploded in a chaos of muzzle flashes and gunshots. Some of the mercenaries threw themselves down to make smaller targets and began returning fire. Others hustled in the direction of Zodiac boats drawn up on the shore, drawing Meredith and Rue with them.

Halfway there, a man wearing Arctic camouflage stepped around a rock, the muzzle of his AR-15 already rising. Meredith shoved Rue hard with an elbow, ripped off her glove, and fumbled with the pistol in her parka pocket. She couldn't clear the weapon.

Snarling, she stopped yanking on the pistol grip, and simply aimed and fired through the pocket. The smells of burning cotton, polyester and nylon slapped her nose as the man staggered backward, disappearing behind the rock.

Rue wrapped both hands around her bicep. "Come on," she urged.

Meredith heard the deep, hollow thunder of an explosion and felt the concussion hit, rocking the earth beneath her feet. She fell on her knees. Her hands—one gloved, one dangerously bared—scrabbled for purchase on the ice as solid ground seemed to drop away, leaving her stranded with a plummeting stomach and senses reeling out of control.

She heard Rue scream and forced her eyes open. The woman was still upright, staggering like her joints had come unstrung. Setting her jaw, she managed to dislodge a hand from its grip on the ice and yank Rue down beside her. She held on to Rue while the tremors weakened and finally died.

The world finally went still and quiet.

"Are you okay?" Meredith whispered.

Rue stared at her. One blue eye, one brown eye, but both held identical expressions of grief. "I…I don't know. It's gone, isn't it? The sub."

Meredith feathered kisses over Rue's eyelids, tasting salt. They both knew the answer.

Less than half a minute later, two- and three-shot bursts of gunfire sounded farther up the beach. Sadiya and several mercenaries guided her and Rue to the shore and helped them into a Zodiac. In the center, two of them carefully placed Catalina Rivas, who lay on a makeshift stretcher with her eyes closed. A bulky, bloodstained bandage was bound to her shoulder.

The Zodiac was pushed into the water. The motor started with a cough and a startling roar, followed by the sound of the second boat's motor. Within a few seconds, the boats tore away from shore and into the floating masses of pack ice.

Meredith tugged on her glove and held on. Her gaze dropped to Catalina. The woman's breathing was regular and deep. Catalina would probably recover, provided the boat wasn't shot or sunk by Grazione's soldiers.

On the other hand, she wasn't so sure about Rue.

CHAPTER FIFTY

The day after their group's return to base camp, Meredith wasn't surprised to find Elliot Velse, his pilot, and a handful of security guards entering the common room. Velse wasted little time calling her and Rue into a corner for a private discussion.

"Tell me," he said simply.

Rue filled him in on the expedition, including what had happened to the U-boat. "Ms. Rivas pulled some strings and got a pilot to do a flyover of the site yesterday. There's nothing there except water and ice. We believe the explosion collapsed the cavern."

"So U-3019 is lost." Velse sighed. "A pity, but at least my family's stolen legacy won't enrich the pockets of a Nazi lover." He spoke the last two words with real venom.

"The ship Grazione hired upped anchor and left the area early this morning. We don't know how many of Grazione's people survived the fight, the explosion, or the collapse."

"Let them rot. What about the submarine's cargo before it sank?"

"From what I saw of the cargo hold, the paintings were… well, not just damaged, but very nearly destroyed." Rue grimaced. "There wasn't time to make a salvage attempt and judging by the rips in the U-boat's hull, she's likely on the bottom of the sea. I'm sorry."

Velse waved a hand, dismissing her apology. "It is enough."

"There is one more thing," Rue said, a corner of her mouth quirking upward.

Meredith presented the wooden box Rue had snatched from the cargo hold before they were forced to flee. Rue had looked at the contents, of course, but refused to let anyone else, including her. Anticipation buoyed her mood. The box might contain nothing important, but its presence made the U-boat's discovery more visceral to her. That part of the expedition had taken on the quality of a fever dream in her mind. She held her breath.

Rue pried the lid open. Inside, nestled in a bed of straw, lay a trinket, albeit a valuable one—a gilt cherub pulling a wheeled cart filled with a softly shimmering gold egg ornamented with sparkling sapphires and white brilliants.

Meredith was struck by the beauty and the blood-soaked history of such a frivolous confection of the jeweler's art, once despised by Communist revolutionaries as a symbol of Romanov excess. The Russian imperial family collected pretty baubles like these while harvests failed and people starved. She longed to touch it, but didn't have the right.

"Fabergé," Velse breathed in the hushed, awed tone of a man standing in front of the Holy Grail.

"The Cherub with Chariot egg presented to the Empress Maria Feodorovna as an Easter gift in 1888," Rue said. "As far as I know, there's no connection to your family, but the history of the piece is pretty murky after the thirties. Go ahead."

With trembling hands, Velse removed his prize. The top of the egg swung open on a tiny hinge, causing a second cherub holding a round, enameled clock to emerge from within. "It's exquisite," he said. "I don't recall my grandmother mentioning an imperial Easter egg to me, but she may not have known everything her father kept in his shop."

"Or Krause could have taken the egg from some other family. There's something else here which I believe does belong to you." Rue moved some straw aside to reveal a flat, cloth-wrapped bundle. She set the box on a nearby table. When she turned around, she held the bundle in the palms of her hands, silently presenting it to him.

Velse put down the Fabergé egg. He flicked aside the muffling folds of cloth and held up a platinum necklace. A teardrop-shaped pendant held a central blood-red diamond the size of a man's eye in a serpentine setting accented by smaller blue-white diamonds.

"My great-grandfather Schilders was commissioned to make this necklace for a Hungarian baroness, but the war intervened." The gemstones glittered as he let the chain slither through his fingers. "He promised my grandmother she could wear the necklace at her wedding. I wish she were alive today. I'd put it around her neck myself." He shook his head. "Nothing brings back the dead except memories."

Meredith stayed at Rue's side while Velse thanked her, thanked Catalina, and said a few more words of general appreciation before he and his entourage left, citing a need to be out of the area before a coming storm hit.

"We'll be leaving for Argentina shortly ourselves," Catalina said as she approached. She'd regained consciousness on the trip to base camp. The bullet wound didn't appear to have affected her adversely. "Be ready. Our transport arrives in a half hour."

Rue gestured. "C'mon, Mer, I think we need to talk."

Meredith followed Rue to a small storage room and shut the door behind her. "What do you want to talk about?" she asked quietly, feeling ill at ease. There hadn't been time to talk about their relationship since the return to base camp. She pressed her back against the door and waited, her stomach in knots.

"Well, I'll be getting a generous payment from Mr. Velse," Rue started, "and I'll be taking some time off to visit Paris. Not the Louvre—I've been there often—but the more out-of-the-way art collections. I know somebody who owes me a favor. He owns a pied-à-terre with two balconies in the Saint-Germain-des-Prés district. Very nice place. There are some lovely period details and he's had the apartment decorated in the Directoire style, and um—" She stopped and gulped, her mismatched gaze suddenly fastened on the floor.

"And what?" Meredith asked, her anxiety beginning to dissolve. She'd gotten to know Rue pretty well and the babbling tended to indicate nervousness.

"Well, I was wondering..." Rue's voice dropped into a mumble too low to understand.

Meredith moved closer, her insides fluttering. "Yes?"

"Do you remember what I said to you in the tunnel?" Rue asked in a rush.

For a moment, Meredith's brain stuttered to a halt. "Yes?" she attempted. A second after the lame reply came out of her mouth, she realized what Rue meant.

Rue huffed. "Oh, for God's sake!" She grabbed Meredith by the shirt collar and hauled her in for a kiss.

Finally, Meredith broke the embrace, her mouth tingling. She grinned and licked her lips slowly, just to see the flush crawl up Rue's neck and stain her cheeks bright pink. "I take it now you won't kill me if I say those three little words?"

"You are such a—" Rue broke off, shaking her head. "Yet I like you anyway. I must be crazy. Anyway...will you come to Paris with me and stay a while?"

"How about forever?"

"Sounds good to me."

Meredith wanted to dance or break into song, but there wasn't room for waltzing in the storage room and her singing voice would make dogs wince. Instead, she gathered Rue into her arms and held on, her heart beating *love-love-love*.

She had found safe harbor at last.

Bella Books, Inc.

Women. Books. Even Better Together.

P.O. Box 10543
Tallahassee, FL 32302

Phone: 800-729-4992
www.bellabooks.com